WHATEVER IT TAKES

www.penguin.co.uk

For more information on Andy McNab and his books,
see his website at www.andymcnab.co.uk

WHATEVER
IT TAKES

Andy McNab

BANTAM PRESS

TRANSWORLD PUBLISHERS
61–63 Uxbridge Road, London W5 5SA
www.penguin.co.uk

Transworld is part of the Penguin Random House group of companies
whose addresses can be found at global.penguinrandomhouse.com

Penguin
Random House
UK

First published in Great Britain in 2019 by Bantam Press
an imprint of Transworld Publishers

A CIP catalogue record for this book
is available from the British Library.

ISBNs 9781787632110 (cased)
9781787630260 (tpb)

Typeset in 11.5/15.25pt Palatino by Jouve (UK), Milton Keynes
Printed and bound in Great Britain by Clays Ltd, Elcograf S.p.A.

Penguin Random House is committed to a sustainable
future for our business, our readers and our planet. This book
is made from Forest Stewardship Council® certified paper.

MIX
Paper from
responsible sources
FSC
www.fsc.org   FSC® C018179

1 3 5 7 9 10 8 6 4 2

'For what can men do when so many have grown lawless?'

Alan Paton, *Cry, the Beloved Country*

PROLOGUE

2016

1

Queenstown, New Zealand
Sunday, 27 November 2016

It's amazing the view just a few million dollars will buy you. Far in the distance, the other side of this never-ending wall of glass and the breathtakingly turquoise infinity pool, which you could swear merged with the lake sparkling in the brilliant sunshine, mountain peaks jutted majestically into the clear blue sky. Speedboats carved their way across the water. Paragliders floated through the air. Locals and tourists alike were having fun on this beautiful Sunday morning, and if I hadn't been up to what I was, I would probably have joined them.

Instead, I turned my back, picked up my bag from the kitchen island, and grabbed a large shiny red apple from a fruit display that looked more like a Cézanne painting than a bowl of stuff to eat. I carried on into the blindingly white room, then deeper into the house. It felt so good to have the place to myself. No family, no gardeners, no cleaners, no cooks, just me, and a few thousand square feet of billionaire's mansion. I'd been waiting weeks to get time to myself.

I passed through one of the large lounge areas and wasn't too happy about the white leather sofas but, considering I'd had no input whatsoever into the décor, I didn't suppose I could complain.

Still munching, I took the wooden staircase down to the basement and pushed through a heavy, bomb-proof door. Everything was just as plush down here, but without the view and the natural light. Clusters of bright seasonal-affective-disorder lights compensated for that by giving the illusion of sunlight, and the high-end air-con did its best to convince you that a window was open, letting in a gentle breeze.

I walked into the den – well, I say den, technically it was the family panic room, dug into the hillside and under the house, and about the size of an Olympic swimming pool. And panic room? It was more like an underground panic complex, complete with bedrooms, a kitchen, food-storage areas, a clean-water facility – everything you'd need to lead a very plush and comfortable existence while, just a few metres of reinforced concrete above you, Armageddon raged. It was designed for the family to live down there for up to a year. Time enough for the world above to finish burning and a new order to install itself.

This first bit had been converted into office space, and a dozen monitors on the walls broadcast round-the-world stock markets in real time, green gains and red losses, updates on multinational trade a constant flow of numbers tumbling down the flat screens, or running horizontally beneath CNN presenters, like digital ticker-tape.

I didn't stop to take in any of the information. I didn't know how to and, anyway, I wasn't down there to see how Marcus Dalladine made even more money.

I was down there to relieve him of some of it.

I swallowed the last of the apple, including the core, so there wouldn't be anything left behind by accident that could eventually find its way back to me. Dalladine was the American hedge-fund guy who'd moved his family there permanently – not for the great weather and views, but for sheer safety. Up till 2008, he'd been making more money than the average third-tier country, and then the financial crisis had hit. After that, he'd made even more as he preyed on people's desperation and fear. He'd ripped off his clients and their pension funds, and walked away from the carnage scot-free by simply telling the world he was suffering like the rest of us. Suffering so much that he'd joined the wolf-pack down here in New Zealand.

So, where was the harm in repatriating just a little of it to its rightful owners?

It wasn't his investors' rage and despair that he'd run down here to avoid. That was just small-fry compared to something he and many others who'd fled to New Zealand considered much worse.

Anyway, that was his problem. Mine lay directly under the desk in the middle of his trading room, covered with an orna-mental rug that lay, like an island of swirling colours, in a sea of grey Italian slate. The desk was dark wood, straight-legged, heavy and substantial. There were castors on each of the legs that were going to make it ever so easy to move away from the rug.

A pretty basic mistake that signals you're trying to hide something underneath.

I pulled the desk aside, very conscious of keeping all the family pictures, the paperwork, the pens and pencils from moving or being displaced. Obviously, it would have been easier if I'd had a mobile with me to take a couple of pictures, the before to compare with the after, but bringing one in was dangerous. The dangers far outweighed the advantages. I needed to be careful. I *was* careful.

I was *always* careful.

With the rug now free of the desk, I rolled it up to expose a brushed-steel cabinet set flush with the floor. It was rectangular and embedded in the concrete – just as I'd known it would be.

2

This wasn't my first visit to the Dalladine household. I had called in twice before, a year ago, while the house was being constructed. I had found out all the details possible from the local authority, all the consents and specs, so I knew what was being built – but, more importantly, how and with what. I knew where all the electrical and security systems were going to be installed, all the plumbing, everything down to the type of locks that would be used to keep out intruders.

My other visits were to confirm that the specs were being adhered to correctly, and no one on-site had batted an eyelid. Construction is a bit of an international brotherhood, and it's amazing how helpful people are when you say you're in the business, you're on holiday, you were just passing by, and you couldn't resist seeing how things were done this side of the world. It all paid off. Once the house was finished, I could come back and access it on a day of my choosing, and take whatever I wanted, just like today. It had made me very happy for months that I knew what was going to happen and the owner didn't.

I had realized years ago that what I did to make money,

these days, was very much like my old business. In what now felt like a lifetime ago, I had been a quantity surveyor. Say the word 'surveyor' and most people think you're the guy a building society sends round to check a house you're buying, and who doesn't even spend enough time to look in the roof-space before approving or turning down the mortgage.

Back then, I used to smile and say, 'Yep, something like that.' I never had the time or the inclination to explain that my job had nothing to do with mortgage applications. A quantity surveyor ensures that construction costs are kept within budget, so he or she has to supervise the entire end-to-end process of a construction development. To be able to do that, he or she needs to understand all the relevant building regulations for a project and everything about construction down to the last nut and bolt, from drainage to electrical systems to insulation. I had overseen the building of everything from a home extension to a multimillion-pound tower block. I knew my stuff. I had a practical, logical mind, a methodical way of thinking, and was pretty creative when it came to problem-solving. I'd gone to university, studied for years to qualify in my old career, and I didn't see why this new one was any different. Any gaps I had, like dealing with the pressure of being caught, were filled by my training and experience in the reserves as a captain in the Royal Engineers, which had included a tour in Afghanistan.

The cabinet was locked, which I took as a good sign. Until now, all I'd known was that the concrete well existed, and I'd been wondering why it was needed.

For sure, it would be to keep stuff safe, and accessible to the family if it was time to use the panic room. But what was in it?

There were no drawers in the desk, so I checked the top: maybe a key in a jar, or under the lamp.

I tapped the cabinet door, and this was no safe. Maybe just a few millimetres of steel that could easily be cut.

Digging into my bag, I pulled out a battery-powered disc cutter. It only gave about fifteen minutes of cutting time but was small enough to carry unnoticed in a daysack, and that would be more than enough time to cut around the one key well that secured the door.

It never mattered to me that I left carnage, as long as I could cover it up long enough to give me time to make distance. In fact, I liked it even more: I wanted people like Dalladine to know that someone had come into their house, violated their personal zone, then stolen from it.

I put on my safety glasses, pulled on my yellow washing-up gloves for a better feel as I gripped the cutter, and started to cut in three straight lines around the lock.

Sparks flew and the disc screamed. This wouldn't take long.

This was my fifth robbery in the past five years. I'd never had much problem getting in, getting what I wanted and getting out. In other words: getting away with it. The hardest task was deciding what and what not to take. For that, I needed to work out the value of things, which was when it paid off to have been a student and therefore addicted to daytime television. Three years of *Bargain Hunt*, *Flog It!* and *Antiques Roadshow* had set me up for life. This life, anyway.

Sometimes I'd look at something nice and shiny, but decide against taking it. I wasn't stealing the Crown Jewels. All those diamonds and rubies – I wouldn't be able to sell them. It's all well and good stealing a diamond the size of a golfball, but where do you offload something like that? I didn't even want to find out. It would mean people being involved in my business, would increase my chance of being found out. No, I just went with things that could be moved on easily or used, and that mainly meant cash and gold.

Besides, I wasn't greedy: it was all about taking what I was owed.

Sometimes I called myself lucky, but was I really? After five years, I still wasn't sure what luck was. My family had spent their lives trying to do the right thing, then gone through hell for it. Luck never entered their lives when it was needed. Doing the right thing doesn't bring luck. Luck is just opportunity and timing. Luck is about being able to identify the opportunity and the right time to take advantage of it. Don't try to do the right thing: just act when opportunity and timing align.

It took no more than ten minutes before I could stamp down the last of the remaining steel around the lock for the door to bounce back on its hinges. I always packed up before opening, just in case anything was left behind. Once it was used it was secured, just like a pocket with a button: if there was one, it should be used.

As I opened the cabinet, I saw what tended to be kept in this sort of container in a panic room. Some cash and valuable minerals of some kind, and assorted paperwork that, for all I knew, could be more valuable than anything else in there. But that would mean understanding what I was looking at, then the effort to find people to profit from it. Inside this particular cabinet were just two items I wanted.

The first that caught my eye was the cash: US$100 bills, still bank-banded in $5000 lots. I didn't bother counting how many, but there were more than ten, for sure. Then there was the gold, a bandolier of twenty one-ounce gold buffalo coins, the US version of sovereigns, and Krugerrands. I was a big fan of gold coins. They were easier to sell than ingots: ordinary people traded them, and collectors bought them.

With my daysack full, I kept control of myself and slowly replaced the rug and desk. Now wasn't the time to rush things just because I'd got what I'd come for. This part of the job was just as important, like descending Everest is every bit as important as climbing it. People nearly always die on the way down, not the way up.

I ensured the legs pushed down on the dents they had already made in the pile, then gently brushed back the grain on the wool that had been made by the castors' movement so all looked normal.

Happy, I moved back from the desk and checked the area for the last time. Did anything look different from thirty minutes ago? Did I have everything I'd come with, and, of course, everything I'd be leaving with? Was everything secured in the daysack, nothing to fall on the kitchen floor on the way out?

It took only a few seconds, but it meant I could sleep that night without worrying what I might have cocked up.

All was good, so I headed back upstairs. I wasn't excited about what was in my bag. It wasn't really about the steal: what I got satisfaction from was that Dalladine would eventually pull back the rug and discover his stuff had been stolen. He wouldn't be worried about its value – that would be pocket change for him – but what would eat away at him and really, really hurt was the thought that, quite simply, someone had intruded on his world. A world that he had spent a lot of money and effort to keep the hoi polloi away from.

I hoped it hurt, and I hoped it fucking scared him.

3

I got back to the ground floor, where sunlight burst through the glass walls into the kitchen, and decided not to grab another apple from the display for the trip back into town. It would have been to do with taking a trophy, rather than needing something to eat. I would have had more fun sticking Dalladine's toothbrush up my arse. That was always a thought when I got into a target's house, but I'd never done it. It would have taken too much time, and I always wanted to be in and out as fast as I could.

I approached the back door, stopped and checked behind me. Had anything fallen out of my bag? Out of my pockets? Had I moved any furniture or expensive *objets d'art* out of place? Thankfully, even though it was a bit of a show house, it was also a house with kids. It wasn't like it was just one person living there, who'd know where everything should be. It looked exactly as it had when I came in. All I had to do was reset the alarm, and leave, just like the cleaner would have done if the family was out. It would soon be discovered that the CCTV wasn't working, and the repair company would come down and do their stuff, but that was never going to flag up as a problem. The alarm had always been in working condition, and had always reset after thirty seconds. By the time that process had taken place, I'd be miles away and not on any footage, so what did I care?

I had found the PIN for the alarm by sitting in the back of a hire van with a telescope that should have been looking at the stars but was focused instead on the back door. It was easy. Why did designers and installers put keypads so close to the door? A few steps into the house wouldn't have knackered the house-owner, and it would have stopped people like me discovering the code so easily.

There were six digits, ending with 09. Probably one of his sons' birthdays.

As I reached the door, I heard the sound of a vehicle approaching the house.

Shit.

I hit the alarm keys and ran back inside, turning right immediately to take me out of line of sight of the door. The beeps echoed around the house as the alarm system ran its checks before setting.

The moment the beeps double-toned I stopped dead. Both my arms were still out, pushing me forward as I jogged to make distance.

I kept perfectly still. Had the CCTV been working, I would have looked like a running trophy on a shelf with an athlete on top, frozen mid-stride. Slowing my breath, I strained to hear what was happening outside. The door would open soon. I hoped it would. Otherwise, if it was the family returning, the kids might run around the front of the house to head straight to the infinity pool, and then I was in the shit. They'd run straight past me.

The door opened. The sound of children's laughter mixed

13

with the beeps of the alarm as it waited for the PIN to be inputted.

I started moving, using the noise to cover me. I knew exactly where I was heading – I knew the house inside out and none of the family would be venturing to the utility room. It was a room of washing machines, driers, cleaning materials. The Dalladines had people who inhabited this part of the house. It wasn't for them.

The kids shouted with joy and the mother told them to calm down. As they thundered inside, I closed the door to the utility room and pushed an ear against it to hear what was happening on the other side. None of the family had lost their American accents, though I supposed the kids would at some stage.

Marcus Dalladine shouted in mock excitement. 'Let's do the pool, kids!'

A woman's voice joined in. 'Grandma's coming too!'

More screams of delight from the kids.

Good, they'd be outside soon. And then I could join them, but running in the opposite direction.

The shouts receded. Maybe they'd opened the glass doors from the lounge.

I eased the utility-room door open to get a bit of an angle. So far so good. I could hear them outside in the distance.

I moved out and slowly along the corridor towards the kitchen, then froze. Plates and cutlery were being moved around. I stayed motionless.

I waited as I listened to the family joy from the other side of the house, as the kids and their father frolicked in the water. One of the kids called, 'Mom!'

She acknowledged. 'I'm coming! I've got cookies.'

I gave it thirty seconds then took a couple of steps. The

only way out was along the corridor, turning left just before the kitchen.

Through the glass walls, I could see the Dalladines at play. Marcus was happy and content, not a care in the world. Well, he hadn't a care in the world, had he? I stayed exactly where I was, watching them enjoy the money he'd ripped out of the hands of families like mine.

4

My father had been a quantity surveyor, like me. He was the first in his family to go to university, worked his way up from nothing, then started a business to support and educate his family. My mother ran the office. Things were good. The harder they worked, the luckier they were. They built a successful business. Then the '08 crisis happened, and suddenly contracts weren't being honoured. The big construction companies held back on their invoices. No one knew what to do about it.

I qualified in '07 and went straight into the firm. We kept going, working as best we could, trying to carve our way somehow out of the mess. Even my sister, Charlotte, sacrificed her career with a London accountancy firm to help. She came back up north to York to run the books. We both worked for nothing to try to get the firm back on its feet. Then the bank stepped in to help us – only, of course, it didn't.

They said they were going to 'restructure' us. They were there to help us, they said, to let us grow. Only they weren't. They just wanted to squeeze us small companies dry while charging high interest rates, high fees, and once the cashflow dried up they kept pressuring.

The bank mis-sold Dad an interest-rate hedging product that he didn't understand. We couldn't keep up the repayments, and he was forced to go cap in hand to the bank. They said we had to transfer to their 'restructuring group', where we were subjected to even more fees and higher interest rates.

The manager at the restructuring group said the transfer was because Dad had defaulted on his loan and, under the contract he'd signed, that triggered an automatic increase of interest. He also added management fees because of the 'additional attention' the case would need. And because this additional attention posed an additional risk to the bank, the loan was subject to an additional exit fee.

'Restructuring group'? Like fuck. The bank said it was designed to help small businesses recover but it treated us as cash cows. Fees and interest rates kept spiralling and ultimately Dad couldn't take the stress. He caved in. They bought the assets for peanuts to sell on later to make even more money, while we sank even lower.

My sister lost her house. My mother was on anti-depressants. Poor Mum – she'd always had dreams of travelling the world when she and Dad retired, but before long it was hard even to get her past the front door.

And then we all lost our father, husband, grandfather – for the simple reason, though this wasn't on his death certificate, that it was just too much for him: the shame of failure – the failure of the business, not being able to support his family. The failure of the system he had believed in all his life and had raised us to respect. Bank managers lent you money to thrive. They didn't stab you in the back.

I kept telling him it wasn't his fault. But in 2011, he overdosed on my mother's pills along with a glass of whisky from the cheap bottle the bank had given him years before as a birthday present, and that was it. He was gone. At least he got the last laugh.

At least he was spared the pain of witnessing his beloved Jean develop early-onset dementia and end up in a nursing home because, much as we wanted to, the family couldn't cope. The nursing home was fantastic – only the best for our mum – but it cost a thousand a week, which was £52,000 a year of taxed income, and that was never going to happen on the salaries we had. We were lucky we lived in a cheaper part of the country – a guy I was in the reserve with lived in London and was paying out £1,800 for his dad's care.

Grandma sat by the pool with the world's biggest floppy hat on. I watched as she acted being frightened as the kids smacked the water to splash her. There'd be no worries about paying for her care – with my money – when the time came.

I knew I needed to get moving, but I remained where I was. This was the first time I had ever seen my targets in their home. I couldn't help watching the watery joy mixed with shouts of excitement from the kids as Dad threw them up out of the water for them to end with a splash, now that Grandma had retreated out of the way.

I remained static for another full sixty seconds, watching and hating, before I gave myself a mental kick to get moving.

I hoped my dad was watching. If he was, I knew he'd be laughing his bollocks off. As for me, I'd join in the laughter some other day, probably with him. But for now, fuck the Dalladines.

PART ONE

2019

1

Akaroa
Saturday, 27 July 2019
09.15 a.m.

'I know you police like detail and hate excuses, but can I ask one thing of you, guys? Can I ask you to hang on to a couple of thoughts while I take you through all this stuff? Yes, I have stolen, but, no, I am not a thief. And no, this is a very big no, I am not a murderer. I did not kill Richard. Please do not define me by what I have done or what you think I have done. Please just hear me out.'

I limped my way across the room and placed the tray on the circular coffee-table. Staring at me from the other side of the marble, the two not-so-welcome visitors' faces were unreadable.

'Look, I never was the sort to break into a house in the dead of night with a stripy jumper on. Come on, I am – *was* – a quantity surveyor, not Tom Cruise dangling from a rope. Do I even look like the kind of person you normally deal with?'

Their look told me I did.

I pushed down the plunger of the cafetière until my palm hit the chrome. These two were hard work. I risked a smile. 'Not the most talkative of police, are you?'

Lawrence tapped the GoPro on the table in front of them with what had to be one of the world's biggest fingers. The small monkey-grip tripod kept the lens aimed at me. 'We're here to listen. It's you that's got a lot of talking to do.'

I sat on the big brown leather La-Z-Boy that Charlotte had bought to help take the strain off my leg, and glanced at Janet. She had sat back in the trendy blue-velvet sofa and seemed content to let Lawrence do the talking. No idea who had designed the thing: the house wasn't permanent, let alone the contents, so why would I bother taking an interest? I should be moving into my new place, not far from here, in thirteen weeks' time. That was if I managed to get this situation squared away, of course. If not, it would be due its first renovation by the time I ever got to see it, unless they gave me time off for good behaviour.

'You're right. I have a lot of ground to cover, haven't I?'

Tony's thoughts on New Zealand's prisons came flooding back to me. Maybe the system here had more going for it than the UK's. I might not get my nose fixed like he'd said he would, but maybe there were classes and I'd learn how to paint like Van Gogh at last.

I should have started talking, but I couldn't help studying just a little bit longer these two who held my fate in their hands. Old habits died hard. Always doing my homework. The question I was asking myself was this: I was holding a get-out-of-jail-free card, but would they see it that way?

Lawrence, like me, was in his mid-thirties. Unlike me, he was a massive unit, big enough to look uncomfortable in a suit and tie. His badge called him Inspector Lawrence Tutavake. He leant forward to pick up a mug of black, turned and presented it to Janet, who was an even higher rank, and maybe ten years older. These two of New Zealand's finest were taking what happened during the build-up to the events in Sanctuary very seriously, and that was why they had flown down from the country's police HQ in Wellington. It seemed they hadn't been hiding their heads in the sand and avoiding a confrontation, unlike some in their government. Some just wanted the whole episode to disappear. I had got an immediate and very clear impression from Superintendent Janet Baranek, when she banged on the front door at exactly 8 a.m. this morning, that she wasn't one of them. My only hope was that they finally recognized they had no choice but to leave me, leave all of us, the whole situation, alone. It was what they'd been ordered to do, for all our sakes. But that was the problem when there were good people wanting to do the right thing, and these two had the power to do it. I knew, because these past eight months I had become just like them.

'Yes. A lot.'

Lawrence didn't use many words, but he had a strong accent. I'd been told the basic New Zealand accent was a quarter Scottish, a quarter Irish, and half broad Cockney, and after spending so much time on both islands over the last seven years I reckoned he was more North than South.

His haircut was universal police issue. The standard always seemed to be short back and sides with a side parting, a bit like mine, in fact. His hair was thick and naturally black; hers was jet black, centre-parted, and cut above the shoulder. Practical, much the same as her makeup. Not much, but enough to let you know she was wearing it. They were both in business clothes, off the peg, the sort you'd buy a couple of in a sale because they were for work. I knew about these things. In my past life I had done the same.

Janet wore a matching grey skirt and jacket with a white

blouse, and he a grey suit, white shirt, blue tie. In this neck of the woods, wearing a suit was strange enough, but a tie was usually for funerals. It must have been the talk of the town when they turned up for an early-morning coffee.

Lawrence gave his mug a splash of milk, then mine when I asked for it. Now he, too, sat back, and they both kept their gaze on me. Janet crossed her legs, displaying practical, low-heeled shoes, black, of course, as one arm went over the back of the sofa.

It was me who was starting, then. I waved my arm around the room. 'So, I'm going to tell you about all this.'

Even though I said so myself, it was a pretty impressive place. This room alone was 26.8 metres by 25.2, and enjoyed an uninterrupted view of the Pacific. I might not know about soft furnishings but the one thing I did know about was buildings and their dimensions. Especially this one: not the furniture and décor, but every detail of its construction, even down to the spec of the filters on the waste-water treatment system that sent only clean water back into the environment.

'But before I start, please keep somewhere in the back of your mind that I've spent my whole life doing the right thing. It's just that sometimes doing the right thing isn't enough.'

I took a sip of the dark roast and wondered if they'd already made up their minds. If they had me down as a bad guy, was I in with at least a shot of changing that? I was sure I was. They didn't know what I knew. Not yet, anyway.

'So, okay. It all started here . . . right here . . . in Parmesh's house. But you need to understand something before that. You need to understand what brought Parmesh to New Zealand in the first place.'

2

'Why do Silicon Valley billionaires buy properties down here in one of the most isolated towns in one of the most isolated countries in the world? Like all of them, Parmesh Subramanian was looking for isolation and security, but at the same time he needed instant access to his yacht, and to be just an afternoon's drive from Christchurch International.'

I switched my focus away from the two faces opposite and into the GoPro lens.

'To be able to do that takes money, and that was why I was here. For his money. He got onto my list as soon as he decided to come down here from the US. But you know that anyway, don't you?'

I glanced up from the camera.

'Can I call you Janet and Lawrence?'

I felt I'd already earned the right to be familiar. After all, I'd made them coffee.

I got a couple of nods.

'Thank you. Look, it didn't matter what I took – it was all the same to me. I just wanted to take from these people. I don't need to apologize. I'm a good guy who's done some not-so-good things, but I have reasons – good reasons. You'll see.'

As they cradled their mugs I waited for a reaction or a question, but I didn't get either. They sat there, staring and listening, with no visible reaction. I supposed it was police training not to be read easily, to put the suspect off balance. But I knew exactly what they thought of me, and I understood why.

'Okay, then.' I placed my own still-far-too-hot mug on the table and sat forward.

'I've always done my homework. My research told me that Parmesh had just turned forty and, like you'd expect from a gazillionaire, he had all the add-ons that made him even worse. He was healthy, good-looking, married with three beautiful kids, all adopted and of all colours.

'He was born in Sri Lanka, but escaped with his parents in 1985 from the civil war that was raging at the time. His family were from the north and among the country's Hindu minority. They, along with Christians, were caught up in the conflict as the Tamils rebelled against the government for an independent state.

'The minorities were persecuted from all sides but the Subramanians were some of the lucky ones and managed to secure a US refugee visa. The family was set to become part of the American dream, but at a cost. Just days before they were due to leave, government forces attacked their village and many members of his family became statistics in the war's hundred thousand civilian casualties. They were killed as they slept or tried to escape into the bush.

'It was tragic, but life had to go on for the Subramanians in their new country. His parents paid for his education by working two jobs each, and Parmesh eventually landed up on Wall Street with an MBA.'

I stopped and waited once more for a reaction or a question.

Nothing.

'What I'm trying to say is that this guy ended up with so much cash, he could have bought his own US state with just the spare change he had sitting in his own bank.'

Still nothing.

I carried on. Of course, they already knew all of this, but I needed to explain to make sure that when the revelations came they were in context.

'So what do you do when you've got more money than the Sinaloa drug cartel and nobody likes you because, one, you have it and, two, because of the way you got it?'

This time I didn't wait for an answer.

'You build yourself a little – or in this case quite big – hideaway here in New Zealand.'

They were all doing it, I told them – the dotcom guys, the bankers, the rock stars, the bitcoin whizz kids, even American politicians. They all had houses down here. Cash was no problem. Parmesh wasn't the only one with a castle in Paradise.

'The thing about billionaire venture capitalists is, they have the time, energy and vision to think about these things. But the difference between them and other thinkers is that they have the cash to be able to do something about it. And they considered New Zealand to be the future. So much so that they bought real estate, and some even became Kiwi citizens to make sure they'd be let in when everything went to shit in the rest of the world.

'Look, the mega-wealthy are not concerned with the world's smaller problems, like terrorism. They know it's been around since Jesus, and over twice as many people are shot dead every year in the US as get killed by terrorists worldwide. What's more, terrorism is containable and can make money. It's the big picture, the planet's nation states collapsing – that's what gets them edgy.

'And just in case you can't think of how many ways we're all going to die, there are people who certainly can. Nuclear war is more likely now than ever before. The threat is more real now than it was during the Cold War. North Korea is on the verge of putting nuclear warheads on intercontinental ballistic missiles that could reach the United States. Tensions are racking up with Iran.

'The Americans have a president who can still be baited with tweets. He has resorted to military force against Syria, which is backed by Russia, after seeing television images of children dying during sarin gas attacks, and he has boasted of building the biggest and deadliest nuclear arsenal. Also, let's not forget Russia has taken Crimea by force, and NATO fears an invasion of the Baltic States. And that's before we start on China. They say, when trade stops, war starts. Not good, is it?'

Still no reaction.

'What about a synthetic-virus breakout? Water wars – all manner of resource wars? Then there's artificial intelligence unleashing a nuclear attack of its own during a conventional conflict. But none of those are as clear and present a danger as the main one that Parmesh had identified.'

Janet and Lawrence looked very bored. I must have sounded like some mad conspiracy-theory guy being interviewed for a late-night documentary on cable. Time to make it up-close and personal.

'I can promise you that people like Parmesh think about this sort of stuff, and when it happens, they'll get on their private jets and fly down here to New Zealand to sit out the collapse of civilization, then re-emerge.'

These two weren't mugs. Like every other local, they knew that, within days of Donald Trump becoming US president, the number of Americans interested in gaining New Zealand citizenship had gone through the roof. New Zealand became the hideaway of choice, not just for Silicon Valley's tech elite but anyone with a vision of the future and the money to prepare for it. And, more importantly for some, a plan as to how to cash in on the aftermath or be part of the planet's reconstruction.

I wondered if resentment bubbled up in these two like it did in a lot of New Zealanders, fed up with the influx of people who didn't even bother to check how many zeroes were on the price tag as they drove house prices to unaffordable levels. I wondered if these two had voted for Jacinda Ardern. Her government had finally shut the door on absentee foreign buyers. They could only buy farms now, and I was sure that that loophole would be closed down in a year or so, when everyone who wanted to had bought.

I wondered, too, if they knew this movement of wealth to the islands hadn't started just because Trump was elected. The tech elite in Silicon Valley had been thinking and planning since the late nineties. Between themselves, they had made many predictions that became true. Things like the rise of cryptocurrencies that made it harder for governments to interfere with private transactions and thus harder for them to tax incomes. Things that freed people from government restrictions to the extent that governments started to lose their power, and, in time, became obsolete.

We'd had years of news headlines screaming at us that multinationals were not paying their share of the tax burden. But why should they, if governments weren't strong enough to enforce their ever-declining power?

'It's not that I have any interest in the apocalypse,' I said. 'I've had mine already. What interested me was the bunch of billionaires who called themselves the "cognitive elite" that I started to read more and more about, who were setting up down here.'

What they had said would happen had started to happen.

They were visionaries. These people weren't like politicians who had more education than intelligence: these people had bucketloads of both. They were planning that out of the wreckage they, the cognitive elite, would rise to power. They commanded vast resources yet would no longer be subject to the power of nation-states. They would redesign governments to suit their ends. They were big enough, strong enough, and had the mental capability and drive to make it work, so why not?

It sounded like a plan to me, and certainly a plan that many gazillionaires had bought into. That was why they had already been able to reshape the planet in less than a generation. Some were already advocating the Valley's complete secession from the US to form its very own corporate city-state.

Scary plan. But already old news.

I stared into the GoPro once more. 'Okay, here goes. My sixth robbery, and it should have been the easiest. This is what happened – and what happened at Sanctuary, and why I'm sitting here in Parmesh's house as if it's my own.'

I pointed down to the floor for the camera's benefit, seeing as these two were more dull-eyed than the lens. 'Like I said, it all started here, November last year, right here in this house.'

PART TWO

Eight months earlier

3

Sunday, 25 November 2018

The locals loved Akaroa. It was small-town New Zealand. Everybody knew everybody else. You could leave your front door open and your car unlocked. There were only a few hundred houses, including Parmesh's, on the Banks peninsula area just outside the town, on the hill overlooking the ocean and yacht club at the southern end.

The Maoris had lived there for hundreds, maybe thousands, of years, consuming their enemies to, in turn, consume their power, but to me it felt and looked like a slice of France – maybe because it very nearly was one. In the middle of the nineteenth century, the area about eighty Ks south-east of Christchurch had been the beachhead for the French attempt to take control of South Island. The peninsula stuck out a thumb from the middle of the island on the eastern side, and they'd used it as a natural harbour for their whaling fleet to get a foothold and install some form of administration. As soon as the Brits had got wind of the plan they'd cleared them out.

The massive inlet for the Pacific Ocean was in fact the top

of a volcano, the ocean side of which had collapsed. Farmers chopped down the forests to make way for sheep and cattle, and now they'd made way, too, for livestock of a different kind. Tourists flocked to Akaroa aboard cruise ships or via the steep, narrow and very winding road from Christchurch, so they could take in the French street names, visit fake French patisseries, admire the views and watch the dolphins. The whales were long gone. British harpoons had made sure of that.

I had studied the day trippers, and now, with my little daysack on my back, along with its plastic water bottle shoved into the side netting, my cheap Craghoppers shorts along with Decathlon walking boots and socks pulled up far too high to mid-calf, I looked like a Brit accountant on his walking holiday. Even though it was a Sunday, I'd shaved. That was what nerds did. I didn't want anyone looking at me twice.

Not that they ever did anyway. Average build, average height, that was me. Short back and sides with a side parting, maybe that was why. Or the colour. Bit of salt and pepper beginning on the sides. Showed I worked hard, and worried even harder. As for looks, Charlotte called me Parker. We used to sit on the floor in front of the TV, me aged eight, Charlotte ten, the two of us watching International Rescue save the world each week, and shouting, 'Thunderbirds are go!' as they took off. I always wanted to be Alan Tracy, the astronaut who flew Thunderbird 3. Charlotte wanted to be Lady Penelope, International Rescue's secret agent. I used to joke that that was never going to happen. Charlotte was never going to be a blonde-haired, blue-eyed Lady P. She always came back at me that no way was I an Alan Tracy: I looked more like Aloysius Parker, Lady Penelope's driver. The names stuck, and I liked it. Nothing wrong with driving Lady P's Rolls-Royce, Thunderbird 1.

As I took the long driveway uphill to where Parmesh's

house was hidden, the sun poked out from the clouds to make it even hotter for me. That was good. The sweatier and more confused the lost tourist, the better.

The fir trees either side of the very smooth concrete drive were getting thicker. I stopped, caught my breath, hands on hips, and turned back towards the sea. There was a stunning view of the inlet, and between us a perfect example of the have-nots and the have-yachts. Parmesh's gleaming white and super-sleek yacht was moored in the centre of the sparkling blue water. Green hills curved 3.8 kilometres the other side of the inlet. I know, geeky, but I like detail. From this distance it was hard to tell if it was a big yacht, or maybe just a small helicopter on the back. But compared to the cruise ship further out in the bay, it wasn't that big.

The liner was in for the day. Smart blue motor launches ferried tourists to and fro to buy their fridge magnets and munch a croissant. I pulled out my phone and took a couple of pictures to send back to Charlotte, and couldn't help smiling like an idiot to myself as I turned back towards the hill and the house. No matter how big, or whatever it is you've got, there's always someone with a bigger or better one.

I carried on up the hill, sweat pouring down my face, and the house came into view. It was old, sixty-eight years, to be exact. I knew because I had found out all the details, like I did on all my targets. But you wouldn't find it on Google Maps, even if they had recorded the area. Part of the local tour guides' repartee was that members of the US Senate owned houses round here, wanting a quiet life when the rest of us started to burn. So why bother showing everyone where anyone with influence lived?

The front elevation of peeling blue paint was of a wide, wooden colonial, with first-floor balcony for the bedrooms and a ground-floor veranda that went all around the house, surrounded by more firs. But the real house, the new construction I was interested in, was being built underground, all nice and safe. Well, I hoped it wasn't going to be that safe. I still wasn't exactly sure how I was going to break in – hopefully, walk in – next spring, but I was in no rush. As long as I didn't stay longer than two weeks at the Top 10 campsite on the other side of town, I would be just one of the many European or Chinese tourists taking in the views and excursions.

Surrounding the house was a standard 2.4-metre-high chain-link fence, protecting concrete mixers, plant diggers and Portakabins, where the workers would get stuck into their bacon rolls.

A few acres of rough ground had been churned up all around what had once been a grand and imposing building. And it would be again, after Parmesh had finished his complete rebuild.

Suddenly I felt at home. All I needed was a Marks & Spencer's off-the-peg suit, white shirt, and tie, along with a pair of wellies and a hard hat, and I could have been back working in the UK.

Today was my second recce of the site to check how far the contractors had got with a particular piece of concrete structure that would house some electrical circuits that were going to be very important to me next year. If the concrete casting was exactly the same as the plans, all was good. If not, I'd have to rethink.

Assuming the best, I could go back to Christchurch and buy what I needed to get myself a nice back-door set-up. But all that was for another day. Today was about checking out all of the construction to see if they were on schedule and following the original plans.

4

The easiest place to push through the fence was right next to a warning sign telling the reader to keep out. It wasn't high security, more about protecting the plant so it didn't drive itself onto a flatbed one night and disappear than keeping any secrets in the house. Not that they'd be able to build in complete secrecy. This was hardly Putin's Russia. But they could go a long way towards it by keeping all the subcontractors separate so no one person or company had the total picture. Some of the contractors would have known about the underground connected rooms, a modern-day version of Hitler's Berlin bunker, but so what? They would also have known it belonged to some American gazillionaire and they were all weirdos, right? It was up to the weirdo what he wanted. As long as they got paid on time, who cared?

Like all summer construction sites, it was a sea of rutted dried mud churned up by heavy plant tracks. These lads were doing a good job. The drainage had just been laid and there were some deep trenches ready to be filled with the soakaway crates piled near the treeline. Sheets of rigid insulation boards were stacked ready to fit. Coils of conduit for underground cables rested against a couple of Portakabins. As I walked past the dusty windows I could see construction-issue drawings pinned to the walls.

Without a doubt there'd be a kettle and some half-gone-off milk on a side table in both of them.

Apart from that, there'd be no consistency. Different companies, different working practices. They might speak different languages. It was just an escalation of the rule for fitting intruder-detection systems to business premises: have one company carry out the first fix on the exterior, and the second, the interior, by another.

Back when I was on sites, nobody knew what was going on in the whole job. That was more to do with inefficiency than security – all Parmesh need have done was get some Brits down here.

In a year or so, he would be sitting pretty in his nice new hideaway and at some stage in his idyllic life discover he wasn't so safe after all. Fuck him and his oh-so-beautiful, smiley, happy UN family.

The old colonial building was, for now, a shell. Its insides had been gutted so only the outer walls remained. It looked like it belonged on a film set.

Once past the façade, I headed for the bare concrete steps leading down, taking care not to trip on all the power cables that snaked below ground level. I tried to work out which was which before I reached complete darkness, and felt my way to a mobile arc light on a tripod and hit the switch.

I got my laser measure out of my daysack and laid it against a wall. When it came to retaining information, I was pretty old-school. Jotting stuff in a notebook always seemed quicker on-site – and, of course, a pencil would still work in the rain.

I hadn't heard any vehicle. How could I, tucked into the side of a hill, inside a concrete box?

It was their shouts I heard at first. A South African voice, out of nowhere: 'We're coming down for you! Stay calm – stay where you are!'

Then I heard boots on the concrete, more than one set. My heart pounded. The combination of multiple boots and that hard, low South African accent got me thinking very quickly.

The voice. It clearly belonged to a man who knew a thing or two about violence. I couldn't run. There was nowhere to go, apart from the stairs that the boots were coming down. All I could think of was hiding my notebook and laser, and I started to shove them back into my daysack to get it on my back as quickly as possible. I'd stand my ground, see what was coming down towards me, then work out what to do about it.

Next thing I saw were two pairs of boots, then grey cargoes, and then black polo shirts.

'Put the daysack down! Show us your hands! Do it before I have to make you!'

The second, heavier, accent came from Leeds, and round that way they can make ordering coffee in Starbucks sound like a death threat. This one was a little smaller but still built like Schwarzenegger.

What could I do? I was cornered. I could fight but this was the real world and I would lose against these two. I was a nerd walker, so why not try to be one and maybe have a better chance of coming out of this in decent order?

I would do nothing, but I had to say something. Saying nothing would mean I knew what I was doing. Playing stupid, I was good at. I had learnt that because it went with the nerd look. Playing scared, even better.

'I'm sorry, I'm sorry. I got lost and came across the house. It's a fantastic house – I saw it was empty and I was being nosy. I – am – so – sorry.'

I didn't have time to say it again. The Brit picked up my daysack and the South African pushed me towards the steps.

'I didn't think it would hurt to have a look.'

I got a finger jabbed into my forehead by the South African. 'Shut it.'

No problem.

And that was it. Caught in the act.

Were they going to call the police?

I hoped so.

5

They sandwiched me between the two of them and forced me back up the stairs. My feet caught on cables but the two of them kept me moving up and back into the sun. My sunglasses were still in the daysack and I squinted like a mole.

They pushed me through the same gap in the fence, and a shiny black Range Rover was parked at the top of the driveway. They halted.

'Hands up.'

Anything they wanted. At least now I was in the open. The problem I had was that these two also knew that, and were never more than an arm's length away.

They gave my clothes the once-over and out of my shorts came my wallet and mobile, along with the few cents' change from a coffee I'd bought on my way through town. That all went into the South African's cargoes. He didn't even bother opening the wallet. Was that significant? It had to be.

I got shoved into the back of the Range Rover, which smelt straight from the showroom. It was just starting to get hot inside – I guessed the air-conditioning had been turned off when they came down to get me.

The Brit sat to my left and the South African fired the engine as the door locks clicked closed. We rolled down the drive-way. It hadn't been at all like in the films, when they bundle you into a car and accelerate down the street with a screech of wheelspin. It got me even more worried. They knew what they were doing and where they were going. There was so much purpose.

Maybe I'd find out what they were going to do when we got down onto the public road, which was good for me. Public meant people, and people have eyes and ears. Maybe they were just going to kick me out or drive me into town and dump me at a bus stop. Of course I was being a total opti-mist. As soon as the car came to the road it turned left, away from the town.

The Brit unzipped my daysack and rummaged around inside. It was then I noticed the black-ink tattoo along his tri-ceps, half exposed as he checked my bag and his polo-shirt sleeve rode up. It was a set of roman numerals, maybe a wife's or a child's birthday. On his skin, it was hard to see at first glance.

'Please let me go,' I pleaded. 'I'm really sorry. I know I did wrong, but I was just walking past and saw the house. I was nosy, I just wanted a look. That's all I was doing. We don't see buildings like this in the UK. I'm so sorry, I won't go back.'

But clearly that wasn't going to work.

The Brit pulled out the laser and the notebook and gave me a look that said, Yeah, right.

I knew I was done for when he flicked through my pages of notes, not only from today but also from last Sunday, the first time I'd gone to the house. He didn't say a word, totally ignored me, just like the South African did up front. Their silence moved me along from so-far-so-good to concerned.

I didn't know why it happened. Maybe it was looking about

me, trying to work out what to do when the vehicle stopped – maybe I could chance it and punch and run – but I couldn't help noticing how perfect the two men were. Just like their car, they were showroom fresh. Pressed clothing. The South African was shaved, with immaculate short blond hair. The Brit had a buzz-cut and a perfectly groomed beard to match.

Maybe getting these two to lower their guard, getting them to think I wasn't going to resist, would work if I started sinking deeper into begging mode. 'I'm so sorry. Please, tell me where we're going.'

The Brit didn't look up from the daysack as he dropped the laser and notebook back inside. He pointed across my chest at the bay to our right. Parmesh's yacht gleamed on the water. It was so sleek and low-profile it looked warlike.

The South African turned into the yacht club and parked. He jumped out and opened my door, like I was a paying customer. The Brit nodded for me to get out. They weren't slacking off at all.

The South African gripped my arm and pulled me in close so his mouth was next to my ear, so close I could even smell his cleanliness. Shampoo and body wash, no tobacco, no alcohol. 'Follow me. Don't try to run. Don't try to alert anyone. If you do, you'll regret it. You understand me, don't you?'

Of course I did. I nodded and he released my arm.

I followed him, the Brit behind me again, towards the jetty where a long slim white RIB was moored. The Range Rover's locks chimed behind us as we stepped onto the wooden jetty.

I tried to control my breathing. I wanted to show I was respectful to their demands, and scared. I took a couple of deep breaths and tried to accept the situation for what it was.

I'd been caught. Now I needed to think up a decent enough lie to get me out of what was clearly a problem.

They didn't have to push me into the RIB. As I leant back

into the plush nylon padded seat around the station two-thirds of the way back that housed the wheel, they even made me put the seatbelt on.

Within moments we were bouncing over the swell, thrust not by big outboard engines but an air-propulsion unit, a bit like a jet ski. The warship got bigger and bigger by the second, just as all the possibilities of the bad things that could happen to me got bigger and bigger in my head.

6

The propulsion unit roared and the wind blasted the South African's perfect hair all over his face. My eyes were slits against the spray and dazzling light.

The RIB manoeuvred alongside the steel gangway that protruded over the side of *Saraswati*. The yacht's name was plainly stencilled along its bow.

The Brit turned back to me and yelled, 'Boots off – now!'

I did as I was told and left them in the boat, climbing the rungs behind the South African. As my head came level with the deck I heard a loud buzzing noise behind me and ducked.

A matt-black six-propped drone the size of a coffee-table swooped overhead, stopped and hovered about three metres above the stern of the yacht, right next to the just-as-sparkling white helicopter. It wasn't small, by any standards. Why would it be? Two young guys waited beneath the drone in jeans and T-shirts. One had the console in front of him with a strap over his neck, like the ice-cream lady at the Odeon in York where our dad took Charlotte and me when we were kids. The second stood by the yacht's guard rail, watching two black metallic legs with four outstretched talons at the end of each arm descend from under the drone. Just like a bird of prey, it had three forward and one at the rear to make its claws. To me the drone looked just like a matt black eagle would have done as it swooped from the sky and gripped its prey with its claws before heading back skywards, except that as it approached the rail it slowed to a stop, and the claws gently wrapped around it. The young guy waiting unhooked it from the rail, then laid it alongside another on the deck.

The Brit led me towards the bow and through a blue glass door. It was like walking into a fridge. There was music playing over the soft whirr of the air-con. From wherever the speakers were, a woman with a guitar was singing Nirvana's 'Come As You Are'.

The South African jerked his head to indicate a plush grey semi-circular settee and coffee-table. On it sat a jug of lemon juice, by its colour, and two glasses.

I took a seat and kept my hands on my knees where they could be seen. The Brit disappeared back on deck, leaving the South African standing and staring down at me. Should I say something to the man now hovering by the door? No. I didn't want to write more words than I had to in this exam: more words could mean more chances for bad marks. I tried to count my blessings. So far, so good.

I hated not knowing what was happening. I was a planner. I liked stuff to be mapped out so all my focus could go on getting the details right. Even in Afghanistan, I hadn't felt as concerned for my safety as I did now. There, I'd had control of my actions and a way to fight back. But I hadn't experienced this feeling since primary school when I was pushed around in the playground. I'd had a KitKat, and the world and his dog wanted a bite. The pushing and shoving had started as I tried to get the chocolate back into my pocket. That was when Charlotte came in and rescued me, two years older and, even then, taking no nonsense from anyone. She had never needed a spine to hide behind. Our parents had adopted her as a baby because Mum thought she couldn't have kids, and then I came along. Having her was the best decision they ever made for all four of us. I just wished she'd burst through the door right now for yet another rescue. There always had been something almost other-worldly about her.

But that wasn't about to happen.

I sat and tried not to make sudden movements or antagonize or look like a threat to the South African, whose short hair was now perfectly back in place since the ride in the RIB. As if I would have been a threat with my socks collapsed about my ankles and exposing the lily-white skin of my dad tan.

I couldn't help but notice the wealth. I could smell it. Inhale it. The interior was as new as the Range Rover's and, probably, the helicopter's.

I tried to resist being lulled by all this opulence. As always, I had to turn it into anger. That was what I had for these people. That was why I was doing what I was doing. I took from these people because they had taken from us.

There were voices from the stairs, coming up from below and behind me. They were deep, both American, and they were talking about seagulls, but not appreciatively. As I turned, two heads and then bodies emerged from below. One, who was doing more nodding than complaining, was in immaculate white uniform, with gold rank on his shoulders. He headed up to a higher deck, and the one who really didn't like seagulls came towards me, and I knew exactly who he was. Homework, right?

He was wearing a pair of flowery Bermuda shorts, and below his skinny, dark brown and hairless legs a pair of green canvas slip-ons. On top, despite being rich enough to buy Armani – and by that I don't mean the clothes but the entire brand and empire – he wore a saggy old T-shirt. It looked like he hadn't taken it off all week. There was a couple of days' jet-black growth below his deep-set brown eyes, and his long hair, centre-parted and just past shoulder-length, was like all the hundreds of pictures of him online.

Only two sorts of people could look like this: him, and the poor.

'Hey, James, good morning.'

My eyes must have been big as saucers. His expression was unreadable. Despite the upbeat greeting, I couldn't tell if he was angry or happy. He just looked down at me like I was some kind of exotic specimen his divers had brought up from the seabed.

He leant down, and poured two glasses of juice.

7

I shook my apprehensive head. 'I'm so sorry for trespassing. It was just that I saw the house and it looked so—'

A glass of juice appeared in front of me. Parmesh wasn't even listening. The hand presenting the drink had perfectly manicured nails, not a callus in sight. Why would there be? His money had come from his brain – or, rather, from his brain knowing how to get the money from the rest of us.

He sat down on the settee, uncomfortably close. 'Please, James. There is no need to carry on with this nonsense. I know who you are. I know what you are. I know everything about you. Your family, your work, even your unit in the military. Engineers, right?'

He tilted his glass in the direction of the South African, who was still at his station by the door. He hadn't said what he knew yet so it could just be words, but that didn't stop my pulse surging. They would have noticed. I would have.

'We both thank you for your service.'

I had done three years as a reservist and, of course, like most of the military, wanted to go and experience the post 9/11 wars. Mine was quite boring at first, building blast protection around the military and diplomatic areas in Kabul. But the second half of my tour was spent down in Helmand Province. There, big clearing operations were happening before the war was handed over to the Afghan National Army and we all came home. The Brits and the ANA would fight their way through valleys and the green zone with the likes of me thirty minutes behind, bringing HESCOs and armoured plant. As the infantry advanced, my team would start to construct a Forward Operating Base. We filled HESCOs, massive defences made from circular bins of galvanized-steel mesh and poly-propylene, with whatever was to hand – usually sand. We then built a square fortification where the ANA would even-tually fight from, and hopefully still dominate the area when we were gone.

With the confusion and closeness to the fight and, of course, the ANA using the same weapons as the Taliban, I never knew who was shooting or firing RPGs at me. But that was now part of another life.

I shrugged because Parmesh's words meant nothing: it was just something Americans said because of their embarrass-ment at treating returning Vietnam veterans worse than the enemy.

'Mr Egbers, he is a very productive person. Our little eyes in the sky were taking a look at the house last week and you were spotted, James. Looking here, measuring there. It is okay with you if I call you James?'

He wagged his little finger at me, like a parent telling off their child, but actually having fun with it at the same time. 'Mr Egbers said not to go and pick you up immediately but to follow you. Find out more about you first. You see, there are some people who do not have what you might call warm feelings for me – not just for what I have, but for what I think.'

He paused and took a sip of the juice, his eyes constantly burning into me. It was eerie. I could feel it and I didn't like it.

'So, that is exactly what our eyes in the sky did. They saw where you went, saw who you talked to and, of course, Mr Egbers discovered everything about you and your family. Technology – it is amazing, do you not think?'

Parmesh took another mouthful of juice but mine stayed cupped in my hand on my knees. 'So, James, how does it feel to be followed by the kind of advanced technology not even the US military have yet? The cameras are so good that lip readers could even interpret what you were saying to your fellow campers.

'And let me tell you, it was so boring. Asking where to eat breakfast in town because the campsite kitchen was too busy? Not what I, or Mr Egbers, was expecting, for sure.'

His free hand gestured to my glass while he gave himself enough time to smile for effect. 'Please, drink. You must have a dry throat. Nerves.'

I did as he suggested, wanting to show I was compliant and not a threat. So far, all that had happened was words, and that was how I needed it to stay. Egbers looked as if he had other ideas.

'So you see, James, I know this is the second time you have been to the house, maybe more – only you know that.' He tilted his head to the side and studied me a few seconds. 'You are here to steal from me, are you not, just like you did in Queenstown?'

He pushed his glass towards me rather than an accusing finger, but at least it was with a smile. There was none coming from Egbers.

'Come on, James, now is not the time for modesty. Marcus Dalladine told me what happened. It had to be you, right?'

I kept staring at his face, trying to avoid the deep-set dark brown eyes, clear, penetrating, confident in every word he said.

My silence confirmed what he already knew. He wasn't worried if I replied or not. He moved in closer. He was enjoying this but, strangely, not in a hostile or even malicious way. He was leaving that to Egbers. Maybe I was the first real person he had ever met.

'You see, James, there are not too many of us down here. The cognitive elite, it is quite exclusive.'

He waited for me to ask, but I didn't need to.

'I know.'

Parmesh was impressed, but his expression suddenly clouded. Was it because I'd said it with such contempt? He jumped up and jerked his thumb towards Egbers and the door.

I jumped up as well, bracing myself for the fight.

Egbers came forward, his eyes dull and focused on mine. This was going to be painful but, fuck it, what else could I do?

At that moment, white-clad crew members rushed past, shouting and wildly clapping their hands. This wasn't about me: it was about the gulls.

I couldn't help but smile as I extended my arms, my fingers spread out as I sat down again. 'It's okay, my mistake, my mistake.'

Parmesh kept his eyes on the scene outside as he addressed Egbers, who was clearly disappointed I was back on my arse. 'We need to find someone who can sort this out. Maybe design a high-frequency device that we cannot hear but irritates the life out of them. There has to be something.'

Egbers gave a firm nod and Parmesh was content. He, too, sat down again and attended to me with a reassuring smile. Egbers returned to his spot, clearly disappointed that nothing had come of it.

'I am sorry to startle you, James. But the gulls, the mess

they leave – I should have brought a grey one, that is all I am saying.' He held up his arms to the sky. 'They give me nightmares. Arrgh!'

I gave a smile and nodded, inwardly very happy for the gulls.

'Word gets around from people like Marcus. He gets angry because he would sell his soul for a shiny stone, so when even a little pebble is stolen from him, well, he takes it personally.'

He wasn't looking at me any more: this was aimed at the South African by the door behind me. I knew he was still there as his voice swept over my shoulders.

'No soul, Mr Mani. No principle, just a husk.'

Parmesh was in total agreement, as was I. Parmesh soon returned his attention to me, now with a smile.

'During Mr Egbers's research, you have been coming to New Zealand every year for the last seven. Walking holidays, were they?' He gave a little smile and looked up at Egbers, who took a step or two deeper into the room so I could see him smile back. A perfect white-teeth South African smile. His focus then moved to me, and the combination meant only one thing as far as I was concerned. He had plans for me.

Parmesh continued: 'The problem with Marcus is, he is greedy. What you took would not even cover his mineral-water bill. But he cannot see beyond his greed. There are many like him, you know.'

He sat back in the settee and it felt like there was a bit more room between us now, even if our knees were almost touching.

'You know what, James? I admire and respect you. I really do.'

Like a spring he bounced forward to place his glass back on the table and gently lifted mine from my hands. Maybe he was trying to unnerve me. If so, I didn't feel he had what was needed within him. Egbers on the other hand . . .

'Too sweet? Coffee?'

I shook my head. 'No, no, thank you.'

He was getting back on track. 'So, James, the question is, why? Why come down here from the UK and take from us? What is so important that you compound all the problems of stealing – on an island, for the love of God? Is Europe not easier for your line of work? Is it the fresh air down here? The scenery? Or is it just people like us you want to steal from?'

I took a breath, tried to hold it back, but it didn't work. He wasn't exactly an admirer of Marcus, so maybe that would help me. Whatever, he already knew the answer. He focused on me and smiled. It felt genuinely warm and even a little curious.

The nerd act wasn't happening any more anyway, so fuck him, why not?

'You one-percenters, you take, and you leave the rest of us in the shit. You fuck up our livelihoods, and you don't care what you leave in your wake. Now you're preparing for when the world that the likes of you have created goes to rat shit. But you don't care. It's going to be okay for you, isn't it? You lot will be down here chasing birds off your decks while the rest of us suffer – again.'

It wasn't the brightest thing I'd ever done but I couldn't help myself. His confidence, the power he exuded, the mere fact he was sitting on a yacht made me think of Mum and Dad, our family, my family. Fuck him, and fuck Egbers.

Parmesh nodded and ran his fingers through his hair. No doubt he had heard all of this before from angry protesters or online attacks. I was sure a lot more than just 'some people' didn't warm to him.

'James, I admire your passion, I really do, but there are two things out of sync. First, I am not one of the one-percenters. I am one of the nought-point-nought-one-percenters.'

He let the fact sink in for a second before his voice jumped up an octave, as if he had startled himself. 'Which is crazy, right? I am not the smartest guy you are ever going to meet. I do not even have any technical skills. But what I do have is a very high tolerance for risk. I love it, cannot get enough of it.

'You see, James, my world is just me diving into the two most risky things out there. Accelerations in technology and the G word . . . Big G . . . globalization. But I am good at it. I can keep my mind open to the big picture. That is why I am crazy rich. No skill, just stuff, crazy, right?'

I nodded, not really knowing if that was a good reply or bad, but it didn't matter. His button was on play.

'I do not know where it comes from, my head, my heart, maybe my parents. My mother, she was a very strong woman, very much a risk-taker to protect her family. Maybe it is my genes, DNA, whatever. They say it is the mother who provides all the good stuff. Who knows? Do you?'

He waited for some sort of reply, but what would he expect me to say? 'I'm sorry. I got it wrong – you're richer than I thought'?

I received a shrug. 'No problem. Would you also like to know the second thing you have got so wrong about me?'

He gave a beat, but continued once it was clear he wasn't going to get an answer.

'Well, you are right, James. There is a big divide between people like me and people like you. And I will tell you what, the problem is getting worse, much worse . . . but I am not going to make the divide even wider. I am going to fix it. Open minds to the big picture.'

He held up his hand, forefinger extended, as if I was going to interrupt. Like that was ever going to happen.

'You see, James, very soon the middle class will disappear,

and do you know where that will take us? Eighteenth-century France. And you know what happened then, do you not?'

He didn't wait for me to answer. 'Tell him, Mr Egbers.'

'Revolution.'

Parmesh's smile evaporated. 'Exactly. And we all know what that means.' His arms waved about, like he was conducting an invisible orchestra.

'You see, James, there is no example anywhere in human history where the level of wealth accumulated by so few guys like me has not led to people like you coming out onto the streets with their scythes. That is what you are already doing in your own small way, James.'

Was he trying to justify what he was doing down here? I braved his eyes again. 'But having your castles down here, you'll be okay, won't you? Fuck the rest of us.'

He gave another shrug. 'Not exactly.' The dark browns flicked over at Egbers, then back to me. 'But, James, the differ-ence lies in what we are going to do once we have packed up and moved down here while you guys burn. I am not one of the Marcuses. I am part of the cognitive elite, in the true sense of the phrase.

'You see, I am always thinking, coming up with ideas – what is the best way to help people on this planet, transform, even amplify their potential? How can the world be a better place for all?'

He paused, waiting for it to sink in. That was no problem for me. The more talking, the fewer problems with Egbers.

He threw a broad smile at Egbers. ' "Cognitive elite"? Where did that come from? What do you think of "hyperleaders"?'

Mr Egbers was all about the words and not using them.

'No imagination. Hyperleaders? I think that is already out there. It has a meaning. But you will be able to change it to whatever you want when the time comes.'

8

I didn't speak, didn't acknowledge any part of their conversation. It sounded like a mutual love-fest to me and, besides, I might already have said too much. Egbers still looked like he had plans for me.

Parmesh pointed at me again with that little finger. I wasn't sure if he was just playing with me, knowing he had total control, or if he was one of those crazies who've always had the inclination but not the freedom that cash can bring. People with money had power, and that meant they could do virtually anything they wanted. 'I know what you are thinking. I bet you think I am one of those banker guys, the Marcus kinda guy, who went and screwed everybody over in '08.'

I didn't answer, but my face probably said what he needed to know. His kind of confidence only came with people already knowing what they needed to know.

'I am not, James. I am so not. I could see the crash coming and got out. Like I said, I can see into the future. The Wall Street gig was just to earn my entry fee to Atherton.'

Parmesh wasn't even bothering now to check if I knew what

he was talking about. He knew I had done my due diligence. The celebrities of Silicon Valley live very private lives. Nobody really knows much about them outside the mega-companies they control. Which, of course, is great for the media: they can come up with whatever stories they want and speculate on what hair product or deodorant they wear.

But the one thing they all had in common was the number 94027, the most expensive zip code in the US. The average house in the US cost about $258K, but in 94027 it's $7 million. Clearly, Atherton is no ordinary small town. It's about forty-five minutes south of San Francisco, and just twenty from the offices of Facebook, Google, Tesla, and all the other companies that make up the digital, industrial complex. Mega-mansions line nearly every block, with fences and landscaping to foil prying eyes. I knew because I went there – and to Wall Street – to try to work out how I could settle my anger.

I wasn't going to become an 'active shooter', killing as many bankers as I could in a Wall Street cocktail bar or an Atherton Starbucks. I'd fantasized about it for months, been and done the reconnaissance even, but it was only to try to make myself feel better. Deep down I knew it would be counter-productive. It would be just a short-term gain that I might or might not survive. After my five minutes of glory, what then? What about my family? Who would be paying the bills? So, once I had a grip on my anger I got back to what I was good at: being logical and precise as I worked out how not just to take my anger out on them but get our family's money back from them.

It had been in Atherton, while carrying out my research on who lived where and how I could access their wealth, that I stumbled upon the Silicon Valley cult that had produced the cognitive elite.

And that was when I'd discovered that New Zealand was where I'd get satisfaction.

Parmesh exhaled slowly as he slumped back into the settee, his face clouded. What did that mean for me? Was it time for Egbers to disappear me? If so, I was going to take a couple of chunks of him with me, for sure.

'James, you think you know me, but not so. Not by a long shot, my friend. I believe nations should tax wealth. Any system that gives wealth can also benefit from it. I do not see any problem in providing free health care, free education, all that kind of stuff. Like I said, with no more middle class, kids will never have the chance to be better off than their parents. Then all those people out there will be looking to burn us down. Look, your gig is more than just the money for you, James. I get it, I really do. We share the same values. You just do not see that yet.'

Parmesh was being inquisitive and trying to bond rather than leading up to revenge. All good, as far as I was concerned.

'Really? It's you, the one-percenters, or the nought-point-nought-one-percenters, whatever you call yourselves, you're responsible for what I do. I have no shared values with people like you.'

Egbers didn't like that at all, and he took a stride forward. Parmesh held up a hand to halt his advance. I had no control of what they chose to do with me, no matter what Parmesh said. My experience had always been that once I'd accepted I was in the shit there was almost a de-escalation in the situation, whether on-site, dealing with aggressive contractors who were charging high and working low, or getting shot at by my own side trying to build an FOB. I also knew that the de-escalation wouldn't last for long. Something else would ramp things up.

Parmesh sat shaking his head. He was either really empa-thetic to my argument or deserved an Oscar. His face seemed to be saying he felt sorry for me not understanding his point, but that wasn't where he was going. 'James, your family, '08 – a terrible story, a very sad story. How is your family now? Are you a good father?'

'I try. I'm part of their lives. I support them and my wife – well, ex-wife.'

'That is good, James, so good to hear. Your mother? Mr Egbers explained to me she needs care.'

He rested a hand on my shoulder to help me dial down. If that was what he wanted, I could do that. 'She does, but that's one of the reasons I do what I do.'

He gave my shoulder a squeeze. 'You are a good son, James. I like that.'

The more of this the better, as far as I was concerned. But I knew there was more than just a friendly talk to come, a pay-off for him confirming that Egbers really had done his checking on me.

'And what about your sister – Charlotte, no?'

'She's doing okay, working part-time, but it's been hard.'

He smiled and I smiled with him. Always good to mirror the client to keep onside. Something Dad had taught me as a teenager, back when the plan had been that I would eventu-ally take over the firm.

'But why have you made so much effort to find out about me? Why do you need to know? Why am I here and not in a police cell?'

He tilted his head and smiled some more as he worked out if he was going to answer. His decision was no, or, maybe, not yet. But that was okay. I didn't mind waiting rather than being thrown overboard by Egbers.

'So, James, as far as I can see, what you have been up to

down here should be thought of as . . . What would I call it? Let me think . . .' His face contorted as he tried to come up with a word. 'What would you call it, Mr Egbers?'

The answer came so fast there wasn't enough time for me to turn my head in his direction.

'Most definitely payback.'

9

'Exactly, Mr Egbers.'

The way he said it, they must have had the conversation many times. Egbers didn't sound or look pleased with himself at having the answer on the tip of his tongue. He just radiated more intensity than anyone I'd come across for a long, long time. Well, come to think of it, ever.

Parmesh, on the other hand, was much more animated as he studied my face, smiling, waiting for a reply from me.

'You could say that.'

He liked that. 'I do, James, I do. You should feel proud of yourself. I feel proud for you.' He leant across and slapped my knee, then refilled his glass. 'James, do you know that I used to give money away?'

I shrugged as he sat back with his drink. 'That's good – but it never came my way. Us little guys . . .'

'You are right. It rarely gets to where it is needed. But you know what? I had to *fight* to give it away.' Parmesh nodded a couple of times – 'It is true' – while playing with a little chunk of ice in his mouth. 'After a billion, I just had to concede defeat, give up the fight. A billion dollars. Most non-profits just do not know how to deal with ten million, let alone a hundred. And then there is the scrutiny and all the due diligence around people like me giving donations. Why did he give it there instead of here? You know Mark?'

I shrugged. There were millions of them.

'Mark Zuckerberg? You taken anything from him? Come on, you can tell me.'

I shook my head.

'But you would want to, am I right?'

He was.

'He gave a hundred million to the New Jersey public-school system – but then was publicly crucified for not consulting the local community first. *What?* The only consulting they needed to do was how to spend the money on their kids. But no – crucifixion.'

Parmesh's arms came out to demonstrate the pose, in case I wasn't up to speed on Christian imagery. 'Crucified. They resent the fact that money makes money. We make money quicker than we can give it away.

'We give billions away but the problems out there – it does not even touch the sides. But, hey, it makes us rich guys feel better because we are all too busy congratulating ourselves that we are self-made – or most of us are.'

There was something about his eyes: they looked almost glazed, like he was on something, or that maybe he was just as dangerous as Egbers. Whatever it was, it didn't stop him talking.

'That donation thing, it no longer works for me. I am a capitalist, a proud and unapologetic one, and you know what? Compassion is not enough. The Big G? It is out there, for now, and compassion? It cannot buy your kids new shoes. Am I right?'

There was no time for me to work out what my answer was. That play button was still pressed.

'So, James, I have to be thinking bigger than just feeling good about myself.

'People like me, James, our existences will not get better until all our fellow citizens feel better. And they are not going to feel better until they actually do better. Would you not agree, James? What do you think?'

I nodded and had to agree, even though it was beginning to sound like he was preaching to me. When that happens there is always a reason. 'So why are you telling me all this? You wanting to justify yourself? Or wanting to sell something? You pitching to me?'

He liked that and it got a big smile.

'You know what, James, we really are more alike than you think. I want both of those things to happen because I have a plan for you.'

I nodded. I was willing to listen rather than get a kicking. Besides, who knew what might come of it?

'You see, James, the problem is that we are never really satisfied with what we have. But it is not just consumerism. It is governments that play on our need for instant gratification of a short-term gain. We get the stuff and we feel good. They drop a tax here, a fuel-price hike is cancelled there, but it soon fades because it is all short-term gain. Governments are short-term thinkers. It is not their fault, it is that of democracy. Short-term tenures mean short-term fixes.'

He looked at me as he talked, but he seemed to be aiming his words over my shoulder.

'Try thinking of governments as Mafias – cartels forcing their citizens to surrender large portions of their wealth to pay for not only protection but roads, hospitals, schools, all that stuff. It has worked for quite a while, but it is slowly coming to an end. I see it, the others see it. We see the rise of tribalism.'

He brought his voice back to me, maybe because he had

lowered it. 'But listen, who am I to tell you? You had your share of pain when the norms were broken.'

His eyes never left me, and I was starting to wonder why I was on the receiving end of this lecture. Don't get me wrong: if this was punishment I was very happy with it.

But Parmesh hadn't finished. 'So, the cognitive elite. We are concerned about what will happen and we are prepared for it.' He paused. 'But, hey, you know that, do you not?'

'Yes.'

'Well, James, the theory is sound. Governments will simply lose authority because they have not addressed inequity. Social media will play its part in making people angry so that they organize themselves, but only to the point that they gather and take action. But then what? Nothing. Nothing.'

Parmesh's expression had slowly morphed from smiling and confident to borderline zealous. 'And that is why it is up to people like me, the cognitive elite, to make the world a better place when the time comes. Our privilege needs to be used to serve people.'

He leant a little towards me, a finger pointing to the sky.

'Because, James, it is not all mud out there. People are creative, hardworking. Hey, in twenty years' time there will be jobs out there we have not even got names for. We just have to make sure people, like you and your kids, get opportunities to thrive. That is all I am saying.'

He paused, like he was deciding whether to carry on or bail out. I knew the feeling.

'You see, James, what started as just Atherton dinner talk in the nineties soon mushroomed into something much bigger.

'It became more than just an inward-looking, self-protecting, geek-populated cult. The cognitive elite will bring order, peace and prosperity to the planet.'

His eyes had become blank and unblinking, yet his smile

never dropped. Either he was mad, or he believed what he was saying. Whichever it was, I found myself having a little respect for him, even though he was my target. It wasn't his history, but his clear determination to succeed.

'I have been thinking for months of a way to explain the business model of the CE, even to some of its members, and the easiest way I can describe it is that we are cardinals in the greatest crusade the world will ever see, and Mr Egbers here is one of our Knights Templar.'

I turned. He had moved away from the door and was staring at me, his face still stone.

Parmesh leant in and put a hand on my shoulder. 'James.' He smiled. 'I am inviting you to join us.'

10

'What? Work for you?'

'James, no one works for me. We are *family*. I am asking you to join us in making the world somewhere that we all can live together and be prosperous. Crazy idea? We think not.'

My eyes darted between them. Egbers's eyes drilled back into mine, his expression impossible to read. An image flashed into my head of an unyielding medieval priest, killing disbelievers because God had told him to. Religious people find it very easy to justify unreasonable and irrational behaviour, just like there had been in the last so-called 'great' crusades. Was I being asked to become one of him?

It was time to protest, but sensibly. 'Look, I'm not one of you people. I'm just small fry. I don't have your money, don't have your vision. I don't—'

He held up his hands, then gave a slow shake of the head and a tut. 'James, James, I understand. I am sure this has come as quite a shock to you. But all you have to do is trust, believe, and you will surrender to hope.'

I knew the CE called themselves a cult, but this was starting to tear the arse out of it.

I jerked my head back to the South African. His cold, pale-blue eyes continued to burrow into me. They were slightly glazed and off-focus, as if he was on medication or, more like it, in some form of trance after Parmesh's performance. Whatever it was, I didn't like it.

Parmesh carried on with enough charm for both of them but was on full evangelical. 'Mr Egbers, he was just like you once. He was sceptical, thought it was all madness, but he soon came to grasp the truth.

'Change is coming, James – and at the right time, people like me, the cardinals, will make themselves known. We are going to help governments regain power, help them make policies that will ensure people feel better about their situations and then start to feel good about themselves. We are going to give society a set of networks to make it better. Improve ourselves through connection, dialogue, collaboration, working together. And the technologies and services that we have and can build will allow us to give back to citizens their lost faith in the system, rebuild the social contract. We will be able to give the world hope. Do you not want to be part of that? After all, James, Mr Egbers tells me you are a builder, and he knows everything. Do you not want to be part of something creative, to build something?'

'I was part of a system once, and look where that got me. I—'

He cut in again: 'Exactly, James, exactly. But we are going to change that. Inequality is unnecessary and self-defeating. If we adjust our policies in a way that, say, Roosevelt did during the Depression, we pre-empt the revolutionaries, the crazies, the ones with the guns, the ones at the extremes, the haters. We stop them in their tracks. You want to be part of that? You want to be the very person who makes it happen?'

The yacht juddered, and I felt a bit of motion. Through the

window I could see the high ground a couple of kilometres away, and it was moving.

Parmesh stood up and pulled his T-shirt down over his start-up dad-bod stomach.

'Think about it, James. I know, a big ask, but what we are going to do for the world is big. Any questions, we can talk later. I have something to attend to now. My daughters, it is Daddy talk time. Feel free to wander round the yacht. Ask the crew for anything you need.'

A knot tightened in my gut. Not about the job offer: whatever that was, he was playing me. And it was working because I wanted to know more. I got off the settee to join him.

'Where are we going? Am I a prisoner? Am I not going back to Akaroa?'

The hand came up again. 'James, relax. All is good.'

He laid both his hands on my shoulders and gave me a smile.

Closing his eyes, he took a deep breath. 'James, you are very important to me. Not that you feel like it right now, I am sure, but you must believe me when I say I need you. I want you to join us in our crusade. Once we act, hope will be everywhere.'

Parmesh slapped my shoulders gently and his eyes smiled into mine. Then he turned and walked, stopping at the top of the stairs. 'Please, James, just sit back, relax, or maybe go out on deck, take in the air and the view of the ocean. Once we are out to sea it will be a bit colder so take a jacket. Any of the crew will show you where they are.'

He began to descend the stairs.

'James, feel free to call your family, call your sister, check that they are safe. Use the cell by the door – yours will not work. I know you are concerned, and will want to hear their voices. But, please, no word of what we have talked about. Not yet, anyway.'

His head disappeared, and Egbers went out on deck.

I was alone.

I opened my phone and saw no bars. Parmesh was right. By the door, on a small stand, a Samsung was charging. It opened without a code and there were four bars. It was only then that I remembered I didn't know Charlotte's house or mobile numbers. It was all speed dialling. I opened the contacts list on my own phone and dialled her on the Samsung.

Now I was really worried. He knew me and he knew my family: was I being made an offer I couldn't refuse?

11

Come on, Charlotte, pick up!

I tried to stay calm and logical, keep some sense of propor-
tion. But just the mention of my family had got me worried
and that fast became fear. Was he threatening my family if I
didn't join his?

I was thirteen hours ahead so it was early morning in the
UK. I just had to hear her voice to make sure everything was
okay.

Come on!

It rang and went eventually to answerphone. The default
voice told me to leave a message. I cut off and tried again.

It was finally answered, the voice gruff and sleepy.

'Simon, it's me. Sorry, I know it's early.'

'It's not, it's the middle of the night. For fuck's sake, what is
wrong with you?'

'I need to talk to Charlotte.'

Bedclothes rustled and the phone was dragged over fabric.
I heard some mumbling between them.

Charlotte's sleepy voice came on, breathy as she tried to get
herself into gear. 'James? You okay?'

'You – you're okay? Nothing's happened to Mum, Pip, the boys?'

It sounded like she was changing position, maybe sitting up. She cleared her throat. 'You're okay?'

'Just had that weird feeling something was wrong, that's all, and wanted to check. The kids – you seen them? Pip okay?'

'Yes, everything's great, we're all good. Unless you count my bag being stolen at yoga. Can you believe that? It was right by me. Anyway, I picked the boys up from school – Pip had a job interview. That's great news, isn't it? Something to do with green energy. She fetched them just before seven and she wasn't too sure how it went. Look, everything's fine.'

'Okay, sorry to wake you.' I worked hard to sound calm and change the tone. 'Tell you what, I took a picture for you today. You'll love it – great view of the bay. I'll send it in a sec. Did the boys get their kiwis?'

'Yeah, they love them. They had them yesterday. There was lots of Daddy this and Daddy that.' She laughed. 'It's okay, they haven't forgotten you. When are you back?'

'Not sure – there's a snag with the build. It might take a while to sort out. What about Mum – she okay?'

'You have to stop worrying about us all the time. You sound like Dad. Mum's still the same. She still thinks I'm her mummy most days, and she wants me to take her home, bless her. She always gets distressed when I leave. But you don't want to hear all that now. What time is it, anyway?'

'Sorry, sorry. I'll call soon after the weekend when you've seen Mum. Just say hello to them all for me, yeah?'

'Yep – and, Parker?'

'Yes, m'lady?'

'Don't forget the picture.'

'Yes, m'lady.'

She clicked off, no doubt to the sound of Simon honking about her irresponsible brother.

It wasn't the first time I'd called so early in the morning, but that was only because I hadn't thought about the time difference. Simon hadn't been a fan of the early-morning wake-up calls then, either. But Simon wasn't a fan of much, really.

I loved talking with Charlotte when I was down here, but I always felt guilty afterwards – even when I called at a civilized hour. I'd been lying to her for seven years about what I got up to. The whole family thought I had a yearly contract in New Zealand. I'd been lucky enough to get a job after our company folded. Work wasn't easy to come by in the UK and these 'yearly contracts' had been a godsend for us all.

I still did bits and pieces back in the UK, mainly because I needed a cover story. But as far as they were concerned, the one thing that was constant and helped us all was a contract I had with a shopping-mall construction firm in New Zealand. I wasn't making millions, but it was enough for a little extra to share round the family. We all needed it and, of course, it relieved the pressure when it came to paying the nursing-home bills. Plus, I got a lot more out of it than just looking after my family.

However, Simon got pissed off with it. In fact, he got pissed off with everything that had anything to do with Charlotte. I'd never understood what she saw in him. He was even pissed off that he wasn't the breadwinner in that house. He should have got his finger out of his arse and worked harder instead of being an 'artist'. Oil paintings of unicorns and castles don't pay the rent.

I opened up the photos and set about emailing the nice shot of the yacht in the bay. I used email rather than WhatsApp because yet another communication app meant it would be easier than it already was for the family to contact me. I felt I needed to be in control of our communications while I was down here.

But I had forgotten: someone else was in control of my communications right now. There were no signal bars on my mobile, just the Samsung.

I had a sudden thought about the family. It wasn't just my mobile signal that had dried up. What about my income stream?

I took some deep breaths of the ocean air. I had to think about what might be happening here. What did I need to be doing about it? What were they planning to do with me? Why was I a 'chosen one' for this so-called family?

For now, I didn't have a choice. All I could do was play along with Parmesh, keep onside.

The land slipped away as we headed out into the Pacific Ocean, and the yacht began to surge up and down as the bow cut through the waves.

I checked my mobile once again. Still no bars. That didn't make me feel good, but then I thought, Why would Parmesh let me use his mobile if any badness was planned for me? That was what I had to keep trying to tell myself.

The yacht crashed into a wave and I abandoned my attempt at logical thinking. I watched the land disappear behind me. Was I on a one-way ticket if I said no to whatever Parmesh had in mind for me?

12

It was cold and windy out on deck, even with the sun beating down. Parmesh had been right. I pulled my socks back up to my dad-tan line, my only bit of comfort at the moment being that the deck wasn't wet and soaking my wool-clad feet.

One of the crew, a small woman in her twenties, with red cheeks and blonde hair in a bun to stop it flying everywhere, ran up to me with a fleece-lined windbreaker, the yacht's name embossed on its left chest. She had a strong American accent. 'She's the Hindu goddess of knowledge, music, art, wisdom, learning – everything that's kinda cool.'

I thanked her and zipped it up to my chin. The world was instantly warmer. The Samsung was still full of strong signal. I continually checked. It made me feel better that I had contact with the outside world if I needed it.

The yacht bounced over the white horses, the coastline three or four miles to my left. We must have been travelling north.

It also made me feel better that we weren't heading out to the open sea. Not that I didn't like ocean, but land felt safer. Having a point of reference made me feel somehow that I hadn't been kidnapped. I checked the Samsung once more.

I heard Parmesh behind me before I saw him. As I turned, a crew member further along the deck ran towards a newly landed gull. The massive grey thing waited until the shouts and clapping were just centimetres away before it fired up its wings and shot away.

Parmesh was multitasking, switching his mobile from hand to hand and ear to ear as he pulled on a windcheater. The wind took away what he was saying so he motioned with his spare hand to stay where I was. He was coming to me.

Like I had places to go.

The call ended and the mobile went into the coat pocket.

'James!' His expansive wave took in the coastline. 'Magnificent, is it not? Can you imagine waking up to that every morning?'

'Absolutely.'

York, in the north-east of England, versus South Island: there never had been any competition. I'd have stayed down here the first time I came if it hadn't been for my boys. They might not be in the same house as me any more, but they still needed me, just like I needed them. There was also the rest of my family. I'd miss them if I didn't see them every so often. My parents were to blame for giving me such a happy and stable upbringing that I didn't want to leave them.

I joined Parmesh in admiring the view, both hands on the guardrail to steady myself against the waves, before the spell was broken. 'So, James, your family, your sister, they are all okay, are they not?'

I fell back to earth. 'Yes, they are.'

I was about to say thank you, but then decided against it. What if he took it as an insult? I was overthinking this. 'Why do you want me to join you? I mean, you don't even know me.'

I couldn't bring myself to say 'your family'. I didn't know if he'd used the analogy to help explain or that was how he really thought of it.

'Oh, James, I really do know all about you, everything. That is why you have become very important to me.' He kept his hands on the rail as he surveyed the coastline. 'What I need you to do and why, I will tell you once we are inside.'

He was playing with me.

'I know you are interested – you cannot help yourself. But trust me, you will like what you learn, on so many levels. All you have to do is have hope and we can make change happen.'

Waves crashed against the cliffs in the distance.

'Where are we going?'

'Christchurch. It is not far, but I love going by sea. Better for the soul than taking the helicopter. Besides, the crew need to do some maintenance, refuel, that sort of thing. And I like waffles. Café Lumes in the city? The best.'

He stopped and smiled to himself, like he was having a private moment. A gust of wind hit him from behind and blew his hair over his face momentarily. 'What do you think, James? Shall we get out of the wind and find out how to put the world straight?'

He was all smiles and I found myself mirroring him. 'Do I have a choice?'

He broke into a laugh. 'Of course you do. But I need you. You are important for our crusade, James.'

'Why can't I use my mobile?'

Parmesh pointed up to nothing in particular among the array of antennas and white spheres. 'We have a bubble, like a Faraday bubble but much better. No Wi-Fi, no cell signal can come in or out except our own.'

He pointed at the Samsung. 'Nothing else works for just over a hundred metres around the boat. Cool, do you not think? Mr Egbers likes to keep control of our world. It is safer that way.'

Just then a gull dive-bombed and got its revenge as a perfectly aimed grey and white squirt landed on his head and continued onto the shoulder of his windcheater.

I stood still, wanting to laugh but not sure what was about to happen. That soon changed as Parmesh erupted into laughter and one of the crew came running towards him with a towel.

I joined in, but not as much as I would have liked to. Parmesh wiped his hair and took off the jacket.

'It is when I talk with my kids and the gulls get their comeback, I think that is Nature's way of telling me not to get so up myself!'

He nodded at the door and the crew member took the towel and jacket away. 'Please, James, after you. Out of the wind. You have a lot of information to take onboard.'

He jumped ahead to open it for me and seemed to realize something. 'Ha! Take onboard. I just made a funny!'

I plugged the Samsung into its charger, took off my windcheater, and we sat in the same places as before.

'James, I need you to know that I and the vast majority of the other cardinals are serious about our beliefs. We really will be able to help and guide governments to reorganize, take back control and so help the people. They will depend on us. But there will be many turbulent waters to cross before we are finally there. James, I need your help.'

The door opened and the sounds of wind and the ocean entered the room along with Egbers and my boots.

'Mr Egbers there, he is my firefighter-in-chief, and I have to tell you, he does not want you to be part of our crusade, not yet anyway. He thinks you do not trust yet, and certainly not believe, and he should be taking care of this situation. He thinks he should be taking care of everything, not bringing in outsiders before they are fully confirmed.

'But I feel you are already a convert, James – you are just practising a different version of the same belief. Besides, sometimes it can be best practice to have a generalist onboard. Do you not think?'

He got a nod and I got a smile in return.

Those eyes were starting to have that medicated look once more, but now I knew that, whatever the drug was doing, it was coming from within him. There was a messiah inside him, pushing itself out through his eyes. Whatever was going on between the two, all I could do was let them get on with it.

'Thank you, James. So. Back to the CE business plan. Think Catholic Church. The top guy? That would be God, right? But we do not have one of those in our religion. Popes always start wars to prove that their imaginary best friend is better than that of the other guys. That is not our gig. We are about saving lives.'

I nodded. I got it so far.

'So, normally below God you have the emissary – number one, *numero uno*, the Pope. This is the guy with the hotline to headquarters. But we do not have one of them, either – not yet. With me so far, James?'

He got another nod.

'Good, James, that is good, because that is the problem I need you to fix. So, back to it. Below the Pope we have the cardinals. That is us guys, the cognitive elite. We are always thinking. We are always working stuff out. Wheeling, dealing, managing the cash – getting ready, doing all the backroom stuff for when the change happens. And when it does, we will be there, ready, just like all good cardinals. You see, the Pope and his cardinals will guide the people via their governments, who will depend on our resource. But when the time comes for us to do our thing, we will need a leader, we will need a pope.

'But that is when the trouble will start for us cardinals. We will be good buddies to each other and talk the talk and show that we are doing the right thing, but just like any religious order, we will all eventually start to fight and claw and scratch and lie and deceive our way to the top. You see, everyone wants to be pope and some of the cardinals, well, they do not have friends, just interests, and being human normally means those interests are just to do with themselves.'

He gave another of his pauses for it all to sink in, and it did. But so what?

'What is it you want me to do?'

Parmesh glanced at Egbers, then back at me. 'James, I need you to steal something for me. A ledger. Here, in New Zealand.'

'That it? Just steal a book?'

I might have been curious, but now I definitely wanted out of this shit. When something sounded simple there was a reason, and that reason was never a good one.

Parmesh nodded with a smile, and I wondered if he knew what I was thinking.

'Just a book. But, James, what is written on its pages holds the key to who I should and need to be – the Pope. It belongs to Eduardo Castro, one of our cardinals, who really does not have the same vision as us.

'Eduardo, in Mr Egbers's words, which are always perfectly matched, is a husk of a man. Mr Egbers should know – he once worked for him. Eduardo reminds me of a modern-day Caligula. A damaged man with a damaged psychology and great power, yet we expect him to behave correctly.

'But he cannot. He is unable to. He can only fill his emptiness with his ego and greed. He has no hope for our futures, just his own. The information, the names, the places he has written in the ledger, together they will give him the juice to become pope. It simply cannot be allowed to happen. I have to take possession of the ledger, and I need you to get it for me.'

Parmesh fixed his unblinking eyes deep into mine. I was making a supreme effort to do the same when Egbers had something to add: 'Mr Castro thinks that just because he breaks all the rules it entitles him to make them. That cannot be allowed to happen. He is not important to us, just the ledger.'

Parmesh didn't relax his focus as he slowly nodded in agreement.

'Exactly, Mr Egbers, only the ledger. James, none of the other cognitive elite know that the ledger exists and we have to thank Mr Egbers for bringing its existence to my attention. I must be the one who has the ledger so that when the change comes it happens for the greater good, as any religion should guarantee – but when has that ever happened?'

I shrugged. Religions are man-made corporate institutions. And, like any corporation, to survive a religion must grow its brand, compete for market share. It had to be on top of its game just like Apple or Starbucks.

Parmesh let that settle in my head, his eyes burning into mine for good measure.

'So, James . . . do you want to be part of something that changes the world, that brings peace and prosperity to all?'

Another pause. I wasn't sure if it was there to fill. I couldn't have, even if I'd wanted to. My head spun. Whose wouldn't?

Parmesh had no problem filling the vacuum. 'You know what, James? You were not a failure to yourself, or even your family, when you got caught today. People like us, we do not fail. We learn, make new opportunities, and move on.

'So far, your journey has been all about payback. But today

you have the opportunity to change the very system that brought your family all that damned misery, James. Now, that is an even better ride. Do you not agree?'

But agreeing to anything didn't concern me.

What did was: *Why me?*

So I asked him.

13

'James, I am so sorry, but now is not the time. You must trust me. You will be very well rewarded, not just for your work but for your trust. For the rest of their lives, your family, all of them, will never have to worry about anything other than how to enjoy themselves. And even the next generation.'

I hadn't expected that: a sense of security, relief, had been presented to me on a plate. Could opportunity and timing be colliding in front of me?

'How much are you offering?'

'I have not really thought that far.' He pushed his hair behind his ears. 'Say, fifteen million US. No, let us say sterling. Now that is also something to get excited about, do you not think?'

Excited? Now I knew what it would feel like to see all your lottery numbers come up. Your head would be buzzing, but you'd be thinking, Is it for real?

Keep it logical. Just for lifting a book? That was a big number, and if it sounded too good to be true, it probably was. 'What exactly am I letting myself in for?'

Parmesh gave the biggest smile yet as he took that for a

yes, and I supposed it was. It had to be: what else was I going to say? But I still needed to get off this yacht and feel some control of events around me.

'I need to know the where and the when – or how can I tell you whether or not I can do the job successfully?'

'Details.' Parmesh pushed it aside with a wave of his hand. 'That is what I like about you, James. Details matter. The best early-stage investments in people appear obvious in retrospect. So many people jump to the money without having the detail worked out first. That is not good, James. But you, you are good.'

He threw a look to Egbers. 'We have the right guy.'

I didn't see Egbers's reaction.

Parmesh leant over and shook my hand. It might have been the Brit reserve in me, but the shake seemed to go on for just a few seconds longer than it should have, and his eye contact was still too far on the messianic side of intent for comfort.

'Thank you, James. Thank you.'

The South African was on his feet and waiting for me between the settee and the door, my boots in his hands.

Parmesh motioned for me to join him. 'James, the helicopter will take you back to Akaroa. Mr Egbers will tell you everything you need to know. We will talk soon and often, James. Again, thank you. This is such vital work. Our crusade is so important. We are willing to die making it a reality. That is how strong our hope is for our future.'

Egbers opened the door for me and stayed a pace behind. It was still windy on deck, but the yacht was slowing. The engines of the helicopter whined into action.

I was pulled in two directions. I felt like I'd been sold snake oil but not even walked away with a bottle of it. Was he a real billionaire philosopher? It really didn't matter. I needed to get off *Saraswati* and onto dry land. For all the smiles, I was still being held against my will. Once I was away from there, I needed to take my time and do what I was good at. Working out situations with a practical, logical mind, thinking about problems methodically. And then I could be creative and innovative about finding the solutions that would get me out of this shit, or not. The money, even if not true, had still got my head churning. I had fucked up and got caught, but first of all I had to get off this yacht in one piece, then find out what I could about the job without too much contact with Parmesh, Egbers and that Brit.

Then decide.

Egbers made sure I had my boots back on and then he strapped me into what was effectively a red leather settee in the rear of the helicopter, facing the cockpit and the back of the pilot's helmet. He jumped into a matching settee that faced me. No seatbelt for Mr Egbers.

The rotors turned and their noise was soon deafening. He shoved a headset into my hands before putting on his own. The rotors were suddenly just faint background noise. His voice was tinny but the threatening tone was undiminished.

He half closed his eyes in disgust, then pulled himself forward on the settee and leant over to me. He adjusted my microphone. 'Speak normal, no shouting.'

I nodded as if he had given me advice on something I didn't already know.

The helicopter lurched from the deck and gained height, then swivelled. *Saraswati* disappeared behind us. Waves crashed against the stretch of coastline dead ahead.

The South African leant over and poked me in the shoulder. 'Listen to me. You're going to Queenstown.' He handed me a white envelope the size of a postcard. 'Don't look at it now, just listen to me. In there is Castro's address, where the ledger is held. There is also a credit card. The PIN is 1234. Use it for hotels, cars, as you want – change the PIN, do whatever you like.'

I nodded.

'In Queenstown, do your recce. I will contact you when I'm ready. Until then, that's all you need to know. You understand me?'

I got the message. Shut up and do as you're told. Fine by me. I just wanted this heli to land and me to step out of it to be alone.

What had taken a couple of hours on *Saraswati* was rapidly being reclaimed as we skimmed over a green mountaintop and into the mouth of the inlet. At the far end lay Akaroa.

I felt the hard plastic of the credit card as I tucked the envelope into my shorts, and very soon I could make out the shell of Parmesh's colonial house, the churned-up earth and the machinery around it. We overflew the property to a field behind, which I knew Parmesh also owned, along with as much surrounding land as he had been able to lay his hands on.

The helicopter dipped its nose, and it wasn't long before two hands the size of shovels undid my seatbelt, but then shoved a hand against my chest to prevent me from moving.

'You have not asked one question. Why? Why not?'

He could read me like a book.

'Mr Mani is a great man.' It wasn't an observation, it was a warning. His eyes seared into me as the helicopter gently settled on the grass. 'A very kind and thoughtful man. He is a visionary. He will save us all.'

His face came to within a couple of centimetres of mine. I could smell his cleanliness again. 'Mr Mani finds hope in everyone, and hope has two beautiful daughters. Anger and courage. Mr Mani has courage to see the way things could be.

If you disappoint Mr Mani, you will see anger. I will make sure you watch us rip your children's mother limb from limb before we do the same to you. Your children – what will become of them? Clear?'

Crystal.

'Mr Mani will never know what has just passed between us. He has more important things to be dealing with. But make no mistake, you will perform whatever task he requires of you.'

The rotors slowed but didn't stop. 'Now get out. Go straight out at ninety degrees from the door. Do not go near the rear rotors. Do not run.' He pulled off my headphones and yanked the door open.

The downdraught battered the back of my shirt and head before slowly dissipating as the helicopter took off.

At last I'd got what I wanted: to be back on firm ground and away from that lot. However, my great plan to work out what to do had just crashed and burnt. Once family are involved, two things happen: anger at them being threatened and the need to liquidate anyone who could hurt them; then, the realization that if you love them you're fucked, because with family no risk is acceptable.

It looked like I was hitting the road.

PART THREE

14

Queenstown
Tuesday, 27 November 2018

Speargrass Flat lay about ten kilometres north-east of Queenstown as the crow flew, except it was such a mega-exclusive area all the crows probably took Ubers.

Not that there was much to indicate wealth, driving north along the two kilometres of Hunter Road in my baby-size rental Toyota. The narrow strip of tarmac with grass and gravel at either side was nothing special, the only display of ostentation the double yellow lines down the centre of the road. Power and phone lines branched off every five hundred metres or so towards where all the money was tucked away in very private estates that were surrounded by manicured lawns and banks of thickly planted fir trees. It was well on the way to becoming the New Zealand version of Atherton.

To an outsider it wouldn't have been obvious why, but the price of real estate had soared round there over the last two years. I happened to know it wasn't just because of the views, even though there couldn't have been many more stunning places to come and sit out the apocalypse. No matter which direction you looked, mountains cut into the clear blue horizon.

This was *Lord of the Rings* country. I knew that because I did all the film location tours the first time I was here, on the Dalladine job, exactly two years ago to the day.

But Dalladine wasn't on my mind now. It was Eduardo Castro or, rather, his house: Sanctuary.

Not that he was the registered owner – they never were. Sanctuary was registered to a trust company, and its registered address was at a lawyer's firm in Auckland.

When I was about halfway along the road, the sat-nav gripped me in a strict New Zealand accent to say I was nearly at my destination. I started looking for a driveway, gate or some kind of sign that indicated the place.

Wooden ranch-style fencing flanked the road on the left, and ahead more tarmac came in at a right angle onto Hunter Road. Very soon, a natural stone wall took over, then thick wooden gates, two metres tall, with all the usual electrical arms and a steel press-button entry box. But no house sign. Was it Sanctuary? If so, the new-looking, light-grey concrete road should snake the 1,986 metres through the grounds to where the front elevation of the house would be.

I carried on, and maybe ten metres past the gate the sat-nav told me I had reached my destination. I continued towards the T-junction, roughly a kilometre away, and the end of Hunter Road. The temperature was in the mid-twenties and I was grateful for the air-conditioning.

I turned left at the junction and headed west, looking for higher ground to have a better view of Sanctuary. I'd been there for two days now and there'd been no contact from Egbers or anyone else. I'd driven down to Queenstown overnight in the hire car the credit card had given me. My time around the lake in Queenstown had been taken up checking Google Maps, online planning permissions, anything open-source about Sanctuary, trying to get an idea in my head of what I'd hopefully soon be looking at. I wanted a steer on the construction materials. Was it timber-framed, concrete, steel-framed, blockwork? What did I have to get through, over or under? And, of course, as on all my jobs, I tried to find out who the contractors were, because once I knew that, I could research their website, blogs and social media for work practices and maybe find a way in.

My problem was that the house was already built, and that was a first for me. This time, I wouldn't be able to create a back door that would wait for me to open it. That worried me: I was entering a whole new world of problems that I'd managed to avoid in the past.

But what really concerned me – well, scared me – was the thought of what would happen if I couldn't get in to take the ledger in the first place. That fear was the prime mover behind me being extra diligent in my research and not calling home. I wanted to keep focused and not give away that there was a major problem. Charlotte would be able to tell: she always could.

On the drive south I had played about with the idea of the family and me just disappearing off the face of the earth. I knew it was a stupid idea – it was a fantasy. I'd have to kidnap Pip, for a start. She wanted to be away from me, not for us to be forced together. Plus, I would be admitting to her that the last seven years had been a lie: she and the boys had been living off the proceeds of crime, and now, because of me, they were in danger. That would put a very firm lid on any chance of us getting back together. If we survived, of course. Where would we go? How would we hide? They would find us. Money buys you influence, buys you power, and it buys you knowledge.

I took Egbers's threat seriously. Even if I felt he and the Brit wouldn't follow it up, I still had to assume they would.

I had to accept that I was caught, and that I had no option but to do as Parmesh wanted. Whatever the ledger's contents did for him wasn't my concern.

I had to stop thinking and get on with the job. It was the only way I could see of getting Pip, the boys and me out of this in one piece. Who knew? The money might just be real.

The road climbed as I followed signs for somewhere called Arthur's Point, and the higher I got the less habitation there was to be seen. The houses were concentrated on the lower ground of Speargrass Flat and around the lake.

I pulled over onto the grass verge and the nose of the Toyota dipped down towards the dry drainage ditch, kicking up a little red dust. Sanctuary was below me now, just over three kilometres away, among the lush greenery of Speargrass.

I fished in my daysack. I was dressed exactly the same as I had been on Sunday, the nerdy Brit walker, but this time, instead of a laser measure in my daysack, I had a pair of 25x70 Celestrons. Christmas was everywhere in Queenstown and it had felt wrong to see Santa and snowmen in shop windows while the sun was melting ice-creams. The salesman who had sold me the telescope I used to recce Dalladine's house, but didn't make the connection as I was dressed normally in jeans, assured me the binoculars I was treating myself to were just as good for watching kiwis at the nature park as for looking at the stars. They were expensive, but he hadn't raised an eyebrow when I produced the card. Queenstown was a holiday town: people splashed the cash there and the locals weren't exactly destitute.

I powered down the passenger window and heard the breeze, then some birds chirping. I took in as much of the house as I could see through the binos, which wasn't much. The new instant garden was doing its job and blocked quite a lot, but from what I could make out, it fitted the plans I'd seen. The light-grey concrete drive was exposed at intervals in the gaps made by the trees and shrubs, and the distance looked correct. It stopped maybe twenty metres from the front of Sanctuary and turned into a dark grey, maybe black, slabbed walkway. Any vehicle then turned left to a set of long, low, empty carports.

The building was clad in dark-green aluminium panelling, a multi-roofed structure, stone and glass elevations, seven beds with baths, and a floor space of just over 780 square metres. Plus, there was the photo-voltaic panel array way to the west of the house. There were seventy PVs on the plans and they all seemed to be in place, looking like a farmer's field that had been turned over to green energy. A few hours of New Zealand sun should provide enough power to keep the house running for days – if the energy was being stored, that was.

Something that hadn't appeared on anything I'd seen stuck out like a sore thumb: a smaller building, detached, two levels, maybe seventy or eighty metres to the west, behind the main house. According to the plans, that area was earmarked for a large water feature – a big pond or a small lake, I supposed, depending on what you're used to. Google Maps showed the main house during its construction, and a big hole that I'd assumed was to be filled with water. Instead, there stood a five-bedroom-sized house – or, at least, a building big enough to be one, had it had any windows. I could see just two solid elevations through the Celestrons, both of the same stone as the main house.

Between the two structures there was grass and ornamental gardens. No driveway, path or even a track worn by footfall across the grass. Clearly there were no plans to throw Granny in the outhouse. Or maybe there were, and they just didn't like her.

No way was I going to try to see the dead elevations, because that would mean entering the grounds – and I wouldn't do that until I absolutely had to. There were other ways – maybe, depending on whether or not the house was occupied. But that would be up to Egbers.

I powered up the window to let the air-con do its stuff as I drove back to Queenstown.

15

As I reached the lower ground I could begin to see Lake Wakatipu, which looked to me like a fat snake slinking along the floor – a very big snake, about eighty kilometres long. On, above and around it were powerboats, paragliders and billboards advertising bungee jumping, mountain biking, skiing, snowboarding, anything the adrenalin junkie needed.

Queenstown was Adventure Central, but it looked after nerds like me too. There were walks and tours, and if I didn't want to wakeboard behind a speedboat I could just sit in the back of a 4x4 on a photography safari or check out Hobbit Land again.

I liked Queenstown a lot. The people were friendly and the whole place felt healthy. It was a long throw from York's traffic jams, homelessness and drug problems.

Soon I was on the outskirts, following the main road along the lake. I looked across at Kelvin Heights, the golf course and Dalladine's house. I could just about pick it out in the distance, but only because I knew where to look. He probably liked it down here on the lake because Kelvin Heights was so close to Frankton airport. But I wondered how he'd thought about his own piece of Paradise these past two years, knowing that he wasn't as safe as he'd thought he'd be. I hoped it still kept him awake at night, even after, probably, renovating the whole intruder system. Or maybe he had moved, the stress just too much. I hoped so.

For all that, as I checked out the lake once more, I felt a twinge of jealousy at the Dalladines' lifestyle. The four kids must have been having an amazing time there. I fantasized for a moment or two about what it must be like to be in his shoes. My boys, just turned ten, would be on water skis in the summer, snow skis in the winter, and at all times of the year living in a safe place. Most importantly, they'd be happy. At the moment, they weren't. Far from it. How could they be, with all the drama – or, more like, the lack of drama – going on between their parents?

Pip and I had met at college and were full of dreams and aspirations. What could be out there to stop us? Three things, it turned out: the crash, and the twins, Jack and Tom, all arriving at the same time. The Afghan tour didn't help. Six months of her being worried sick about me that turned to resentment. After all, I was doing something for me, but what about her, left at home with two babies? She had a point, though I didn't see it that way at the time.

It ended when I'd come home from work very late one night and was so exhausted I went straight to bed. Pip came up maybe two hours later and I was still awake. I could never shake off the worry of trying to make the business work, make ends meet. She asked me what I wanted from my life because I was nothing more than a squatter in hers.

I didn't blame her for packing her bags. I was consumed with trying to keep the business going – for all of us, I'd thought. Unfortunately, I hadn't understood then that Pip also had a life and wanted to do more with it. We tried to get back together and make a go of things, but with my anger at the world and travelling to New Zealand every year to satisfy that anger, it didn't work and we drifted apart. I couldn't blame her for wanting to end with a clear-cut divorce.

She was an excellent mother and let me try hard to be a good father, so maybe there would be a time when we patched things up. As the years went by, I missed her and the kids more and more. Pip was still close to Charlotte: they had clicked from the very first day they met, about a month after we had started to go out with each other. There had never been any conflict about my seeing the boys, but . . . it wasn't the same as being together as a family.

Anyway, maybe that was for later. Right now I had to get a grip, didn't I? Once again, I had to force myself to think of real things, things that mattered, things I could do now. There was only one item on the agenda, and that was finding out how to get myself inside Sanctuary. There was no other business.

My little Toyota suited my socks-pulled-up-to-the-knees look, but as I pulled up at the Crown Plaza next to the ranks of 4x4s and big touring cars it seemed a little out of place. The hotel was a concrete eighties-style building overlooking the lake. It was large, anonymous, perfect for me. I liked such places. The last time I'd stayed in Queenstown it had been at the holiday park on the outskirts of town, with the rest of the campers. The hotel was just as big and impersonal, but armed with a credit card and having no idea of how long I'd be there, I'd thought, Why not take the spa option?

The card was a regular MasterCard with my name on it. The bank's motif, embossed in the top right corner, was a gold pineapple with the initials SIB. I wondered what they stood for, not that it mattered. The only thing that did was that it worked.

I locked the Toyota and slung the daysack over my shoulder to a background of shrieks coming from an adrenalin powerboat hurtling its passengers around the lake. Then, as I turned to head for Reception, I heard a pair of vehicle doors slam shut behind me.

Egbers and the Brit were leaving the sides of a gleaming black BMW X5 and making straight for me. All the happy fantasies of skiing with the kids evaporated.

16

There wasn't a lot to say to them as they came closer – nothing to say at all, really. Not yet, anyway. I could have asked them how they'd found me, but why bother? I'd just get on with what I needed to do. I had to accept they were the masters; but that wasn't a problem for me. Just get on with the job.

I followed them, a couple of steps behind, as they approached the automatic glass doors into Reception.

I'd been racking my brain but still had no idea why Parmesh had chosen me for this instead of using these two, or all the other resources he no doubt had at his fingertips.

I didn't like the negativity that the two Templars brewed up inside me. What happened when I had delivered the ledger? Why would they need me alive? Maybe that was why I'd been chosen: because I was expendable. But why take the chance of me failing? Why not use someone much more skilled at this stuff? There was nothing I could do but hope that Parmesh really did have a reason, a non-expendable reason, for picking me.

Almost in the same breath, I had to tell myself it wasn't worth thinking about. Knowing my fate wouldn't change anything.

We rode the lift in silence and they didn't so much as look at me. It wasn't until we got to my room and I had opened the door for Egbers to enter first and the Brit to come in behind me that the South African started talking – even before I'd been able to place my daysack on the bed.

'How long will it take?'

I was hoping for a question I could answer. 'It's impossible to say yet. I need more information. I've looked at all the planning, all the surveys, and I've been trying to find a way to—'

Egbers wasn't interested. 'What is it you want?'

He took in the view of the lake beyond the glass sliding doors and small balcony, and the Brit had perched himself on the edge of the settee.

'First off, is the house occupied? Does Castro live there?'

Egbers didn't bother to turn and face me but kept his gaze on the lake. 'It's unoccupied.'

'Do you have any details on intruder systems?'

'No. You'll know as soon as we do.'

'What about the ledger? You know where it's kept and how?'

'No. You'll know as soon as we do.'

'You don't know much, do you? How am I supposed to give you a time frame when—'

The Brit's mobile buzzed. Egbers turned back to the room and thrust his hand up, like a traffic cop, for me to stop. He pointed to the bed. 'Sit. This might help.'

I complied.

Directly opposite me, the Brit spoke into his mobile. 'We've got him. You ready?'

Egbers moved close to me and bent at the hip, his hands on his thighs, his face right into mine. 'Ask what you need to know. Do not say anything about the ledger. Just ask about the house. Do not ask over-complicated questions.'

The Brit held up his phone screen to me and I saw what

looked like a wide passport version of a man, South East Asian, maybe.

But this was no passport picture.

His face was bloodied, bruised, his lips swollen. One of his cheeks was split. He was crying.

The Brit turned up the volume to make sure I heard his sobs and gasps as he tried to breathe through the mucus and red saliva streaming from his nose and mouth. 'He can't see you. Ask him what you need to know.'

I could see this guy's pain, hear his fear and sheer desperation as he whimpered, totally dominated and defeated.

My eyes flicked between the two of them as they checked me out for a reaction.

It wasn't the first time I had seen pain. It might have come from someone who'd been shot, blown up, or was under fire, but the look in their eyes was always the same.

Egbers was impatient. 'Ask him.'

I took a breath and thought about what was important. 'Is there a safe? A strongroom? Anywhere that valuables would be kept?'

A voice in front of the Asian, belonging to whoever's hand was holding the smartphone, translated. Sharp. Aggressive. I didn't know the language, but the shouted commands made the man wince, trying to protect his face with every syllable blasted at him.

He hesitated. It was obvious to me that he was thinking, not trying to avoid.

More shouts flew at him from the translator, angrier, more threatening.

The man spoke, blood-stained spittle flying from his swollen lips to hit the camera eye. I couldn't understand what he said, but it was clear to me he was begging. His shoulders trembled.

The smartphone holder translated what we had heard. 'He

doesn't know anything about a safe. He was brought in with the rest of the Filipino crew to work on the underground construction, the basement.'

The poor man was now in full flow, but the tone was still begging, desperate to please.

'That's all he did. One room and a toilet. But they were sent home before they finished it.'

The translator wasn't satisfied with the last piece of information. It didn't make sense to him.

The Filipino pleaded, looking not at the camera but at whoever was holding it.

The smartphone holder's free hand, dark-skinned, swung into shot with a sharp slap to the side of the man's face. He fell off his chair, his imploring magnified tenfold over the speakers, and collapsed onto pitted concrete, wherever in the world he was.

This was getting out of hand. The state of him was enough for me to grasp that he would have told us by now if he knew anything.

I turned to Egbers, who was still close so he could also see the screen. 'Tell him to stop. He's telling the truth. The guy doesn't know anything else – he's not meant to. I believe him. Just let me talk to him.'

Egbers and the Brit looked at each other and the Brit gave instructions. 'Get him seated.'

We all watched as the hand pulled at the blood-stained grey shirt to get him back onto a wooden dining chair.

His head was pulled back, with what was obviously a sharp instruction to look straight ahead at the camera lens.

Tears mixed with mucus and saliva dribbled from his face onto his shirt.

I spoke into the mic. 'Ask him if he knows anything about the other building – the one behind the main house.'

The translation was almost simultaneous. A reply came back, eager. Anything to stop the pain. He kept saying the same thing, trying hard to impress, show that he was helping.

The translation came back over the speaker. 'He says he wasn't there when they worked on anything above the ground. All he worked on was below.'

'Okay. Ask him what he didn't finish building. Maybe the drainage. What was left to be done below ground before the house was built?'

The translation began and the tears and begging intensified with each of his answers. The translator got angrier, demanding he talk more. It felt things were about to get out of control again.

'Just back off the guy and let him talk.'

The Filipino stared into the lens at me. I didn't need an interpreter to tell me he was pleading with me to believe him.

What I finally heard confirmed I was right.

'He says they just laid the concrete for the basement. He says all that was left to build was the basement wall at the back of the house. He doesn't know why – they were told not to ask questions or they wouldn't get paid.'

I turned to Egbers. 'That's all I need.'

The Brit closed down and sat back to relax in the settee. Egbers went over to join him. Once he was seated, he continued talking about the ledger as if the past few minutes had never happened.

'Do not open it, do not record it, do not ask what is in it. You will enter and exit the house covertly. There has to be a long delay before anyone discovers that the ledger has gone. You understand?'

I shrugged. It was what I would have expected. 'Castro? What about him? Is he a wanker-banker, then? I'd just like to know what might happen to me if I get caught in there.'

The Brit laughed as he dug inside his leather jacket. He threw a large plastic Jiffy-bag at me, big enough to take a box folder.

Egbers had started to kick off his boots and socks to reveal that both feet had been burnt. The creamy white and hairless skin stopped at his ankles. He pointed down at them as he tried to wiggle his toes. Maybe six or seven moved. 'I worked for him as a young man. I was loyal. He thought I had stolen a pair of his new four-hundred-dollar sneakers. So I was held down and he used acid to make sure that when I was finally able to wear them they would be out of fashion. That answer your question?'

I nodded as he put his socks back on. The move to Parmesh with the ledger intelligence made sense. Revenge. But now he was a fully paid-up member of the Parmesh family.

'Completely.'

Egbers could see my confusion as I held up the envelope. 'The ledger will be sealed in that before you leave the house with it.'

I dropped it on the bed, wondering what there was to stop me checking it out, maybe even copying the pages of whatever was so important.

Egbers was ahead of me.

'Don't even think about it. We'll be with you all the way.'

'I need your help to recce Sanctuary.'

'Depends.'

'Can I use the drones? Then I could look at the house, particularly the outbuilding. I still don't know if the grounds have alarms – if I walk in there and set something off . . .'

There was no reply from Egbers: he wanted me to sing for my supper.

'Do they work at night? They have night vision? I was thinking that we could go there—'

Egbers shook his head. 'No. Daylight. Better resolution. They'll be here tomorrow. Give me your cell.'

I pulled it out of my shorts, very conscious of the Brit's dark brown eyes staring at me with total disdain. I got off the bed holding the mobile in front of me, and it was the Brit who waved his hand. Egbers was finishing off getting his boots back on.

'Open it up.'

I keyed in my password and handed it over. He started tapping on the screen.

'Can I ask why I was chosen? Parmesh has the world at his disposal.'

Egbers's eyes drilled into mine – with boredom or indifference, it was hard to tell. Either way, they were telling me to shut up.

The Brit passed me back my mobile. 'You're now on Whats-App. Keep the app updated at all times, and keep a signal, and you'll be called. Any of the two numbers in the group, okay? You got that?'

'Can I call them if I need something or there's a problem?'

'Any of the numbers you call will be answered.'

They didn't wait for me to acknowledge. They stood up in unison and headed for the door.

'That builder, what happened? Aren't you worried someone could have seen that?'

If they didn't even care that there'd been witnesses, how was that going to play out for me?

The Brit sighed, almost like he took pity on me. 'It's secure – if you keep it updated.'

'Will he be okay? He's just a worker, nothing special. He knows nothing of value.'

They stopped and turned back from the door. It was the Brit who spoke as he pulled out his mobile and started to tap.

'You understand that was done to help you?'

He jerked his head at my mobile on the bed. 'This isn't a game. Open the link. And if Charlotte is still worried about her bag being stolen last week, it's okay, I didn't use her cards. I just needed to know I had the right Charlotte.'

They left.

I waited until they had gone and picked up my mobile.

I opened the link, and dropped to the bed as if a boulder had hit me on top of the head. A supermarket tannoy was making an announcement about the day's discounts. It was our local Tesco. Jack and Tom were holding the sides of a trolley and jumping with excitement while their mother checked out the freezer cabinet. I knew exactly what Pip was looking for: it was the milk lollies they both loved.

I sank deeper into the bed as the Brit appeared onscreen. He walked up to her, asking her something, I couldn't hear what. She pointed across the aisles and he thanked her with a smile and moved on.

The screen went blank.

And so did my brain as I collapsed back onto the pillows. I knew I was right about Egbers and the Brit, but it didn't make me feel clever.

17

Wednesday, 28 November 2018

It had been a very long and restless night. I'd kept replaying the Filipino's screen images in my head, then carried through with different scenarios of how to get out of this nightmare. Every one of them ended with Egbers and the Brit following Pip and the kids out of Tesco and carrying out their threat, but that still didn't stop me going over it again and again.

In the end, I'd given up trying to sleep, and that was why, two hours too early, I found myself parked further along the road than where I'd stopped to check Sanctuary through my binos. But as Dad used to say: if you can't sleep because you keep waking up worrying, then sleep less and you won't worry so much.

On the high ground two Ks short of Arthur's Point, which I now knew because I'd killed time driving to have a look, there was a small suburban area. Just short of it, at the base of the mountains, was where the drone people wanted me to be.

Thirty minutes to go.

The sun was so strong I had to pull down the Toyota's visor

to shield my eyes. Pity my brain didn't get the same respite from my worries. I carried on thinking and overthinking, and generally being scared. Not on my own account: I accepted I'd fucked up by being caught. It was everyone back home I was fearful for. My thought had been that leaving the hotel early and driving to meet the drone-heads would clear the demons, but no such luck. I landed up with a long wait that only intensified the Armageddon inside my head.

I thought maybe I'd just tell Parmesh what had happened, that Egbers was making me do this whether I liked it or not. Obviously he'd made the offer but the harshness of what followed – did he know? What if he didn't? Parmesh jumping up and down and throwing a wobbler at Egbers, would that make things even worse? Where would that leave me – and, more importantly, my family?

It crossed my mind for about the fiftieth time that maybe I should go to the police. But I had the same answer all fifty times: Then what? Get arrested for seven years' worth of bur- glaries, jailed and leave the rest of the family unprotected? No.

There was absolutely no way round it. I came to the same conclusion every time: I was going to have to man up and get on with this quest, crusade, whatever they were calling it, get it done, hope they kept their end of the deal and we were all safe, maybe even rich, afterwards.

A red Seat 4x4 trundled past and stopped about a hundred metres further down the road, did a three-point turn and, as they drove back towards me, I could see it was the drone people. They stopped parallel to me, with the driver's win- dow down. I did the same, and there was a smile.

'Hi! Morning, you remember us?'

Very West Coast American.

I nodded.

'Okay. Come on, man. We've got a place to go.'

The Seat moved off slowly, giving me time to turn the car and follow. I wondered if they knew the big picture, or just the little bit of it they were helping with.

It wasn't long before we veered left onto a dirt track and started to go uphill. I drove into a rooster tail of red dust, but only for a minute or two. They stopped on the edge of a copse of pine trees, and the front doors flew open. Both were in the same tribe, shoulder-length hair, maybe late twenties, early thirties at a push. They wore jeans and T-shirts, the skinnier one in black, the driver in blue, an Old Navy.

It was the driver who started the conversation, his hand extended, maybe because he was the same side of the vehicle as me.

'James, right?'

I flinched. 'Yes.'

'I'm James, too. And that guy there,' he thumbed as he let go of my hand, 'he's Jamie.'

I nodded at Jamie, not believing a word I was hearing. He waved before lifting the tailgate to expose a large aluminium box.

James joined Jamie at the tailgate and I followed.

'What do you want to look at, man?'

'Everything, basically. The house, the outbuilding, all around the grounds. You able to show me close-ups? Window frames, that sort of thing – maybe even the locks?'

They glanced at each other and laughed. James turned to me. 'Man, we can give you whatever you need. We got you talking on your cell – Lady P, right, comes up on your screen with a small *p*?'

They fist-bumped each other and I mirrored their smiles, acknowledging that they were right to be proud of their work.

The unloading was finished and the drone was on top of the closed box. The camera beneath it was much smaller than I would have expected it to be, given the kind of power and clarity they were talking about. The battery rack contained two large packs that sat on the tailgate, and the console strap was going over the head of James – the driver and now the pilot.

Jamie picked up the drone with both hands and held it above his head. The thing sprang to life, its six rotors buzzing like a very angry food mixer. The drone lifted, then stopped less than a metre above his head, motionless and obedient.

James played with the controls. There were two joysticks and two small screens, with gradients for level, balance, that sort of thing, I presumed. The drone's legs slowly emerged from its belly before the claws opened, closed, and turned 360 degrees as if the eagle had woken up, which I supposed it had. Then the camera under its belly copied and also spun a full 360, and the buzzing got louder as the rotors increased their effort. The eagle leapt into the air, the legs retracting into its body. I tried to follow its movement against the bright blue sky but within a couple of seconds the machine had disappeared, and so had its noise.

Jamie, job done, perched himself on the tailgate and offered round a tub of gum, but there were no takers.

James concentrated on his console. 'Not long now. Just a few more checks and we're ready to rock 'n' roll.'

He stopped in his tracks. 'Whoa! We got some jamming.'

Jamie was off the tailgate like a scalded cat. I stood the other side and looked at the screen. Somewhere out there was a lake, a very small one by New Zealand standards, but it was enough for a couple to have parked their RV and be enjoying breakfast. A table was out and two little chairs, but now they had moved on from the croissants. Beach towels were laid out on the grass by the water's edge and they were hard at it, totally oblivious to the drone high above them. The detail was amazing.

James grinned at me. 'I love this job, man.'

'I bet you've seen it all?'

They fist-bumped. Another group, family, whatever, I didn't care to join.

'Clock's ticking and all that.'

They looked reluctant but the camera zoomed out and the drone travelled.

James was back to being professional. 'Okay, thirty-six minutes before we have to change batteries. After that you've got another forty. And that's it, my man. You get it all on a stick – including the jamming, if you want?'

'The house is all I need.'

'Still, more fun for us than chasing gulls.'

The drone was flown around Sanctuary, and the forty-eight acres of its grounds before it returned for its battery change. Its next flight was all about the outbuilding.

I watched in amazement as Jamie held up his arms and the eagle zoned in on him at speed, its legs and claws out, like it was about to grab him and fly him away to its nest. Then it stopped in its tracks above his outstretched arms before ever so gently descending until its claws gripped Jamie's hands, like two trapeze artists meeting mid-swing. As soon as Jamie's hands made contact, the rotors stopped and there was silence.

Jamie put the drone on the box and the two battery packs were replaced, much the same as I did with electric hand tools.

My head had been full of questions. I kept telling myself it would be wrong to ask any of them just yet: I should keep my mouth shut and my head down until the job was done.

But it wasn't working. These two were approachable. Maybe they had answers.

'You guys worked for Parmesh long?'

James didn't bother looking at me as he checked his console and kept a casual tone. 'Not *for*, man . . . *with*. Five years and counting. He funded our start-up and we've been with him ever since.'

'You like him? He seems a good man.'

Jamie had the drone back above his head and the rotors burst into electrical life. 'Sure, he's cool. He even bought our company after seeding it from the get-go. Our first meeting with him was, like, trying to get some funding, but in a couple of minutes he turned it into a working session. He gets things, man.'

'The drone looks like something out of a sci-fi war film.'

Both of the Js were very happy with that remark, but James got in there first. 'Thank you! That's exactly what they are – or will be soon. We've just armoured them up with some cool carbon-fibre composite so they can be used to carry wounded guys out of the battlefield, people from burning buildings, all that kinda stuff.'

Jamie was still on the tailgate, chewing away. 'The future of life-saving, man!'

The drone didn't bother hovering or even getting its claws out this time: it immediately zoomed up and gained height. The noise died.

It wasn't the answer I'd been after, but maybe it was the way I'd asked the question. I must have paused a bit too long because James jumped in.

'Ah – you mean our family, right? You still unsure? That's cool. We all were. But you know what? Mr Mani has his head-space where it needs to be. He can see round corners, man. You'll understand soon. Just go with the flow. He's the man with the plan.'

He nodded slowly to himself rather than to me as I concentrated on the screens.

'So Egbers and the British guy – what about those two? They scare me.'

He didn't look at me as the camera zoomed in and out of the countryside, showing the veins in leaves, then the gentle ripples as the lens crossed over another water feature.

'Don't worry about them – that's their job. We don't have much to do with those guys. We're the worker bees. Those guys, they're way up, man. They're, like, Knights Templar dudes.' He nodded again. 'But you, James, you're going to be at the top, man. You've just got to get your head where it needs to be. You just have to have hope, man – *faith*.'

Then the house came into view and his tone changed. 'Okay, man. Where do you want me now?'

18

I turned my head and checked the bedside alarm: 9 p.m.

The laptop on my chest had been on overdrive ever since I'd got back from the drone session. The Tesco nightmare had played its course, but no doubt the next would be along soon enough.

I'd tried everything I knew to find out more about Sanctuary, and had got nowhere – apart from the video discovery that the PV energy was stored in six Telstar Powerwalls, stacked three deep at the rear of the house.

Still tired after the sleepless night, I had dozed off frequently. The laptop would slip off my chest onto the bed and join escaped peanuts and crisps from the minibar. I woke with a jolt each time an adrenalin powerboat spun around and got everyone whooping and screaming.

Sanctuary was the most secure build I had ever come across. Every avenue of information seemed to have been sealed off. Whoever was the brains behind it had even gone to the extreme of bringing in foreign workers to cut off any last possibility.

It was dark now and quiet. I had to get back to thinking. The drone had shown the place to be physically secure too, and why wouldn't it be? The footage had shown the gardens were well tended, but I hadn't been able to find out online who the contractors were. So, no information coming from them.

Every single online search had drawn a blank. Beyond Google and the normal local-government sites, I was out of my league. The Filipino had referenced the unfinished wall. Maybe it had been completed by a different contractor because there would be even more underground construction.

The drone footage showed me that the blind elevations from my recce had a concrete pad on the western side, and that that elevation was completely shuttered, apart from an access door on the right-hand side as the footage viewed it. But even on the dead side there was no access route to and from via footfall or vehicle: the building was an island, and the only reason for that had to be because access was via the air. It had to be, hadn't it? But how did anyone get to or from the house?

Maybe underground?

I picked up my mobile, thinking about the WhatsApp group the Brit had given me. They were only going to see a call for help in the event of a failure, but so far I was failing anyway.

Decision made. I hit WhatsApp and dialled. The ringtone echoed in my ear before it stopped sharply. There was rustling for a couple of seconds as the phone went up to an ear. Charlotte was clearly in a good mood. 'This is all new, isn't it? I thought you liked old-school?'

After I'd had my little bit of tuition from the Brit I'd checked out WhatsApp's security. I learnt about its end-to-end encryption, and WhatsApp's claims that not even they could access message content. Even if they could, and some said they could, they had over a billion users every day. So, if it was good enough for the crusade, it was good enough for me. All I had to do was keep the encryption secure by making sure I always updated it.

'Just trying to count the pennies. How are you?'

'All good. Just walking the dogs. You?'

I turned over so the mobile was now sandwiched between my head and the pillow. 'Yep, all good.' I smiled to make my voice sound happy. 'I do need a favour, though, if you're up for it.'

I got the standard response when I asked her for favours, a long and curious: '*Okaaaay . . .*'

'You need to keep this just between us two, but there's a problem down here I need help with.'

She'd always loved a challenge. And, luckily, she'd also always liked bailing out her younger brother. It was like having collateral in the bank. '*Okaaaay.*'

'Could you use that geeky copies-of-everything mind of yours and find out about a new-build down here? I have all the normal open-source docs but there's the house, and then an additional building that isn't on the plans and has no consent. It's on the spot where the water feature should be, and maybe there's a tunnel between the two.'

She was shouting to the dogs to go fetch. It sounded like they didn't want to cooperate that morning. She laughed. 'Sounds like something out of *Thunderbirds*. Where are you, Parker? Tracy Island?'

'Ha-ha, something like that.'

'Why? What's going on?'

'My boss down here is having some hold-back on money owed for jobs done, and it's to do with the new-build and planning consent – who did what build, here, where, and allocation of cash. All the normal crap. I thought, If I do him a favour and find out who else has been on the build, I could get some creepy-creepy points out of him. Always good to have.'

She laughed. She knew that was how it worked.

'Great. Listen, I'll send you the address and a couple of

links to the local-authority planners' site, everything I've got. The outbuilding's big, maybe a hundred and seventy square metres – and it's just talk of a tunnel between the two but I can't find anything.'

I got another elongated '*Okaaaay*.' She was hooked. The favour involved investigation and checking details, making copies of everything said, read or done. Of course she was interested. It was what she did. I'd been making fun of her geekiness since we were kids.

'You'll send me the links? You're definitely okay, are you?'

Clearly, as always, she could hear behind the smile.

'Yeah, just tired. It's been a long day. I need an early night – I've been driving myself mad trying to find this stuff, and it'll take you about five minutes.'

The Brit jumped into my head.

'Your bag. You okay? Your cards cancelled? Bank account still good? All safe?'

'Yes, all good. The gym called last night – they found it behind the lockers. Money, cards, everything still there – well, apart from my brush, but who cares, right?'

'Maybe someone's got a hair fetish. Anyway, as long as you got your stuff back.'

"Kay, then, go get your head down. Send me the stuff first and I'll see what I can do.'

'Perfect. One more thing.'

'*Okaaay?*'

'You need to update your WhatsApp. My mobile's telling me you're using an old version.'

'Thank you, Mr Zuckerberg. I'll get on it!'

She shouted to the dogs again and cut off.

My smile lasted a millisecond before it dropped. I'd done it again. Even more lies, and she knew it. But this time it wasn't just lies. There was danger attached.

19

Thursday, 29 November 2018

The next seven or eight hours passed very much like the last ones. Still in all my clothes, I tossed and turned, but this time all my worry was about Charlotte.

I tried watching TV, but all I could find was shopping channels selling stair-steppers and ab-crunchers. I finally gave up and went online to see what Eduardo Castro was all about. He turned out not to look at all how I'd expected. Maybe I'd been watching too many drug Mafia movies, where the leaders all seemed to have exotic names and looked like axe murderers. Eduardo was in his early sixties, with wavy silver hair brushed back. The face staring at me from the screen looked well fed and benign. His life was a steady stream of private jets, yachts, mansions and beautiful women. If the web was to be believed, he'd started life in the family furniture business in Pasadena. It seemed he didn't make real money from the family business, though. He used the business to make money for himself. Castro was arrested in the early 1980s for drug-running, using the business's delivery fleet to smuggle cocaine from Mexico. The family had a factory down there. But he was acquitted, and by the late eighties he had met the founders of Silicon Valley as they designed hardware and the software to go with it.

He was an early drug-money investor in a bunch of twenty-somethings and had been reaping the rewards ever since. But the money just hadn't been enough. He wanted to know people in high places and had worked hard to insert himself into the Washington political circus. He had backed politicians and funded initiatives to reduce state tax and ease employment laws. He had funded the anti-minimal wage lobby, and the campaign against California's same-sex marriage laws.

He was still involved in the tech world and was very angry when Toronto's residents rebelled against plans to create a city zone that was 100 per cent connected. It would have had robots collecting rubbish, self-driving buses, and public services powered online. Castro couldn't see a problem in a tech giant influencing the zone's residents and its workers' behaviour.

I had to agree with Toronto. The residents were against a plan that involved them handing over sensitive personal data to a private company. Castro liked the idea that the zone's humans might suddenly find that their whole life was being engineered. He called it 'just a Fitbit for your whole life'. Maybe as pope his dream would come true.

Castro liked power, had the cash to help him to grab more and more. He might be a husk, but he was a husk who had whatever it was that Parmesh wanted.

Daylight broke through the blinds and the thrill-seekers' whoops and screams wouldn't be far behind.

I'd been wearing the same clothes for a couple of days and I needed to clean up. My normal gear would be fine – it wasn't like I'd need to blend in any more.

As the hot water hit my head and sluiced down my body I felt like all my problems were being washed away. The only thing I needed was a shave, but that could wait a little longer. Five minutes of peace, that was all I wanted. Then I would work out what I needed to do – and how. I'd thought about going to the town hall and physically searching for the records, but had abandoned that idea. Leaving an electronic search trail was bad enough, let alone popping up on CCTV.

I was about two minutes into soaping myself when the mobile rang. I grabbed a towel and went through. No point checking who was calling, might as well just get on with it.

I put it to my ear. 'Hello?'

'Morning. Or evening, I suppose.'

She was bubbly. I couldn't hear any background noise. She was probably at home, sitting in the kitchen with her laptop on the pine table. That room always stank of Simon's oil paints. The fumes gave me a headache, just like his paintings did.

'It's a very good morning for you, Parker. I've found something.'

I perched on the bed, the towel collapsing onto the duvet. 'Oh, have you now?' I tried not to sound too enthusiastic, tried to settle into the lie. All I was doing was earning some brownie points from my boss. No biggie.

'Something very interesting. There were five contractors on that build, but never on-site at the same time. What on earth was going on? And there were no applications or any building regs signed off on an outbuilding or a tunnel.

'Everything was in order on the main build. All the regs were signed off at all stages. Everything was correct. No retrospective planning, no restrictions, no appeals. It was as if someone was just building a three-bed, not that monster. Nothing untoward. But one weird thing jumped out at me when I was checking the companies. One was incorporated the day after planning consent was granted, and then it ceased trading six months after completion. Don't you find that strange?'

'Maybe.'

I wanted to know the company's name but I let her carry on. This was her moment. She liked dragging everything out and explaining all the ins and outs, whether it was something like this or how she'd found the coat I'd left at her house the weekend before.

'Maybe? What? So . . . New Zealand law is based on UK law, right?'

'I guess so.'

'Okay. I checked the company's online revenue records and there's nothing fancy, just a clean close-down of a limited company. So . . . that must be the outbuilding firm, right?'

'Maybe.'

'Of course it is, and maybe they dug your mystery tunnel.'

I could imagine her grinning from ear to ear, waiting for me to congratulate her. It made sense to me. But she wasn't about to get what she wanted – not yet, anyway.

'What about the company? Who owns it – owned it?'

'Haven't had time to find out yet. I do have a life, you know – well, the dogs do.'

I bent down, picked up the laptop, and placed it beside me on the bed. I logged in to the New Zealand Companies Register website.

'What's the name?'

'Paracoast Constructions Limited.'

The details came up with the headers that Charlotte had already explained. They'd ceased trading in September last year.

'So, I have a Richard Rayner as, or who was, the director, right?'

She went into very smug mode, like she always did. 'If you say so.'

'I do, and the company's registered address is the same as the director's. It's a place called Para something or other. Para-para-umu.'

She waited. No doubt she could hear me tapping away.

'I think you found him.'

'Yes, of course I found him.'

'Well done, Lady P. And thank you.'

While she had a moan about how much time and effort she had put into bailing out her brother yet again, I quickly checked Richard's company history. 'Hey, little worker bee, I bet you don't know the name of the last company Richard was director of?'

'No. I didn't need to look, did I?'

'Lightweight. Steadfast Civil Engineering LLC. A limited liability company that traded for almost twenty-five years in Auckland. He's a civil engineer. He closed the company down at the same time as Paracoast. So, what I'm thinking is maybe he did this no-planning job with the newco and it was worth so much to him because he would have enough money to retire on.'

Charlotte was impressed. 'Quite the detective, aren't you? I've taught the geekiness in you well – welcome to the dark side. And even better – you've got brownie points for the boss.'

'Yep. All is good.'

Her tone changed suddenly, as I'd been sure it eventually would. She knew me so well.

'I don't believe you, James. I know you won't tell me, but I'm going to ask you anyway. And then I'm going to say, if you need help, call, and please be careful. You ready?'

'Yep.'

'All right, then. Is everything okay?'

'Of course it is.'

'Good. If you need anything, you will call, won't you?'

'I already have, haven't I?'

At least we both ended on a laugh. Sort of.

I forced myself into the bathroom and got back under the hot water. What was a big civil-engineering firm doing on a residential build? Rayner's website showed pictures of government contracts for schools and sports centres. But maybe I had the answer. If not, at least it was a start.

I squeezed soap from a container attached to the tiles. But the start of what?

PART FOUR

20

Paraparaumu
Friday, 30 November 2018

The flight to the island's capital last night had been uneventful, and so had the picking up of another Toyota at the airport. Hertz had a great deal going at Wellington, though why I was trying to save a Silicon Valley billionaire a few dollars, I wasn't sure. I'd driven straight to Paraparaumu, about fifty-five kilometres north, and checked into a mid-range tourist hotel. I'd woken up in another sun-drenched corner of Paradise.

I had to find out for myself if my theory about him and what he had built was right. Richard didn't need to go through the pain the Filipino had.

What was I going to do when I found him? Watch him for a while? Talk to him straight away? I didn't have a clue. First and foremost, I wanted to see the kind of man I was dealing with, or hoped I was going to be dealing with, then work out how to find out what I needed to know. For all I knew, he might want to help me. Maybe his company had closed six months after completion because Castro had defaulted on payment, putting Richard out of business. If nothing else, doing this made it feel like there was movement, and I might at least find out if there was a tunnel.

Kapiti Coast District was a dormitory settlement for daily commuters into Wellington, or so I'd read in the in-flight magazine, and Paraparaumu was its main town. It was a magnet for young families who wanted a better life for their kids and better schools, and for retired people who wanted to put their feet up with a sea view. Peter Jackson, the *Lord of the Rings* director, and Dane Coles, the All Blacks rugby player, had been educated there, and the first thing I discovered as I drove along in the Toyota was that any visitor would be taking those two pieces of information to their graves. You couldn't turn a corner without seeing a tribute to the famous sons.

The less famous inhabitant I was more interested in lived on Country Ridge Close, a road about two kilometres in from Raumati Beach and on the ridgeline paralleling the coast. Google Earth showed me Richard had a fantastic view of the sea from up there, and Street View showed he'd done incredibly well in life. None of the civil engineers I'd ever come across had made the kind of money he obviously had, but good luck to him. I felt I could have been right: one secret build and the rest of his life was going to be easy.

I'd finally got to shave and that completed my nerd look of shorts, boots and daysack, with socks to cover the lily-white calves. I couldn't help thinking that, being so borderline boring, the next step for my wardrobe was going to be socks with sandals. I wandered uphill, hoping to get a better view of Kapiti Island, about six kilometres off the coast. The ridgeline was green and lush, and each of the large houses poking out above the treeline was surrounded by its own little bit of New Zealand. The place I was looking for was Palm House.

He was fifty-nine years old, I knew from the register's record of directors' dates of birth, and unless his online pictures had been Photoshopped, I knew what he looked like. He was a lot bigger than me, maybe just over six feet tall, and certainly wider, with well-groomed salt-and-pepper hair and Hollywood teeth. He was an all-round picture of health and beauty, and that was probably just one of the many boxes you had to tick to live in this neighbourhood. The 4x4 in every driveway was immaculately shiny. The yummy-mummies power-walking past me could have starred in the infomercials I'd been watching.

I finally got onto the flat and took a breather. Down to my left, towards the sea, was the town, and beyond that the longness of Kapiti Island. At night the view would have been just like those Hollywood movies where the hero is on the high ground overlooking LA and the lights seem to go on for ever.

Palm House was coming up on my right, and nothing had changed in the years since the Google van had driven past. It was very white, with lots of glass-and-steel balconies, and flat roofs to ensure it didn't cut into the natural high ground behind.

I stopped every few paces, turning away from the house to take in the views, as if I couldn't believe the beauty I was seeing. I didn't have to try too hard. As I came nearly level with the driveway, I could see the triple garage shutters were up and a Lexus hybrid 4x4 sparkled on the drive next to an equally gleaming Ford people-carrier. There was one other vehicle in the garage: a motorbike, a Harley that had everything on it apart from a kettle. I wasn't big on bikes, but I knew one like that wouldn't have come cheap.

I started to worry: against one of the walls was a line of small kids' bikes with wheel stabilizers, and a big basket full of different-coloured balls. I hoped he'd started a family late in life, maybe with a new wife.

The house eventually disappeared behind me and I continued to play the tourist until I came to the turnaround circle of tarmac for the end of the close. Tracks led off in all directions, some by design, with little signs pointing along the ridgeline, and some because the dog-walkers and yummy-mummies cut corners. They all led down to a track that paralleled the road, with wooden benches sunk into the ground for people like me to sit and enjoy the view.

I followed it and turned back the way I'd come, trying to work out exactly where Palm House would be above me. Three benches along, a quick jump up showed I was just short of the house. I was looking at a forty-five-degree angle, but I could see the driveway, and the top floor over the perimeter hedge of the garden that backed onto the road.

Sitting on the bench, I did what all walkers do. I got out a flask of coffee and sandwiches and took in the view, trying to look contented and happy for anyone passing.

21

An hour, maybe an hour and fifteen, went by, with the odd vehicle moving above or someone shouting for their dog to come back, before there was the sound of young children and a woman telling them to jump into their seats because Daddy would be at the station very soon.

I quickly packed away my Tupperware and flask, got the daysack back on, and moved swiftly back along the track before popping up onto the turnaround and instantly changing pace. I sauntered along towards the house, just as the Ford came out of the driveway on the left. The kids – two girls – were in booster seats in the back with a yummy-mummy in her mid-thirties at the wheel. She sort of semi-stopped, glanced right, saw me, but didn't give the nerd a second look as she turned left.

There was a quick double tap on a horn. I quickened my pace and came level with the driveway to see Richard, and the middle-aged woman I guessed was his wife, both on the driveway as a set of garage shutters started to wind down.

His hair was much greyer than it was in his online photo, but still brushed back. He looked just as fit, in jeans, a polo shirt and trainers. She was a perfect match, dark-haired and just as immaculately turned out as her husband. She inspected a pristine flowerbed as Richard closed down their perfect garage, beside their perfect car, at their perfect house.

I felt my face turn red and burn, overheating as I walked past and the shutters slowly rolled out and down, imagining that the couple were staring at me, wondering who I was, why I was there. I couldn't help myself. I heard the shutter motors grind to a halt and had to look left, up the drive. I had to know he wasn't on his mobile, telling whatever to whoever about me.

Both of them were now heading for the front door.

I stared.

My eyes caught Richard's, and it was he who gave the smile and friendly wave. 'Morning!'

I nodded and cracked a smile, as his wife looked to see who he was talking to and gave a smile back. I was sure I wasn't genuine-looking, but turned back to face the road, soon, with luck, to be out of his sight – and, with luck, he would have gone inside. Or was he up on a balcony checking out the nerd in the shorts and long socks, and wondering?

I wasn't going to look behind me. I carried on, face still burning, sweat coming through my shirt.

I reached the Toyota and sat with the air-conditioning going full blast and even felt a bit cocky. I'd found him.

My moment of triumph was interrupted as the mobile rang. I pulled it out of my pocket and the number showing was one of the two in the WhatsApp group. I thought about shutting down but I knew it wouldn't go away.

'Hello?'

The other end of the call wasn't as soft a South African voice as I would have liked.

'What the fuck are you doing in Paraparaumu?'

'I'm trying to find out how to access the house. Trying—'

He was straight in. 'Shut the fuck up. Go to the airport!'

'Okay, but I'll have to check out of the hotel.'

'Now – do it now.'

The line went dead.

I sat deflated, wanted to wait just a couple of minutes more for the air-conditioning to work on me, wanted it to freeze the worry in my head so it wouldn't boil over into fear. I added a couple more minutes of CO_2 into the atmosphere before getting myself, then the Toyota, into gear and pulling away from the kerb.

As I got myself onto the correct side of the road, the Ford people-carrier approached me, now with one extra passenger.

Daddy was sitting in the front, turned back to face his daughters, and whatever was being said was very funny because all four of them were in stitches.

At least some would be enjoying the rest of the day.

22

Paraparaumu Kapiti Coast Airport was the smallest regional set-up I'd ever seen. Abandoning the Toyota among the half-dozen other vehicles in the car park, I rushed into Departures with my luggage in one hand and the daysack in the other. I was drenched with sweat. I hadn't changed: it had been straight back to the hotel, grab the bags and go.

The departure board was dead ahead, and I looked up at it without knowing why. Maybe I was just trying to normalize what was going on. Staring at departure boards is what people do at airports, right? The next flight was to Auckland. From there I could get back to Queenstown. I was in fantasy mode: if I made an effort to get back to Queenstown maybe somehow everything would be all right.

In the back of my mind I knew that Egbers was in the building. He'd told me to get there: he'd be there himself. I dropped my luggage on the floor and glanced about me at the bored-looking people with their trolleys and bags.

Then I saw him, sitting in the coffee shop with a large paper cup of whatever. He was talking into his mobile. He would have seen me the moment I'd come in. I didn't know much about him but I'd have bet the farm on the fact that he didn't miss a thing. He finished the conversation, stood, picked up his cup and headed towards me, shoving the mobile back into his jeans.

What should I do? Was I supposed to walk towards him and greet him like a long-lost friend? Or formally with a handshake, like a business acquaintance? Just to stand still felt the right thing to do: let him be in control of events.

It was then that I noticed how he walked. Even with his fucked-up feet, he glided over the tiling. There was a fluidity in his movement, the total confidence in their physical ability you see in top athletes. When people stopped and didn't know they were in his way with their trolleys, he didn't bother looking at them, he moved round them without breaking step. Maybe, rather than an athlete, he really was a warrior priest – maybe this thing really was a religion, and he'd been sent down from wherever their Heaven was to fight the good fight. I imagined him in brown monk-like robes that flowed out to his sides as he moved towards me, revealing his sword and dagger hanging from his belt. Maybe there'd be a Netflix documentary about them in twenty years' time.

I cut away from the stupid thoughts. What did he know about what I'd been doing here? Did he know about Richard?

Egbers closed but didn't stop his glide. 'With me.'

I grabbed my bags and followed.

Egbers exited the terminal and walked through the throng of smokers in the shade by the glass exit doors and kept going. Did he think I'd been trying to do a runner? Had they been chasing me to bring me back?

So many questions churned in my mind that I just couldn't help myself. 'I was trying to find some information about the house, that's all. I should have told you. I realize now – I should have called, and I should have explained. I'll do that from now on, call and explain what I'm doing.'

No answer. He turned the corner of the terminal and carried on towards *Saraswati*'s waiting helicopter. The Brit was standing by the sliding door, his hands held in front of him to beckon, his eyes down at the concrete, one foot on the step that would get us into the back of the aircraft. For some reason that concerned me more than if he'd stared angrily at me.

The starter unit whined as we approached, and the two large exhausts on the engines just below the rotors pushed out the hot aviation-fuel smell you get when you walk up the steps of a budget airline. Beyond the helicopter, the view of the terminal and small commercial aircraft became hazy in the fumes.

I pushed my bags inside and climbed in just as the rotors began to spin. Facing the front, I sat exactly where Egbers had placed me last time. Eager as a puppy trying to please, I was hoping they would appreciate that. I put on the seatbelt, then the headset, and even remembered to move the microphone closer to my mouth.

Almost as soon as the Knights Templar had jumped in, the helicopter lifted and there was a loud rustle in my earpieces as the other two positioned their headsets.

Egbers sat back, his eyes burning into me, and the Brit kicked out at my bags to make room for his size-eleven Nikes.

Egbers leant forward and poked my shoulder. It might as well have been a punch. But it didn't matter. My head was all about how to keep Richard safe.

'What are you doing here?'

The Brit was stretched out and had his trainers crossed and resting on the seat next to me.

'I was trying to find out if there's a tunnel. If there is, maybe I can get into the house that way.'

There was no reaction from either of them, physical or in the form of a follow-up question.

'Look, I'm doing as well as I can, I really am. I want to get the job done. I'm sorry if I didn't let you know what I was doing. I'm not running. I used the card you gave me – I'm using my mobile, for fuck's sake. Look, I'll make sure you know what's happening in the future – if that's what you want.'

Egbers looked across at the Brit, who now had his head back and his eyes closed. His headphones might as well have been playing him his iTunes favourites.

Egbers, though, wasn't resting. He leant forward as if to share a friendly whisper, only it wasn't. 'So what did you find out?'

'Nothing. I didn't have any time to—'

The Brit didn't even open his eyes as he cut in: 'Mr Mani has the gift of forgiveness, but we haven't. Stop lying, or I'll go back to Tescos.'

I jerked my head back to Egbers as if he was a saviour. His expression hadn't changed, but I knew mine had. And Egbers knew they had me.

'Look, I should have told you. I'm sorry.'

The Brit still hadn't moved. Egbers decided to sit back. It was as if the last five seconds didn't exist.

'What do you now know?'

I explained about the new company formed just for the new-build, and closed down immediately afterwards. It would have been an amazing coincidence if the company wasn't the one doing the outbuilding and maybe a tunnel. 'And if I'm right, that would be a good way to get me into and out of the house without anybody ever knowing.'

Egbers was hearing me, but he wasn't listening. 'Companies

this, companies that, they're just bits of paper. It's people we need. Have you found anyone? That's why you're here, right?'

The rotors thudded in the background through my head-phones. I tried not to make it look like I was avoiding, but the two or three seconds' delay felt like a lifetime in my head. In the end I just nodded, as if not saying Richard's name meant I hadn't exposed him. It didn't work. I had to say something.

'But I haven't spoken to him yet. I don't even know if he's the right man.'

Egbers leant towards me, so as to hear me better. 'Who is he? What does he look like? Where do we find him?'

He sat back and listened to me while the Brit was on the move. Eyes now wide open, he twisted behind me and tapped the pilot's shoulder, spinning his forefinger in the air.

The helicopter's nose dipped at once and we turned back towards Paraparaumu.

23

Neither of them paid me the slightest attention as they talked into their headsets, and that was fine by me. I wanted to become invisible. Egbers had taken mine off my head so they could talk privately, and my forehead rested against the window, vibrating as the rotors roared above me. I stared at the landscape as it rolled past below.

It wasn't long before the lush greenery became the habitation of Paraparaumu and, almost in the middle of the town, the airport. I could even see the roof of the white Toyota. Within seconds, the helicopter was coming in to land, but before the wheels had touched the ground the Brit was pulling the door open and he jumped out, striding towards the terminal building. Egbers talked to the pilot, whose matching white helmet nodded away in front of me.

We landed with a gentle jerk, the left wheel hitting concrete slightly before the right. The two of us in the back stayed put as the rotors slowed and the engine noise died, then finally cut. The only sounds came from the two prop engines of a light aircraft as it got the power up before taxiing down the runway. That, and the faint sound of the public-address system leaking out of the terminal building. Maybe it was announcing the flight to Auckland, and although I knew it wasn't going to help me, in that moment the little bit of normality was welcome.

What was I supposed to do now? Talk? Sit up? Jump out? I looked at Egbers, but he still wasn't taking any interest in me. He pulled out his phone and held it in his hand, waiting.

It must have been my guilt.

'Look, you two are scary – maybe he'll warm to me. Why don't I just talk to him as I planned? I need technical details, intricate stuff. If he's in shock or battered to shit, it's going to be hard for him to concentrate.'

Egbers turned his head. His eyes were very clear and blue and unmoved.

My mobile rang with its old-school tone. I reacted and went to my pocket, then realized it was coming from his. As usual he was short and sharp. 'Okay.'

As the mobile was closed down and shoved away in his jeans, a small Holden Combo van rounded the corner of the terminal building, two seats in the front, the Brit driving, the sort of thing a painter and decorator or electrician would use, or someone who'd had it converted to take a wheelchair on a ramp in the back. It was hired.

Egbers jumped down onto the concrete, an outstretched hand telling me not to follow. 'Do not move. Do not talk to the pilot.'

He climbed into the passenger seat and the van swung round, disappearing back behind the terminal.

The pilot got out of the helicopter and pulled off her helmet but kept her aviators on. She was maybe late thirties, and her natural blonde hair was short and practical. She bent to what I presumed was a luggage-area door somewhere in the fuselage beneath me, then pulled out some lengths of aluminium tubing. I sat and watched, transfixed, as the tubing became an arm outside the door, with a bracket looking like a hangman's gibbet and an angled bracket giving it support. When a small electric wiring rig went on, it was clear she was setting up a winch. She finally sorted it out and took off her sunglasses, looked into the heli at me.

'It's okay, you know. You'll be fine.'

I nodded at what was a strong Italian accent.

'Mr Mani has a strong sense of social justice. It sets him apart from the others. You just have to have hope, that's all. It's a powerful thing. You want coffee?'

I nodded once more, and she walked off towards the terminal. No way was I going anywhere. I certainly wasn't going to nick her helicopter, that was for sure.

24

Three coffees later, and two trips to the terminal toilets – the pilot explained that not returning would be really stupid – the only other time I'd been outside the helicopter was when she was getting it refuelled. That hadn't taken long. It was just a top-up: it had clearly been filled before the last flight.

I sat on the red settee seating where I'd always been, directly behind the pilot and facing the back of her head. As the light started to fade, she flicked on a small cabin light so she could continue turning the pages of *Wuthering Heights*. It didn't seem right: the two didn't mesh, just like Christmas in 20 degrees centigrade-plus. It was a long time since I'd had to read it at school, but I could remember Mr Burton teaching us the main theme: that the capacity for love and hope contrasts with the ability to hate. Because of his hate, Heathcliff resorted to revenge, another major theme. It had struck a chord with me at the time because I still wasn't over the KitKat incident.

I did have hope, but only that they wouldn't find Richard. I knew I was kidding myself: they would turn up with him here tonight, tomorrow, whenever. It wouldn't go away because they'd got bored waiting.

Her mobile sounded, and she answered before the second ring. I sat bolt upright, as if instant action was needed. As if I had anything to do with anything.

It was as terse as any Egbers call.

'Roger.'

The phone was put away, then switches were flicked and instruments lit up the gloom as she pulled on her helmet. I kept my eyes on the corner of the terminal and, sure enough, it was no more than ten minutes before the white van appeared. As the headlights moved out of my line of vision I could see the Brit was driving. The passenger seat was empty. It drove under the stationary rotors and the side door opened.

Richard stared out, his eyes wobbling with fear. Egbers told him to grab his bags and get into the helicopter. He fumbled around with two plastic carriers and clambered out. As the van drove off, the helicopter's starter motor began to whine. I put out a hand to take the two Pak'nSave bags of groceries and help him climb in, and it was then that he recognized me. It couldn't have been hard, the way I was dressed. He looked at me as I imagined I'd looked at Egbers when the Brit had spoken about Pip: as if I was going to be a saviour. I didn't know what to say. I hadn't a clue if he knew why he was there. He probably didn't know he was looking at me as the saviour – it was just fear, and I knew that feeling. But I wasn't his saviour, was I? I was the reason he was in the shit.

The stench of aviation fuel filled the cabin. Egbers cut the silence with a shout above the slowly turning rotors. He pointed to the seat immediately next to the far door. 'Sit.'

Richard obeyed, and was now right beside the winch.

Egbers sat directly opposite him, and pulled the sliding door shut, maybe to eliminate the fumes and some of the noise. He strapped Richard in, exactly as he'd done with me, and Richard was as compliant as my boys were when I fastened them into their car seats – but, unlike with my two, there was no fun, smiling or joking.

Richard looked at me and his eyes welled up, silently begging me to show him a sign he was going to be okay. I tried, but it didn't work for either of us.

I shuffled towards Egbers as he finished adjusting the strap. 'He's scared. We can do it by just talking.'

Egbers sat back and I had to lean in to him so I could hear what he had to say. 'You'll have your chance. Get your belt on.'

The rotors screamed at full power, and as the door slid open again, the Brit pushed his way past Richard and Egbers. The downdraught rammed more fumes into the cabin. I kept my eyes down, focusing on the tops of the carrier bags flapping frantically in the wind so I wouldn't catch Richard.

There was calm the instant Egbers pulled the door shut and we lifted into the air. The Brit positioned himself next to Richard and strapped himself in. I didn't want to look at the three of them. Instead I rested my forehead on the window and watched the lights below me as we gained height into the darkness and gently turned. At any other time this would have been a great sight. I used to like taking off from the compound in Kabul: as we gained height, the city lights would sprawl out across the valley. But not tonight.

The lights of the town grew smaller and we headed towards the ones defining the coastline. Vehicle beams moved along the main highway, and then they, too, disappeared. Below us was total darkness, and around us was the red glow of the helicopter's interior.

I got a kick from the Brit as he threw my headphones at me.

25

Richard's laboured and very erratic breathing filled my ears.

Egbers's face was bathed red in the glow of the overhead light. 'So ask him.'

I tried to move closer but had forgotten about the seatbelt. 'Richard, your old company worked on Sanctuary last year, just outside Queenstown – right?'

The best he could give me was a nod. Confusion and fear had taken hold. In the earpieces, all I could hear were his sharp intakes of breath. He sounded like he was about to hyperventilate.

'Richard. Calm down, mate. It's okay, I promise.'

My arms did a mime, as if that was going to help.

'All I need to know is what work you carried out at Sanctuary. Just tell me about it.'

I needed to bring him onside gently. He might have information about more than just the tunnel and the outbuilding, and who knew what I could do with it?

I thought I'd open on wide, then bring it down to specifics, exactly as I would on a site. You start with the big picture of what the client is trying to achieve so you can narrow it down to what needs to be done. If, of course, there actually was a tunnel.

He was eager to please. 'I was just the general management there. Setting out, quality control, keeping the subbies in check – all the normal things. Look, please, I'm just a civil engineer. That's all, just an engineer.'

It didn't sound convincing, even to me.

'Richard, you need to help me here. We know you opened a new company just for the Sanctuary job. Why did you do that?'

His eyes bounced between the three of us, wide as saucers and glistening in the red glow. 'Please, I just did some work on a new-build. It's what I do. Normal stuff. I want to help you but I don't know what you want from me.'

His hands came up to his face in despair. Egbers and the Brit burst into life. The Brit jumped aboard him and pinned him down; Egbers leant across the gap between them and pulled open the door. Noise and cold wind forced their way inside. Richard begged through screams and sobs. Soon that sound was lost because the headset was yanked off his head. I recoiled as far as I could into my corner.

Richard had a strap, maybe a loose seatbelt, I couldn't tell, wrapped around his chest before the winch clip was attached. Then they grabbed an arm each and pushed him out of the door.

I yelled. 'Stop! Don't! Don't! I need him to talk!'

It was too late. The helicopter tilted to the right and the pilot corrected.

Richard dangled from the winch. Below him were hundreds, maybe thousands, of feet to the sea.

His arms and legs flailed as he tried to hook just one of them over the step. His screams were loud enough to penetrate my headphones.

Once again I concentrated hard on the loose handles of the Pak'nSave carrier bags as they flapped in the gale.

The helicopter slowed. The rotors changed pitch: they were doing a different job. The downdraught and his screams still dominated and the handles were in a frenzy. I stared at them even harder.

The screams got louder, but only because Richard was being hauled in. Between him snatching drowning-man gulps of air and his head thrashing around like he was plugged into the mains, they had to work hard to control him. He'd totally lost it. I had no idea what words he was screaming, but until he was sane again it didn't matter.

His headphones got shoved onto his head but the mic wasn't on his mouth properly. I heard parts of 'Oh, my God, oh, my God – thank you, thank you.' And as soon as the winch cable was taken from his chest, his hands shot down between his legs and gripped the seat for dear life.

Egbers pulled the door shut and Richard's head fell onto his chest. His grip on the seat got tighter. His sobs filled my headphones.

Egbers took control again. 'Richard.'

There was no response so he leant forward and pulled his head up. 'Richard. Do not lie to us again. Do you want to see your wife? Your family?'

Richard's eyes closed and he nodded. He battled to take in more air but his nostrils were blocked. Saliva drooled from his mouth. His face was a glistening mess.

Egbers removed his hands from his chin and wiped them clean on Richard's jeans before sitting back. 'That's very good, Richard. So, to achieve that, all you have to do is what I told you to do in the van. Answer the questions. Do you understand?'

There was a slow nod of acceptance. His bottom lip quivered.

'That's good, Richard. Now clean up your face, take some deep breaths, and get your head straight.'

The helicopter clawed through the darkness, the sound of the rotors now louder in my headphones than Richard's raspy breaths. He coughed, trying to clear his throat. He would have been thinking of his wife. He wanted to go home.

I stared out at the darkness as Richard tried to compose himself. If they'd only given me a couple more minutes I would have got him talking and we wouldn't have had any of this shit. Pinpricks of light shone way below us, two or three in a cluster. Were we going out to the yacht?

Egbers cut into my thoughts. 'Richard, answer the questions. If you tell the truth, all will be good. You will go home.'

Richard was in full begging mode, but some element of control returned. 'I'm sorry, I want to – I will do. I'm sorry. I'm just scared – those people, they said they would make sure there were consequences if I ever told anyone what I did there. I knew what they meant.'

Now was the time to jump in and get this all over and done with. 'It's okay, Richard. They will never know. And if you tell me what I need to know, these two guys will take you home so you can carry on with your life.'

His head dropped again and the heavy breathing returned. I thought he was going to faint.

Egbers looked at me and sat back.

My turn.

I didn't bother looking at the Brit. He was number two. I was starting to understand the dynamics here.

'Listen, Richard, just breathe, it's okay. Not long now, and this will all be over.'

He turned his mess of a face to me. 'My wife. She'll be . . . Oh, fuck. I just went for some fucking milk.'

He started to cry.

Egbers was getting impatient. 'Richard, dry up, man. Your mobile and wallet are in your car. We stopped your life at the store. She will spend the rest of her life never knowing what happened to you. Killed? Or maybe you just deserted her? Maybe she'll blame herself. So just get on with what you are here for and your world will be reset to normal.'

I had seen his life – his beautiful house, his beautiful wife, his beautiful child and grandchildren, all the things and people he had worked so hard for all his life, supporting and nurturing. Success story – and now this. He wouldn't have known what he was getting involved in. Sanctuary would just have been a job for one of those mad, publicity-shy foreigners who were pushing up the real-estate prices. It made sense to me, and it had clearly made sense to Richard. He didn't deserve this but, at the same time, I wanted to know what was inside his head. Life is shit, isn't it?

'Richard, it'll all be over soon, mate.'

He looked up at me. At last he'd found a saviour.

I unbuckled my seatbelt to get closer but Egbers stopped me with a hand. What did he think I was going to do – grab Richard and both of us jump out? I stayed where I was, but leant in, as if that would help me understand him better.

'Richard, you opened up a new company just for the job, right? Just nod.'

I got what I needed.

'That's good. So what I'm thinking is, you had only one part of the construction to do. They were using different firms for different parts of the build, right?'

Another nod. His chest rose and fell more rhythmically as he got a decent reaction to his answers, and his hands came up to his face to clean up the mess.

We were getting somewhere.

26

I hated to admit it, but the Templars had got him where I
needed him, and they'd done it efficiently and quickly.

'Okay, Richard – what is it that your firm built?'

'We put up a building away from the main house, and a
tunnel between the two of them.'

He flinched, realizing he might have dropped himself in it,
laid himself open to more pain. 'I don't know what for. We
got the job done, and then left. Just a building and a tunnel,
that's all, I swear.'

'It's okay. Tell me about the build. Do you still have the
as-builts?'

He shook his head. 'They took the drawings, they took everything. Look, I was given the job and I didn't ask questions. They
said all the planning was taken care of – but I knew it wasn't. I
knew because of the money they offered. They paid enough for
me to get my kids houses, get my grandkids educated.'

The thought of his family made his whole body shake. He
was going to spiral, and I couldn't let that happen. There was
still a lot to talk about.

'Richard, mate, it's okay. Who wouldn't have taken the

money and run, right? It was just a job – I get it. What about you start with the building? Tell me all, and I'll come in with questions now and again to help me understand or maybe jog your memory. Would that work for you?'

We talked for about thirty minutes, starting with the outbuilding that had replaced the water feature. He told me about the tunnel's construction and where it met the basement of Sanctuary. Richard had completed the final basement wall that the Filipino builders had left unconstructed. He had done a good camouflage job, constructing the tunnel even while inspections were being carried out on the main build. Planning inspectors came at different times to check different parts of the build, and while they were doing that, Richard was busy digging a tunnel right under their noses.

A builder might have constructed a tunnel in the old-fashioned way, but Richard couldn't dig a massive trench that all the world and his uncle could see, even on Google Earth, then crane in circular tunnel segments, joining them together and finally backfilling the trench. Instead, he dug underground from the water-feature excavation and installed interlinking trapezoidal and expanded segmental smooth-bore tunnel linings a metre at a time until he finally had a concrete ring 2.44 metres in diameter all the way to the lookout – enough for most to walk along standing upright, even with a level board at the base. It was perfect. This was the same method used to build the London tube system, but the Victorian engineers did it so it didn't disrupt the city above; for Richard it was to keep the project safe from third parties.

The waste material was simply loaded onto trucks first thing each morning and was soon en route to being disposed of as normal construction waste. If an inspector had come early and spotted the piles of spoil, they would have said it was from the basement excavation.

The outbuilding was constructed of concrete block and stonework, with a zinc roof, much the same as the house. Richard said he had built no internal walls. There was nothing inside, just one big void. There was a concrete base, and a stairwell that gave access down to the tunnel. He didn't know what had been built since he'd left.

That was disappointing. But it meant only one thing to me: that it had to be for one of these machines we were in. There was enough hard-standing outside for a helicopter to land before getting a tow past the shutters.

I got so engrossed I had to kick myself to make sure I remembered where we were, why we were there, and why we were talking about Castro's house. Parmesh and the ledger had dropped completely out of my head. It was as if I was in my old office talking to a colleague about a job, getting all the technical geeky details and the background before pitching in. I was disappointed in myself – but what was even more disappointing was what Richard then told me about the tunnel segment that joined to Sanctuary. Three rings back from the basement wall, he had set a 200-millimetre concrete bung to prevent any entry or exit. It was prefabricated by the same manufacturers as the tunnel lining so its spec could easily be found. There was then a section of just over two metres, two rings' worth, of void. The outer basement wall of Sanctuary that he had built to complete the underground area was concrete block, and its internal side had been stud-walled and tiled.

That was all he knew, and I believed him. 'Thank you, Richard. You've helped me so much.'

Egbers butted in. 'You finished?'

I nodded and he yanked the headphones off Richard. The

154

Brit turned back to the pilot and once again gave her a tap on the shoulder and a twist of his forefinger in the air to get us back to Paraparaumu.

The nose of the helicopter dipped as she tilted to the right and we started a slow turn. I leant back in my seat and Richard did the same in his, taking a deep breath of thank-fuck-for-that. He looked over at me and his face tried a smile. I nodded and gave him a full one back. He mouthed a thank-you.

I tilted my head back, closed my eyes to try to digest what had been said, and as we continued a gentle turn right, the tension seemed to drain from my body.

I jerked upright to the sound of Richard's screams and the roar of wind and rotor noise.

The door was open and the Brit was pushing him out.

One second Richard was struggling to keep himself aboard, the next he was gone. He plummeted into the darkness.

Egbers went to pull the door closed again, like all he'd done was let the cat out. But the Brit stopped him for a few seconds more as he fished in his jeans, pulled out a bunch of keys held together by a Lexus keyring, and threw them into the darkness to follow Richard.

I lost it. 'What the fuck are you doing? You said he was going home. There was no reason! What is wrong with you fucking things?'

They looked at me, not a flicker of reaction in either pair of eyes. A terrible realization hit me.

'The Filipino guy. He's history, too?'

There was no reaction physically, but at last Egbers communicated: 'What we are doing is far greater than the sacrifice of just two lives. Both of them died to serve what you needed. Nothing more.'

27

Saturday, 1 December 2018

For three hours there hadn't been a word spoken between the three of us in the back, and the window was smeared with greasy skin marks where I'd been resting my head. Most of the flight, I had stared out at the rhythmical bursts of the navigation lights puncturing the darkness. I hadn't noticed at the time, but now I realized they hadn't been on before Richard was killed. Apart from the glow of the instrument panel, the only other light came from a small town or area of habitation way below.

I was angry, and I was pissed off with myself. No matter how helpful the Filipino and Richard would or wouldn't have been, they were never going to be left breathing. I should have known that.

The rest of the time, I'd stared down at the floor and my shoes bathed in the red glow. The other two had opened the contents of Richard's Pak'nSave bags, eaten the fruit and drunk the milk. They offered me an apple but taking it would have made me one of them. I had killed a couple of people and seen many more dead, but it was impossible to get the image of Richard's terrified face out of my head. Maybe it was guilt, I just didn't know. After all, I had tried to keep Richard away from these two, but failed. The guilt of failure?

I tried to cut away from it by concentrating on the job. I had the Filipino's information, and I had Richard's, but it didn't amount to much. It certainly wasn't enough to act on. It wasn't a big enough picture if I had to be in and out and leave no trace. Despite that, no way was I going to try to find out more from anyone else. I needed to know about intruder systems, for example, but that would come at too high a cost.

The job was going to happen, no doubt of that. I had no choice. But what would happen after I'd found this ledger for them? Would I join Richard in the Pacific Ocean? No matter what Parmesh had promised about the good life, I had nothing that guaranteed it, no insurance. All I had were his words . . . but I had seen those two actions. The more I thought about it, the only way I could see of ensuring everyone's long-term safety was to find out what was so important about those pages. Only then would I know why time, energy and lives had been taken to possess it – two already, and maybe more I didn't know about. If I had a copy of what was in the ledger, would they risk it being exposed?

Far below us, the ribbon of lights along the lake meant we were coming in over Queenstown. Another ten minutes and we would be on the ground at Frankton. It couldn't come too soon: the pilot had put the heating on after we'd refuelled at Christchurch and the cabin was hot, claustrophobic, stifling, horrible. I wanted out.

As we descended over the lake and made our approach, the first glow of dawn was pushing itself over the mountains. I could make out the town and the lake, a few boats bobbing on it, and as I looked across at the men opposite me the wheels gently nudged the concrete. The helicopter settled and the rotors slowed.

I waited until they'd taken off their headphones. 'I need to talk to Parmesh. I can do the job, but it's complicated. He needs to understand. He needs to okay what I'm thinking.'

The Brit wasn't listening. He opened the door and jumped out, but Egbers stayed looking at me, curious. 'What is that?'

I hesitated a second, enough for Egbers maybe to think I was worried about how he was going to react, but he was wrong.

'That's for Parmesh.'

28

Same hotel, different room, whole new set of problems.

The air-conditioning hummed gently above the desk near to where I was sitting, as the thrill-seekers whooped and screamed on the lake. In each corner of the room stood a small, tubular-shaped 3D camera on a tripod, all at different heights and angles, with microphones and speakers. My chair had been positioned by Egbers to face the end of the bed, about a metre away from it.

Egbers stared at his watch. 'Not long.'

On my lap rested a set of HoloLenses. They were like a virtual-reality headset and, apparently, I was about to 'holo-port' with Parmesh. It was a brand-new word to me, but not to Parmesh or the engineers in Cambridge who had developed the technology. Parmesh was out there somewhere in the world and, no matter what, he and Egbers always communicated in this way. Parmesh liked the human touch, which was strange considering his techie background. Egbers explained that he was a hands-on leader: he liked to be involved.

The Brit had set up the cameras, three silver and one black, about ten minutes ago, then left. That was good. He made me feel uncomfortable, and I had asserted myself a bit, which made it worse. The fact that I wanted to speak to Parmesh and no one else didn't mean I was in control of those two. Far from it: the looks on their faces when I told them in the helicopter were very clear.

Egbers checked his watch again. 'Stand by. Get the lenses on.'

I did what he said. Everything looked exactly the same as before: as I turned my head, everything was where it should be, including Egbers sitting on the settee to one side of the bed. It was like they were just clear glasses. A lot heavier, but the view was the same.

Parmesh's voice then entered the room via the speakers. I moved my head around trying to look for him and he instantly appeared at the end of the bed, directly in front of me.

'James, what's up?' He raised his hand in a high-five and I half got out of my chair to respond, but we missed. He laughed. 'Oh, no, still not working. Early days, James. Early days. But really cool, don't you think?'

It was.

He sat on the end of the bed – or, at least, it looked like it. I followed, so we were both sitting and facing each other.

'If I'm not embarrassed by our first product release, I've released too late, right?'

It was like he was really in the room. I hadn't known what to expect, maybe some slow, wavy materialization, like in *Star Trek*, and then a hazy image that faded in and out.

Parmesh had his hair pulled back in a ponytail and was dressed in a green V-neck sweater, jeans and, no doubt, the world's most expensive multicoloured Nikes.

'So, Mr Egbers says you need to talk to me. Anything wrong? Is there anything I need to fix? Anything you want, just say the word.'

Parmesh was his normal self, from what I'd seen of him.

Big smiles, big hand movements, which was strange through the goggles because they felt like they were coming too close to me. He became distracted by something to his left and beckoned someone in. 'Hey, little baby, of course, of course.'

A small child in a pinafore dress and thick tights, who I knew had just had her fourth birthday, ran in and clambered onto his lap. I couldn't help but think of my own two, and how much I used to love them doing exactly that. All they wanted was a kiss from their dad, and she was the same. Parmesh did as requested: he kissed her forehead and turned his attention to me.

'Say hello to Mr Egbers and my new friend, James.' He pointed over her shoulder in front of him, and I got an embarrassed wave and a 'Hello' before she was directed to Egbers and he also got a wave.

At last there was some humanity in the South African's voice. 'What a lovely dress.'

Parmesh finished off the introduction for me. It wasn't needed, as I knew all about his family as part of my target research, but it was easier for us all if he just got on with it so I, in turn, could get on with what I wanted from him. 'And this is Jing. It means "quiet, still, gentle".' Another kiss on top of the head. 'And, as you can see, that is not the case!'

I waved back. 'Hello, Jing.'

Parmesh gave her a kiss again, this time with encouragement to go and play with her sister.

'She could hear you but not see, because she didn't have the lenses on.'

I pointed to my chest with both hands, as if that was going to help the question. 'But you can see me, right?'

'Sure, you're sitting in the chair.'

Then he realized what I was trying to work out. 'Ah, yes, but you see me without my lenses on, right?'

I nodded.

'Yes, I know. So cool, isn't it? It only works with the lenses on, but you never get to see them. Face recognition takes care of all that. Even cooler is that you get instant memories. Mr Egbers – hiya. Morning.'

Egbers stood as he was addressed.

'Can you show James what I mean after this?'

'Yes, of course.'

He stayed standing as Parmesh switched his gaze to me, his tone still upbeat. 'Mr Egbers tells me you have made some progress. So, James, what is happening? What do you need?'

My head flashed back to Richard disappearing into the darkness. I bet Parmesh hadn't a clue how the progress had been made.

'I have, and now I know I need help. This job is complicated.'

Parmesh nodded to himself. 'Okay. Please elaborate.'

I explained what I knew so far about Sanctuary and the lack of knowledge by any one contractor. 'It's been constructed just like your house has, and that means it will take far too long in discovery, and I get that you want this done ASAP. And, of course, the more discovery that has to be made, the higher the risk of the whole operation being compromised. That's something none of us wants, isn't it?'

Even now, mid-conversation, I couldn't stop what was happening in my brain. I couldn't erase Richard being swallowed by the darkness. He flashed in front of me again and this time I heard the scream.

Parmesh was concerned. 'James, you okay?' He turned to his left. 'Mr Egbers, can you please fetch James some water?'

I raised my hand, trying to show him everything was fine. 'It's okay, thanks. I haven't had much sleep in the last couple of days, that's all – trying to come up with a plan.'

Egbers materialized with a bottle from the minibar anyway. I looked at his expressionless face bearing down and thanked him.

Parmesh joined in with the gratitude. 'Thank you, Mr Egbers. So, James.' He leant in, wanting to hear more, elbows on his knees to come closer to me. It really felt like he was there in person.

'With the information I have at the moment, I think I've found a way to get into Sanctuary, find the ledger, and get out again without them ever knowing – until they discover the ledger's gone, or they eventually open up the tunnel.'

Parmesh's smile broadened. He liked that one. 'Tunnel? What do you mean? They have a tunnel?'

'There's an outbuilding that wasn't on the planning details. The tunnel has been dug from the outbuilding to the inner wall of the basement. There's a concrete bung, and then a gap between the bung in the tunnel to the wall, a two-metre gap.

'So, what I need are three sets of skills. Technical first, so we can overcome any exclusion technology that the house possesses – and we have to assume that it does. Why wouldn't it?'

Parmesh was nodding away and thinking about it.

'The second skill is physical. I've got to get through that concrete bung.

'And the last skill set I need is aesthetics. I have to get through that tiled wall to access Sanctuary, retrieve the ledger, go back through the wall, and replace the inner wall tiles from the tunnel side so nobody knows we've been there.'

Parmesh was enthusiastic. 'That sounds cool.'

I had to agree with him on that one. 'Physical, technical, aesthetic. But also I need skill sets that they can cross-over, because we don't know what we're going into. And that's just to get in and out of Sanctuary – I still don't know where the ledger is and how it's protected. Are you able to tell me yet?'

Egbers interrupted from the settee. 'Mr Mani, I think it's too early to explain.'

Parmesh didn't look at Egbers because it didn't matter. He couldn't be seen anyway.

'Okay, so how many people are you thinking of? Are we talking just the first chairs or a full orchestra?'

I felt confident but I knew not to overstretch. 'I need three people. I know them, and I trust them. They're like me. But I'd have to make sure they'd want to work on this for me. Can I offer them the same incentive you've given me?'

He didn't hesitate. 'Sure – but I will have to take Mr Egbers's advice and his guidance about the ledger. No, we do not know where it is held yet. We will soon. But how we are getting that information, I cannot tell you just yet.' He smiled at me more intently to show there were no hard feelings.

I shrugged. No skin off my nose: all I needed was the detail.

Parmesh sat up and slapped his thighs, all smiles and happiness. 'Of course, everyone will get their rewards. But collecting your merry band, and how you plan what you guys do, must be under Mr Egbers's direction. You okay with that, James?'

It was going to happen regardless, so what would I do but nod and agree?

'That is great, really great. How is everyone back at home? Sons, yes?'

I nodded, while worrying what was coming next. Maybe he knew exactly what the Templars did for him. 'Yes, all good.'

'That is great, James. And your sister – Charlotte? She good?'

'Yes, Charlotte's good. Everything's fine.'

He nodded away to himself, slowly and deliberately, his eyes now focusing on the windows. He couldn't see anything but sky at this height. Maybe he was on gull watch. Then, just as quickly, he was back with me.

'You have to understand, James, if we get this right, one day there will be statues of you because of the amazing thing you did for our world. We –' his fingers pointed between the two of us '– we can do great things. We are all family now.'

There was a pause as Parmesh collected his thoughts and made sure his head was back to normal after his little outburst – or whatever normal was for someone like him.

'Okay. James, it was great to see you and we will talk again soon.' He brought his hand halfway towards a shake, then had second thoughts and laughed. 'We have to get that glitch sorted out some time.'

I joined in the laughter as he stood and turned, then disappeared. I went to take off the goggles, but Egbers shouted for me to keep them on. He went to the black camera, pressed a button and, at once, the 3D playback commenced on top of the bedspread, in an area about half the size of the bed. The hotel room became miniaturized with all three of us in the room interacting, even Jing jumping onto her father's lap and saying hello.

Everything was replayed before it then cut out and it was clearly time to take off the goggles.

Egbers sat back on the settee. 'So – you've had the replay, you've seen the instant memory as offered. That is now deleted. Remember – everything you do, everything you say to these people, I will be in control. If you screw it up and your people get damaged because you have not controlled them, or they have compromised our crusade, that will be your fault. It will be because of you, because you're the one who wanted them in. It will be your fault. Do you understand?'

I nodded. He was right.

29

It was past midday by the time Egbers and the Brit had packed up the holoport kit and left. While they'd worked, I'd tried to get my thoughts together on the best way to recruit the three people I wanted for the job – three people I could trust, and who I knew trusted me. That might change once I got them down here, of course, but there was no point in crossing that bridge before I had to. I had to be professional, and the best way of doing that was to remember that the most important thing about the three I had in mind was their own professionalism.

I picked up my mobile and called Charlotte on WhatsApp. I'd made sure Egbers knew I was going to call, and how I was going to approach these people.

Simon answered and I gave my normal apologies. I hated being the nice guy, but he lived with my sister, so what else could I do? At least he sounded awake. The TV blared in the background.

'Sorry, mate. I'm still getting my timings wrong. It's not too late, is it?'

Clearly it was. I knew it was midnight in York. He didn't reply.

I followed him as he climbed the stairs and the TV died, then got the creak of the bedroom door and 'It's him.'

She was straight into her normal big-sister stuff, even though she'd just been woken up. 'You okay?'

'I'm fine. First, the good news. You did brilliantly finding out about that new-build.' I fought to block the vision of Richard falling from the helicopter, did my best to remain calm and normal. 'I'm so much in the good books, I've been given my own job down here on that very same build. No more than two or three weeks, but good money.'

Charlotte was impressed. 'Wow, that's great! But you'll definitely be back here in time for Christmas, won't you? We have the boys this year. Remember? They're so excited.'

My brain had blanked that out. 'Yep, of course. All good. But listen, I've got work for some others as well. Could be really good for a Christmas bonus. Do you know if Tony Bradley's still about? Is he even still alive? I was also thinking about asking Gemma and Warren.'

'I saw Tony last week in Morrisons. He's very much alive, considering it was only six, seven months ago.'

'He was always nagging Maureen to quit. She was so nice to us. Especially to you.'

'Yep, but always smoking in the car with us in the back, remember?'

'And with the windows closed.'

Charlotte gave a very low 'Aw, yeah, but still a lovely woman.'

I cut in. There was still more I needed to know and I wanted to get this bit over with as quickly as possible. 'I think Gemma moved away from home. Joyce and Gerry, they'll know how to get hold of her, and Warren, well, he'll be at home, won't he?'

Charlotte was doing her normal 'Okaaay' as she waited for the punchline and the inevitable request for help.

'So I was thinking . . . could you call them, tell them I've got some work down here, and it's worth fifty K each? No more than a couple of weeks.'

I'd plucked the number out of the air but it seemed to do the trick.

'That's some job! You got any work for me and Simon down there?'

We both laughed. She, because she knew I wouldn't be after a bookkeeper; me, nervously, because I wanted to keep her out of danger's way. As for Simon, it would probably interfere with his artistic contemplations. 'No, I need masters of form, not bean-counters and a shit painter.'

It got a laugh out of her. 'And after that you expect me to help you?'

'You wouldn't have it any other way. Can you get them together for a conference call? Quick as you can. Flights paid, business class, nice hotel, nice Christmas bonus, what could possibly go wrong?'

'Only you would know that, wouldn't you?' Maybe I was trying too hard to be upbeat. 'You okay, Parker?'

'Yes, m'lady.'

'Okay.' She knew not to go on. 'So you want me to sort them out and get a call together with you?'

'That's about it. How're the boys?'

'All good. Pip didn't get the job but she's not too down about it. Mum came round for lunch at the weekend. She actually remembered who you were. She was asking about you.'

'Quite right too. One more thing.' I heard a big sigh. 'Hurry up with that call, will you?'

'Only if you send me those pictures you promised.'

She was still laughing as she cut the phone dead.

I sat on the end of the bed where Parmesh – or his hologram – had sat, and started to worry again. Had I done the right thing?

Bringing people here on a lie and expecting them to help when they learnt what they were really down here for? What if they said no? What would that mean to Egbers?

I felt shitty about everything, including having asked about the boys. I'd made it a policy never even to speak to them while I was away because I didn't want to lie to them. I knew my thinking was all fucked up and illogical when it came to them, but I wanted something between us that wasn't based on a lie, that was clean – pure, even.

I sat there trying to find the heart to justify this little bit of cleanliness after very likely putting others at risk. But what other option had I had?

I fell backwards onto the bed, my eyes drooping with exhaustion, and liking the feeling very much. I would soon be rid of the guilt for a few hours, and that was good enough for me. I'd take any relief I could get. Besides, it was going to be a busy night.

I brought up the mobile to my face, its glow just a little too bright for me to focus clearly. I'd better send those Akaroa pictures or I'd never hear the end of it.

30

It was getting dark on Speargrass Flat. Somewhere up ahead, on the same track where we'd met a couple of days ago, I'd be meeting the Js. I needed to have another look at the outbuilding, maybe find a way in, even investigate the entrance to the tunnel. Ever the optimist, right? A worried optimist. But the more I knew, the less I would worry.

They weren't there. It was only twenty long minutes later that a set of headlights carved their way up the hillside and their 4x4 finally drew up alongside my Toyota. I wasn't happy, and not only because they were late: this was supposed to be as covert as possible and they'd been on full beam and now kept their sidelights on.

James jumped out of the driver's seat and Jamie went round, opened the tailgate and unpacked their child.

James was all apologies. 'Sorry, man. The power's down in Queenstown. They've had an outage.'

Jamie had clearly enjoyed the experience. 'Hah, it was like a real-life zombie apocalypse. The whole town down – stop signs out, people wandering around in the dark with flashlights. We should go back down and film it. Make a crazy zombie film.'

From our vantage point I could see sporadic pinpricks of light in the darkness of Speargrass Flat, but thankfully none in the area of Sanctuary.

James had his ice-cream tray strapped over his neck and as the screens came to life they illuminated his face. 'Yeah, the radio news guy was going crazy. Said it was all about the energy company not investing, fat cats making big cash while everyone sits in the dark. The outages keep happening, and the politicians do nothing about it. Makes me kinda feel at home.'

The drone came to life in the red glow of the sidelights. James got suddenly animated, too. 'Mr Mani? When the time comes he'll be putting stuff like that to rights. Know what I'm saying?'

I did. And in a way I hoped he would. Somebody had to sort things out.

Jamie approached with a thick black nylon webbed belt that he buckled loosely round my waist. 'Don't worry, man – it works. I use this all the time.'

'You do this all the time? What – for fun?'

He held the belt out at my waist so it didn't fall into the dirt. 'Hah, sure, don't worry. This Mark Three dude can lift a combat soldier, even wearing all that army stuff.'

That was a lot of weight. Body armour, ammunition, water, it all added up. I decided not to tell them why I thought this was a great piece of kit, but anything that got a damaged body out of the fight was a very good thing in my book.

Jamie told me to keep hold of the oversized belt around my waist, then went back to the drone. James took over the instructions.

'All you've got to do is be cool. Just hang there, man, and enjoy. This is a neat idea of yours.'

The drone was now above us, lost in the darkness but low

enough for James to have to raise his voice. 'You'll be directly under the camera. We've got infrared, so all's good, man. We'll let you down on the concrete, you do your thing, call when you're ready to be picked up. Dig?'

Dig I did, because this was the only method of entry I'd been able to think of that meant no tracks in the grass or any perimeter intruder-detection systems being activated. I'd land outside the shutters of the outbuilding and see and do whatever I could. Maybe I'd be able to get inside, check it out, even into the tunnel. I wouldn't know until this thing got me there – and out again. I double-checked my phone. I'd tapped James's number into WhatsApp and done the same into his Samsung so he'd know who was calling. I wanted him to answer and get me out as soon as possible once I was done down there.

The high-pitched buzz of the drone got louder and I could soon feel the gentle downdraught from its six rotors.

James got me to pull the belt up from behind my head so it was tight around my chest and under my armpits, and produced a loop of belt for the drone's claws to grab. I looked up, and it was now no more than two metres above me. The eagle's legs and claws were extended and ready to grip its prey as it very slowly descended so it could grip the belt and take the slack. Then I could let my hands go free. Meanwhile, James moved the lens around, and its electrical pitch changed as it went up and down, 360 degrees, as James gave me one last piece of detail. I liked detail.

'If you want to abort your ride at any stage, for any reason, just keep waving your hands above your head. No cell, you might drop it. Got it, dude?'

'Got it.'

A second later the belt got even tighter round my chest and under my arms and the drone lifted me above the height of the 4x4. It moved forward, and I instinctively grabbed the webbing each side behind my head, as if that would stabilize me. But after the initial shock of being airborne, the dominant feeling was almost excitement. The drone slowed, I guessed as James checked the route, and we cleared some trees by just a few feet. It came down lower and flew between the next set. I was glad he didn't decide to overfly everything, not that the distance of the fall made much difference, I supposed. It was making contact with the ground that did the damage. I was still high enough for a malfunction to kill me, but staying at just above tree height made the whole experience feel strangely thrilling as the wind rushed past my face.

Eventually the dark shapes of Sanctuary's zinc rooftops came into sight, then the outbuilding. The drone turned as James steered me towards it. My mega Alton Towers experience was soon over, and I was looking forward to the return trip.

Back in the real world, I switched on. Something ahead caught my eye. A gentle red glow, just enough to be seen as I got to maybe twenty metres away. It pulsated on the outbuilding, probably at about gutter height.

Ten metres away now, slightly higher than the building, and the drone began to slow. I checked above me. The camera was looking to my half-right, trying to find a way of skirting the building to get to the dead side for the shuttering and the concrete pad.

The red glow kept pulsing and I had to make the decision. There was no way of knowing what the glow was about. Why would it be there? The one undeniable fact was that the light was there for a purpose. And red to me was a warning: it could have been linked to something that normally wouldn't be checked inside the building, and this was an external indicator. A build-up of gases, maybe, or something had overflowed, perhaps not rebooted. But it could also be a warning not to go further: *We've got you. We see you. Stuff is going to happen.*

Like an external sounder and strobe clearly visible on the outside of a house: would you really take the chance of it being a dummy unless it was worth it? For me, for now, landing on the concrete was a risk not worth taking. That wasn't to say I wasn't frustrated, and the journey back was less exciting than I'd been hoping.

I waved my hands above my head. The drone stopped dead and I dangled for a second or two before it turned.

Ten minutes later, James was lowering me next to the 4x4. My tiptoes touched the ground, and then I was down. Jamie attended to the drone as its claws released me and the strain from the webbing fell away from me. The belt hit the dirt and I kicked it off.

James still had his eyes on the console but managed a smile. 'Hey, I thought you were enjoying it, man. You were almost there.'

'There was a light – maybe an alarm. I couldn't risk it. Bit of a waste.'

James had rested the beast and joined me. 'No problem, dude. We've got Zombie Town to check out – plus it's not chasing those fucking gulls, is it, man?'

I had to join in the laughter.

'Will you guys be seeing Mr Egbers or talking to him about tonight?'

'Sure. He's due to call tomorrow. You want us to speak to him tonight and say what happened?'

'Thanks. Tell him about the alarm – it's a good thing I noticed. Can you also tell him I should have the UK calls organized by tomorrow? I'll let him know when.'

'Sure, man.'

As I opened the door of the Toyota, James shouted, 'Maybe see you in Zombie Town! Remember, if they come for you, just take them out with the car. They bounce real easy.'

I left the two of them to fantasize about destroying the population of Queenstown and headed back towards what I supposed was going to be a very dark hotel room.

PART FIVE

31

I sat facing the hotel bed, as if I was waiting for Parmesh to holoport into view again. He wouldn't have been on the end of the bed this time, though. My mobile sat there, ready for the conference call with the three in the team and, of course, their project manager.

And I was about to betray all the trust they had in me. Was I any different from the bankers who had crushed my dad, all smiles in the light, but in the dark a very different agenda? What could I do but suck it up and get on with it? Besides, this was about giving them something, not taking it away. Well, maybe their lives if it all went wrong. But I cut that thought out of my head very quickly because that just wasn't going to happen.

Egbers was on the settee, really close to me. He had moved from his normal side to the other to escape the sunlight pushing through the window. I knew, because he had told me, what I could and couldn't say to get them down here, but he was going to stay just to make sure.

I'd been getting through the bottled water from the mini-bar while waiting as I kept running through my lie – or what I had decided to call my 'sales pitch'. I kept telling myself I'd done this hundreds of times before when trying to win contracts. All I had to do was take out the real emotion, and make sure I gave them a very excited James, who just wanted his old friends to have a share in his good fortune.

It shouldn't be hard, I kept telling myself. I actually did want them to share in the good fortune – if it really existed. Just like my family and me, they had also suffered during the crisis and all we could do was try to help each other. That was how my head was trying to justify pulling them into this. But what if it actually worked? That really would be helping each other out of the shit.

My mobile rang. Charlotte had called me into the group. For whatever reason, I checked first with Egbers if I should answer or not. His answer was a bored flick of the hand.

I put it on speakerphone. A jumble of voices jumped in at different times, cutting across each other with their greetings. Finally it was Charlotte, all chirpy but taking control, of course.

'Good morning!'

It was in Queenstown. It was 7 p.m. where they were.

'Okay, we're all here. I thought if James just elaborates on what I told everyone about the job, we can ask questions after that. Sound good?'

Three yups, and it was clear from the varying quality of the voices they were all in different locations.

'Okay, good morning. First of all, just to make you really jealous, the sun's out today, well, every day, and it really would be great to see you all down here. As you know, I've been coming and going from here for the last seven years and a job's come up out of the blue. It's to sort out a cock-up of a new house-build. A big one – seven hundred and eighty square metres.'

That drew a whistle from Tony. Houses, generally, are getting smaller. The average UK home is about 76 square metres and has 4.8 rooms. This place was ten times bigger.

'I know, more like a hotel. It's the same old story – contractors going out of business, bad subbies, not enough quality control. Anyway, I don't know if there were backhanders involved, but it was all signed off. The owner is a friend of my boss down here and he doesn't want to move in until it's put right. He's suing individuals, suing firms, all the normal good-ideas-gone-bad stuff, same as it happens where we are. But he clearly isn't short of a few quid and is willing to throw money at it. He just wants the problems to go away.'

I let it hang for a second or two, just enough time to sink in but not enough to ask questions.

'So I suggested there should be an objective team to survey the problem. Otherwise, if money was just going to be thrown at it, firms would come up with massive quotes that wouldn't necessarily make good the job. I said I could get people down here who'd be able to look at the work and know how to get it sorted. He almost kissed me.'

I pushed straight on. I knew I mustn't give them any time to start talking or thinking about anything other than what I was telling them. 'So what I was thinking was that, Tony, you take a look at the electrical system. It's a complete mess. They want a new plan of what they can keep, what they need replacing.

'As for some of the structural work, they'd have done better with Lego. I told them I knew someone who knows what's what. But the real reason I thought of you, Gemma, was because there's rugby on the telly twenty-four/seven down here.'

Gemma had to laugh. Everyone did. We all knew that would

have been the first thing she thought about when Charlotte mentioned New Zealand.

'You, Warren, came to mind because everything about the aesthetics, the tiling, the veneers, the plastering, has been slapped on by subbies who are basically pirates in both senses of the word – rip-off work, and they obviously had hooks instead of hands.'

There was a little laughter, but that was okay. I'd wanted to keep it light until now.

'So, look, he's offering fifty grand each, sterling, cash in hand, for maybe two to three weeks at the most. Report what you see, and say how to fix it. Then we're done and back for Christmas.'

I'd been keeping my eyes on Egbers, who hadn't reacted to anything I'd said so far. Why would he? It was all lies he had agreed to anyway.

I knew they liked the sound of it because there was no reaction from any of them. If I was in their situation, my mind would be running down the list of debts that could be paid off.

'Like Charlotte said, we're talking business seats return, food, accommodation – plus Queenstown is great, and the rugby's still on. Guys, I need you here. What do you think?'

Gemma was first off the blocks. 'I'm in. Where do I sign?' I was sure she could hear my sigh of relief, but that wasn't a bad thing. I kept my eyes on Egbers.

'Charlotte's going to sort out the flights, everything your end. No need for work visas. Just come in on a tourist visa – if anyone asks, you're going to see the *Lord of the Rings* locations, all that sort of tourist thing, and you're here for three weeks.'

Nobody balked at that: it went with cash-in-hand. The black economy had been part of the construction trade ever since the first caveman had called in the decorators.

There was still no reaction from Egbers. Why would there be?

'How do we get paid, mate? I trust you, but . . .'

Warren had a mortgage, wife, 2.4 kids, and a green Citroën people-carrier on finance. I had to overcome his negativity fast. He was a good mate, but could always be counted on to look at the downside. 'Melancholic' would be the polite word. I gave myself a big smile and took my eyes away from Egbers. 'Not a problem, mate. I get it. Tell you what, I'll tell him every-one needs ten upfront. That way, if you don't like the feel of it when you come down here, at least you've had a nice trip and got some spending cash. We've never let each other down, have we?'

'True.'

I checked with Egbers, who gave a nod. I felt pleased with myself for coming up with an answer to satisfy both of them, but deep down I knew the money was much more about soothing my guilt. These people – or at least one of them so far – would have to be told the truth eventually.

There was still nothing from the last member of the team.

'Tony, it must be tough . . . you know, Maureen. I'm so sorry.'

'Thanks, son. A sad day, but it wasn't unexpected. She'd suffered a lot. Anyway, fifty K, you say?'

'Yep. Not bad, eh? All you need to do is what you've done all your life. Suck your teeth, shake your head and moan about the state of the wiring.'

It got the biggest laugh so far.

'On the plus side, there's no need to bring your wellies. There's no mud down here, mate. The sun's out – did I men-tion that?'

He ummed and aahed a bit. 'I've never been further than Spain. So, why not?'

'Ha, why not indeed?'

I had to move this on, for two reasons. First, I needed them here as soon as possible. Second, the more I had to talk this up, the bigger the punch would be when I'd got them down here and they learnt the truth.

'Great. Charlotte will sort tickets and organize cash to you once you give her your account details. It's going to be great . . .'

32

The Brit had joined Egbers and they'd set up the holoport equipment again. When Parmesh had said we'd be talking to each other a lot, I hadn't expected to be doing it like this. I was just too old-school.

Parmesh wanted updates from me. So, as before, I sat on a chair facing the end of the bed. At exactly the allotted time, as I put on my goggles, Parmesh appeared, just about to sit down in front of me. He had a different sweater on, blue this time, but there was no high-five attempt. His smile, however, was as big as always.

'They have not got the glitch sorted out yet, James, but soon. Soon.' His tone switched from happy to very happy. 'We have got good news, I hear?'

'Yep. They're all onboard – well, they're onboard with what I've told them. But how it's going to pan out once they know what they're really coming down here for . . . well, not exactly what they're doing, but enough to get them doing it . . . I don't know what the reaction will be.'

Egbers and the Brit were both with me this time and had taken their places on the settee.

Parmesh's mind was on other things.

'Do you trust them, James? Do you trust them with your life?'

I wasn't sure where this was going. Maybe I was wrong. Maybe he did know what the two Templars got up to. Was this the moment they swapped roles and he was the one who issued threats? Had I got the dynamics wrong between these three?

'Yep.'

Parmesh put his forearms on his thighs as he leant in, listening intently. His eyes didn't blink as they stared into mine, and he nodded along with every bit of sentence I spoke.

'All their families suffered during the crisis. We all have that bond, trying to help each other out during that time, so, yeah, I do, I trust them.'

Then the thought pushed into my head: I wondered if that would be reciprocated when they found out I'd brought them down here on a lie.

Parmesh's expression was still intense. 'That is good, James. That is really good – and deep. I know you will have no problem at all convincing them if you have hope in the future and believe, deep down, that what you are doing is right. It is not about the money – it is about making a better world. I have faith in you, James. You will come through for us, no doubt about it.'

His arms waved in the air, like an evangelical preacher's. But he couldn't have been praying to a god because he didn't have one. They didn't even have a pope yet. That was what this was all about. It was what at least two men had already been killed for.

'I will try, Parmesh – I really will try.'

I had to bite my lip to stop myself asking what would become of them if they refused. I had to ensure I picked my battles, and so far, making a copy of whatever was in that ledger was my only battle winner. Not just for my family, but the team's families now – if it came to that. I still kept just a little bit of brain power aside that said maybe all would be good and that we would even get our money.

I pushed on: 'Charlotte's also onboard. I need a project manager, someone to organize and carry out research if need be.'

Parmesh seemed surprisingly happy about such a small thing. 'That is so cool! This really is a family affair, is it not? I like it!'

He turned to the other two. 'Hello there, gentlemen. You hear that? Charlotte is on Team Sanctuary.'

The pair of them jumped to their feet to acknowledge their invisible boss, then resumed their seats.

Parmesh turned back to me. 'So is Charlotte going to Queenstown?'

'She doesn't need to. It's just the three skills I need here. Besides, I'm not sure she can be apart from her dogs for more than a couple of hours.'

I was making light of it, but there was no way I wanted her down here. I wanted her in York. Apart from keeping her out of harm's way, there was Mum to think about.

Parmesh was genuinely disappointed. 'That is such a shame, James. It would have been so cool to meet her. Even if we could not high-five.'

I joined in with his laughter but was puzzled. Why did he keep asking about her? Just because he was weird? Thankfully, his weirdness had kept him focused and driven him. It could have taken him to its darker side and had him bouncing around out of control.

My head was full of so many questions, but one stood out and had been on slow burn for days now. I thought, Why not give it a go? He's happy.

'Parmesh, may I ask you a question?' I was mega-polite, not only for Parmesh but for the Templars also. What I was about to ask I didn't want them to hear second-hand.

Parmesh leant back into what to me was his invisible chair, making him look like an acrobat with his back almost at 45 degrees on the end of the bed. 'Shoot, James, shoot.'

'What is in the ledger? What information is so important that you're going to all this trouble?'

Parmesh clasped his hands together, as the Templars jumped to the edges of their seats. 'It is okay, gentlemen, it is okay. I understand your concerns but, please, relax.' He came back to me. 'James, it is something that is so important to us – and Eduardo Castro, of course. You see, James, those pages contain the names of important people, people who make things happen. They contain the names of places, where those important people will be at the precise time the CE will need to take action.

'Castro has spent years and a considerable amount of money compiling the information on those pages. He knows how those important people think, and so how to press their buttons. When the time comes, Castro will immediately be in their ears, giving them comfort from their fears . . . offering them the CE to change the world. But the problem is that the change would be the way Castro and some of those important people *want* it to be, not how it *should* be.'

'Okay, I get it.'

Parmesh gave a very broad smile, something the Templars certainly didn't.

'These people, James, these important people, they will be needing our help. I must be the one – I must be the first one of the CE to be in their ears . . . I must be the Pope.'

Parmesh turned to the Templars and maintained his smile

for them, not that they could see it, of course. 'Gentlemen, James is becoming one of us. We should show him some trust as we bring him into our family.'

They didn't look completely onboard with that one. And, for me, the problem with half-answers was that they always led to another full question. 'But, Parmesh, if it's so important, why leave the ledger in an empty house? Shouldn't there be more protection? Why not leave it in a bank or somewhere safer?'

Parmesh convulsed with laughter as he turned back to me. It eventually subsided to a smile. 'Because, James, this secret is so important it cannot be guarded conventionally. Banks, guards, high-security fences, all can be defeated, and the more people who know where it is, the more vulnerable it is to theft. The biggest weapon in protecting the ledger, protecting anything of great importance, is concealment. Anything of great value to the world has been treated in the same way. Ancient texts in the walls of churches or in desert caves, religious artefacts hidden in plain sight of their persecutors. Banks are just for tangible commodities that this world has to offer. Not for items of real, true value.'

Parmesh stopped and stared. He was analysing me. I was uncomfortable – even more than I normally was when he got into cult mode. He turned to the Templars. 'Gentlemen, I am sure James is entitled to know some of the details – do you not agree?'

Both of them rose to their feet once more. Egbers wasn't as progressive with information as the boss. 'Mr Mani, I agree but I think he knows enough for now . . . I feel that is as far as the information should go. His team, these Brits he's bringing over, they must never know.'

I nodded in agreement. It made sense to me and, besides,

the less the team knew, the safer, I hoped, they would be from these two.

Parmesh slapped his thighs and stood to signal the session was at an end. 'Okay, then. Onwards and upwards!'

He swung back to me. 'James, we will talk real soon, once your guys are with you.'

33

For a couple of very long seconds the only sounds coming out of my mobile were of dogs barking and the wind howling. Then things went muffled. She must have brought the mobile up to her face.

I was straight in. 'Did you update your WhatsApp?'

'Yes. And I looked up the reason you were so arsy about it.' Her voice was thick with concern that I knew ran deeper than anything to do with encryption and cyber security. I was so easy for her to read. 'What's happening down there, James? This isn't right, is it? Is the job called off? Do I need to cancel flights?'

'No, no. The job is definitely on. But . . . I've messed up big-time. I think I've found a way out, but I'm going to need your help.'

'Way out of what? What are you on about?'

She shouted at the dogs and I heard the exertion of her chucking a ball for them. She had one of those long holders you pick up the ball with and hurl it. The barking receded.

'Is anyone with you?'

Her concern turned to annoyance. She never suffered fools

like me gladly. 'No, I'm walking the dogs and it's raining. Just spit it out.'

'Okay. There are two things. One . . . I haven't been working all these years down here.'

'What have you been doing then – lying in the sun?'

'I've been stealing.'

'*Okaaay.*' She sounded calm, but I knew exactly what was being screened. It was: '*What? Idiot! Why? Get back home!*' But instead I got 'So you lied to me. You lied to us all.'

They weren't questions, they were statements, and I understood her anger. It was reckoning time. I needed her. I needed some back-up, and she was the only person who could and would do that for me. The whole situation was now so much more than just stealing a book. I'd known that would be the case from the start: there had been way too much shit happening. Two deaths, and now with 'important people, important places' added to the mix, it had become much more. I simply didn't know where this situation was headed, and I had no control of events around me. But Charlotte had my back: she was a strong woman and had never let me down. Maybe it was in her genes, her DNA, whatever. She might never talk to me again after all this was over, but she would not leave me stranded.

I explained what had been happening these past seven years, and why.

Payback, pure and simple.

'Someone had to be responsible for the family once Dad had gone.'

Charlotte breathed a bit heavily into the mobile, trying to keep control of herself. 'That isn't being responsible, shit-for-brains. That's just having shit for brains. What if you'd got caught?'

'Ah . . . that's the second thing. I did. That's why I need your help.'

And now she lost it. 'Oh, my God – are you in jail? Is this your lawyer call? Do you need me to come down there? What do I have to do?'

The real Charlotte had pushed her way past the anger and I was so glad. 'No. I'm okay. There's been no police, no arrest. But I was caught last Sunday.'

I explained what had happened and that I now had to do a job for the man whose guys had caught me. I had to steal something. 'Just commercial information, that's all. An accounts book. But it's important enough to him to pay the team fifteen million each. Think about that.'

There was a pause as she took stock. With a normal person the pause would probably have been due to shock at the amount of money on offer, then thoughts about how it would change lives, but Charlotte wasn't like that. 'I don't believe it – it's too much. It's just words. Why don't you walk away? What's the risk? They going to hand you over to the police? If you get back here, that's not going to happen.'

I took a breath and formed a set of words in my head. 'No, it's worse than that. Much worse. They've threatened to hurt Pip and the boys if I don't get the job done.'

She lost it again, but this time she was angry. 'Oh, my God, what have you done? What the fuck have you done?'

I let her vent for a few seconds and tried to bring her back down. 'I overextended. I fucked up and got caught. But we are where we are. I need your help, Charlotte.'

There was no answer. I heard what might have been snuffling. She was trying to hold back a tear. I heard the pad of trainers on tarmac and laboured breathing. Then the dogs were close up to her and barking for more ball-throwing.

'Look, all this started because we got ripped off. Dad paid the price. I just wanted to make them pay. That's all I wanted to do. I was taking back what they took from us.'

She had no answer for me. Again, I was listening to the wind and the dogs, then a couple walking past, waffling away.

'I'm sorry.'

'Shut it. No more, James. I need to get my head around all this. They fly tonight – you know that?'

'I know, I know. But I can't stop it. It has to happen. I'm sorry for lying. I'm sorry for putting you in this position. I'm sorry that—'

She wasn't listening. 'Pip – does she know? Should the boys go away, hide?'

'No. Don't say anything. Don't do anything. They don't know and they're safe where they are. Same goes for the team – don't say anything. I'll sort them out when they get here. I just wanted you to know, that's all. I need your help.'

'Okay, I'll fly with them tonight and then maybe I can—'

'Whoa! No! Don't come. Stay home. Pip and the boys – keep an eye on them. And there's Mum, of course. That will help me feel better.'

'Okay. But what are you going to tell the others?'

'I'm not sure yet. I'll work it out. I'll need your help, though. Will you help me?'

There was a long pause before I got the answer, which was: 'You're a fucking idiot, you know that?'

Of course I did.

'I'll meet them at the airport.'

PART SIX

34

Tuesday, 4 December 2018

The arrivals doors opened and closed every few minutes, spitting out people pushing trolleys piled with suitcases and daysacks. This airport was much bigger than Paraparaumu, for sure. There were jets coming in from Wellington, Auckland, Melbourne, full of excitement-seekers. Out on the pan there were private jets and helicopters. It was a much bigger deal, maybe because there was a lot more money in this part of the island.

The plane carrying the team had landed at 21.20, five minutes late. But they were here. All good. They'd flown via Singapore, then Auckland, connecting to their final flight. They'd been in the air well over twenty-four hours, and I hoped they were knackered. More time for me to think while they rested.

People dribbled through from a Nelson flight. Then about ten minutes later two men came out whom I recognized instantly, leaning on their trolleys as they pushed, hair sticking up, red-eyed. Warren and Tony looked too exhausted even to talk to each other as they scanned the crowd. Warren had been skinny as a kid and still was. He looked even skinnier nowadays, with his full-blown dad-bod and thinning brown hair. He'd always been a bit thin on top as well. He'd been trying to grow a beard since we were teenagers but it had never really worked out. In his thirties, he still had bum fluff. But what stood out about Warren, even at a distance, were his bowed legs. Dad used to say that none of the men in his family would ever be able to catch a greasy pig.

We'd known each other since primary school. Like mine, his parents had made sure he went to school. Leg falling off? That's all right, have a paracetamol, go to the doctor's tonight. He married young and, for him, local: Jackie, who was a year above us. Warren was her toy boy. When we were kids he wanted to be a pilot and I wanted to be a vet, but life never turns out the way you hope. He had responsibilities; young wife, young family. Luckily, he was brilliant at art and design: tiling a bathroom, laying a floor, anything that needed a straight line, Warren was the man.

Then 2008 came along and, like everybody else on the team, business went down the toilet. The only blessing was that Warren's was a new one, a one-man band with a van. He didn't have to lay off staff like we did, but his big dreams had evaporated. Ever since, he'd had to work as a subby, scrabbling around for scraps. If you needed a few tiles over your bathroom sink, he'd take the job. His two girls were at a Montessori school and that costs, but it didn't matter to him: his whole focus was on Jackie and the kids. He had kept his family together through thick and thin, and I admired him for that. Maybe I felt just a little jealous of that success. I just wished he'd cheer up a little. Otherwise, for him, it'd be just moan . . . moan . . . moan . . . moan . . . dead.

Uncle Tony and his wife, Aunty Maureen, had been part of

my life for as long as I could remember, though we weren't related. Great friends of Mum and Dad, the four had grown up together, and that was why, as kids, we'd called them Aunty and Uncle. They'd never had a family. I wasn't sure if it was Tony or Maureen, it just wasn't spoken about. Tony always looked the same to me. Short, stocky and solid, even though I'd seen him go grey, have a hip replacement, and grow ever more reluctant to buy a round. Certain things, though, never changed. His amazingly bright blue eyes always twinkled when he saw Charlotte and me, even when times were bad. And his nose was still very flat and very soft. As a kid I used to poke it, and as I pushed it in, he'd stick his tongue out. I'd press it again and the tongue would disappear. I had never thought to ask him how it had got so smashed up. Maybe he'd been born with it that way.

Tony had never stopped being good to us kids, even when we came home from college on holiday. And Maureen: I was twenty-one and in my final year and she was still digging me out a KitKat, a Yorkie or an Aero. She used to work at the old Rowntree's factory and the contents of her handbag depended on what run she was working on. The thing was so heavy that every time she drove with it on the seat next to her in their Škoda the warning alert beeped that the passenger hadn't put on their seatbelt.

But everything had changed during the crisis. Tony's electrical company had gone the same way as ours, and now, of course, the double whammy: Maureen dying of cancer.

The two made a beeline for me and there were handshakes and hugs. Then I stepped back and looked at both of them. It was unbelievably good to see them.

'You two look terrible.'

Warren had to agree as he checked his watch. 'Twenty-six hours, thirty-four minutes of terrible.'

Tony was just as I'd expected. 'James, it's really good to see you, boy.'

I looked him up and down with mock disgust. 'I wish I could say the same to you.'

One more hug to him and then to Warren, all the while checking the arrival doors over his shoulder. 'Where's Gemma?'

Tony was busy fishing a wet wipe out of his bum-bag and freshening himself up. 'They stopped at the toilets.'

'They?'

Before Tony could answer, the arrivals doors opened and a trolley came through, followed by Gemma, who was pushing it. There was another trolley just behind her, and this one was being pushed by Charlotte.

35

I went to Gemma first: big hug. 'Brilliant to see you!'

Then I stepped back to take in both of them. 'How come you two look so much better than this pair?'

I gave Charlotte a hug and a kiss; there was nothing to say in public, apart from a big hello and great to see you.

She took over the conversation to make sure it stayed that way. 'Because we ate right, we didn't drink the plane dry, and we didn't try to watch every single film they had onboard. Even the kids' ones.' That got a laugh and then, as we started pushing the trolleys towards the exit, Gemma was straight on it: 'Right – so what's the scheme, Captain Calamity?'

'I've got a minibus to take us back to the hotel. It's a great place, views of the lake, room service – but unfortunately there are minibars.' That got a laugh. I wanted to keep it light: I knew Egbers was out there somewhere, watching, checking their faces, making sure they matched what he had already discovered about them. He probably knew more about their secrets and lies than I did.

I held back from the trolley group and Charlotte also lagged to the rear so we could walk together.

'Have you got a room yet? Have you sorted something?'

'Of course. And before you start, the best way for me to help Pip and the kids is to be here and help you. Mum will be fine. They're looking after her really well and she's happy in her own world. She thinks three weeks is three minutes anyway. So, if there's a problem they'll call me, and I'm just a day away. Okay?'

I nodded because it was.

'Good. So we don't need to talk about it any more. Let's just get on and sort this mess out.'

There was nothing to disagree with.

'What did Simon have to say?'

She looked straight ahead. 'What you would expect. But so what? This is important. This is about my family.'

We exited into the bright lights outside and the darkness beyond, and I finally caught a glimpse of Egbers, standing by the taxi booking desk. He would have worked out who the extra one was. It wasn't that hard.

We packed the bags into the minibus. I collected the trolleys and steered them into a bay before we headed off, all four with nodding heads as they tried to keep awake and take in the not-so-good-at-night view of the lake.

36

The team were handing over their passports for photocopying and receiving their door cards in return. Their faces and body language said all they were thinking about was clean sheets and a shower. That wasn't going to happen as quickly for Charlotte as for the rest of them.

I got up close to her as Gemma was handing over her passport and Tony and Warren were piling their bags onto a trolley. 'I'll come to you. We need to talk before tomorrow morning.'

She resigned herself to the inevitable. 'Give me half an hour?'

I couldn't help but smile. 'No matter what, it really is good to see you.'

'I know.'

Gemma was all set and it was Charlotte's turn to check in. Gemma was a little younger than the rest of us, early thirties, and she was one amazing plant and machine operator – much to her parents' disappointment. They had always wanted some upward social mobility in their family.

But the army loved her for it. She, too, was a reservist, and we both served in the same Royal Engineers unit based in

Catterick, a garrison town north of York. We'd done our Afghan tour together and she was my sergeant. It wasn't in her official job description, but her main job seemed to be to sort out all the shit for me – hence Captain Calamity. But Gemma was more than just a reservist: she was a hero. She was driving a Combat Engineering Vehicle to build the FOBs during one of the clearing operations in Afghanistan when the infantry about a hundred metres forward of us came under heavy fire. There were two dead and four wounded, and the patrol was pinned down. What she was driving had a fancy name, but it was effectively just a wheeled excavator to scoop up sand to fill HESCOs, with a bit of armoured plate around the cab.

She saw what was happening and, with the bucket up and front, she went for it towards the Taliban position about three hundred metres ahead. Not only did she take rounds into the cab, but an RPG took out the excavator when she was just fifty metres from the enemy.

I was positioning HESCOs at the time and, standing on a section of wall, could see the whole thing unfold. I thought she was dead when the vehicle took the RPG, but soon the infantry moved up and pulled her out of the wreck. She wasn't standing straight for a day or two, but she was alive.

It was a proud day for her parents when they joined her at Buckingham Palace where she was decorated with the Conspicuous Gallantry Cross by the Queen.

But that day of joy at the Palace was quickly wrenched from them. Gemma's parents owned a construction firm just outside Ripon, building mainly houses and small industrial units. Just like the rest of us, she, too, had been trying to save the family business. Despite everyone's best efforts, the firm was forced into bankruptcy, and Gemma took out personal loans to buy some of the old company's plant and set up on her own. She dug foundations, knocked down houses, laid tracks, moved earth, broke out concrete, drilled manholes, prepared ground for anything like pipework or ducting that needed to be trenched. Whatever had to be dug up or pushed in, she was the one to call, and the business grew and grew. At the same time, her sister, a year older, became a landscape gardener, and between the two of them they seemed to have cornered the market. If earth needed shifting for a fancy new garden it would be Gemma's machines on the case, and if her clients needed a landscaper, her sister would magically appear.

They worked hard; they made a go of it. Gemma, more so: she worked in a totally male-dominated, Wild West environment. Some very strong-arm tactics were employed in her line of business, with heavies coming in to persuade people to use certain plant firms. But Gemma stood her ground. She had chosen to study sports psychology because she was good at people and she was good at sports, rugby especially. And with a mouth and an attitude like her father's, she had been just as tough against the heavies as they were and prevailed.

Gemma wasn't only a hero to the country but to her former captain. It wasn't just the action I'd seen her take but the fact that she never talked about it. That didn't come from having a stiff upper lip – far from it, she was all lip. It was the way she looked at the war and thought, Been there, done that, what's next? She was the one who taught me to think exactly the same. It really was in another life.

I addressed all three of them: 'What about we say eleven o'clock tomorrow morning, in my room, two oh nine, and I'll explain what we're doing, then maybe go into town for lunch?'

There was a general smile and agreement about it, rather than a laugh. They were probably saving that for tomorrow when they'd got some energy back. Not that there'd be much of that in the room after they'd heard what I had to say.

Charlotte joined us and, as they steered the trolleys towards the lift, I peeled off to the right.

'See you in the morning, eleven, two oh nine.'

A quick wave and I disappeared up the stairs. I wanted to get away from them for now, let them sort themselves out and enjoy the last few hours of thinking I was the good guy.

As I cleared the last few steps before pushing through the fire-doors and onto the second-floor landing, my mobile vibrated in my jeans. It was WhatsApp, and the message was clear: Mr Mani wanted to be introduced to Charlotte in forty-five minutes.

37

Shit.

I opened my door and the Brit was already inside, rigging up the holoport equipment.

My first reaction was: *How did he get in?* And then it dawned on me. Of course he could get in. He didn't even look up, just carried on setting up the second camera, the black one that was used to show instant memories, running its leads to the power.

I launched straight into an explanation. 'Look, I didn't know she was coming. All she knows is what I've told the others. Nothing more.' He wasn't interested, but I felt better trying to say something.

At last the Brit acknowledged me. He stopped pushing the power cable into the wall socket and stood up to face me. Then he checked his watch. 'Forty minutes.'

I was straight out of the door and heading for the fourth floor. What did he want with her? To get her to join the family? Would he tell her the truth? That would mean I had no control over it, no context to try to soften the blow. How would she react? First of all, in front of Parmesh and the Templars, and even worse, in the face of more lies from me.

I knocked on the door far too many times without a reply, then rushed back to the lift and picked up the hotel phone on the wall. 'Room four one nine, please. My name's James, and it's for Charlotte.'

I didn't have to wait long and finally the operator joined us together.

'It's me.'

'I was—'

'Listen, this is very important. You've got to let me in right now.'

She was matter-of-fact, but wary as ever. '*Okaaay.*'

This time, one double tap and it opened. Charlotte was in a bathrobe and brushing her wet hair. 'We said half an hour?'

I went in and pushed her jeans and sweatshirt to the side so I could sit on the end of the bed. She knew something was wrong. 'James, everything at home will be okay. It's better for me to help you down here. That will help Pip and the kids more than—'

I put both hands up to halt her. 'Yep, yep, I agree with that. But . . . there's a lot more you need to know. We've got under thirty minutes for you to get dressed and also throw a really big one at me while you're doing it.'

'*Okaaay.*' She braced herself for the next bout of garbage. She came and sat next to me and stopped brushing.

I kept my eyes fixed on the black screen of the TV in front of me, then homed in on the little red standby light to avoid her gaze.

As if. She was centimetres away. I was going to have enough problems with my ears being so close when she kicked off, let alone avoid watching her do it. I might as well get on with it.

I let out everything I'd been holding back: about the cognitive elite, Parmesh, the 'family', the Templars, the ledger, why whatever was in there was worth him giving us millions. And, finally, that I needed her help getting the team onside, without them knowing what she now knew.

And, on top of that, Parmesh wanted to meet her. In less than thirty minutes' time.

I stopped and waited for the big one coming my way.

But nothing.

I turned and she had started to brush her straight, shoulder-length black hair with slow, deliberate strokes. I carried on: 'All I can think of is to try to get a copy of the names, the places. Then maybe we have some protection. But don't forget, if he's telling the truth, we are rich.'

She carried on brushing. 'Maybe. But if everybody else wants it and they know we have a copy . . .' She looked at me and her head tilted. 'I know what you're going to say – that's for another day. Right?'

I nodded and tried to raise a smile. 'Exactly – we worry about that some other day.' I was actually feeling good. Not only had I just emptied the barrel of all my lies, but also her reaction so far hadn't been too bad.

She stood up and pulled a drier from the desk drawer. 'So, you're only telling me this now because Parmesh wants to talk with me?'

I had to admit it. 'Yeah, sort of. Tomorrow I was going to get the team onboard with cash and that what we were stealing was just an accounts ledger, exactly what I told you the other night. But, yeah, I had to tell you. I didn't want to. I didn't even want you down here, remember. I didn't want to put you at risk.'

The drier came on deafeningly and her hair jumped all over the place.

I checked my watch. 'We've got fifteen.'

She turned off the drier and over-concentrated on brushing her hair once more in the mirror.

'I promise you, all he knows is that you're here on the same lie I gave the rest of them. I didn't ask you here, but you came anyway.'

I stood to walk over to her as she inspected herself in the desk mirror. Still no reply: she was too calm. This was worrying, as I knew what was about to happen next. 'I'm sorry. I know I fucked up.'

She just listened, and I knew it was going in one ear and out the other, but I still had to try to make a positive. 'But between us we should be able to get out of this with a lot of cash, and for the others. Just think about that.'

The brush came down from her hair and I sensed it was time to take cover. She turned, and used it to push against my breastbone, her black eyes burning into mine. There wasn't even a blink.

'Do you really think I should be excited about money when you've put your family – *my family* – at risk? Do you?' She pushed harder and I took backward steps. 'Do you really think I want to be here? Sorting out your mess once again? Do you?'

I took the shoves and eventually we were both through the bathroom door and standing on tiles.

'Well, I don't, but I'm here. We are family, and we will sort this out. But don't think you and me are good. We're not. I don't care what you've been doing down here, but what I do care about is your lying. Don't you lie to me ever, ever again. You understand?'

The brush kept stabbing at me as I nodded and took it.

She stopped and pointed the brush right at my face. 'Wait here. I'll call when I'm ready.'

She turned on her heel and slammed the door.

As far as I was concerned it had gone well. At least, much better than I was expecting. The door was immediately reopened for her to hand me an A4 envelope. 'From the boys. They miss you.'

The door was closed again. I sat on the toilet and pulled out the A4's contents.

There were two felt-tip pen pictures, the sort that would normally be stuck on the fridge. Jack had always been better at perspective than Tom, and the drawing of me with wellies, hard-hat, shirt and tie standing on a pile of rubble with a digger in the background was almost correct. I couldn't help but notice details. Jack's, on the other hand, was all over the place and more to do with plant than me. I was standing in the world's biggest digger's bucket with no hard-hat on. It didn't matter: it never had.

Their scribbles were both of the same message.

Daddy we miss you and *Daddy we love you.*

38

We got to my room with five minutes to spare, and I opened the door to find Egbers and the Brit standing in their allotted positions by the settee. Two pairs of eyes studied my sister.

'This is Charlotte.'

As if they didn't know. They gave her a polite hello and a good evening. Actual words.

Egbers handed her a set of goggles. 'Please put them on when you sit.' He indicated the two chairs facing the end of the bed, where there had usually just been one. It was clear which one was hers. My goggles were waiting for me on the seat.

Egbers remained very polite. 'Please take your seat from the back. The gap between the chair and the bed, I need to keep clear. Thank you.'

Charlotte looked at me, her goggles in her hand, and raised an eyebrow. I'd forgotten to tell her how we were about to meet Parmesh: there had been more important things to think about at the time. Anyway, she was probably about to find out.

Egbers guided her round to the back of her chair, like a waiter at the Ritz, pulled it out for her, then pushed it back in as she went down, as if he was about to hand her a menu next.

This was all very formal and I wasn't sure how worried I should be.

As the goggles went onto her face she gasped. I still didn't have mine on, but I knew what she saw in front of her. 'Whoa! You must be Parmesh!'

The speakers came to life, but he must have been sitting, waiting, watching us since we entered the room.

'Yes, it's so wonderful to see you at last, Charlotte. James, please come and join us.'

I put on my goggles as I sat down, in time to see Parmesh explaining the technology to Charlotte and why we didn't see each other's goggles. 'I was trying to get the high-five glitch rectified for the next time I spoke with James. But, sadly, no luck yet. We need to fine-tune the perspective on each side so that hands can meet.' He clapped his hands together. 'But, anyway, such a pleasant surprise you are here. I just wanted to say hello.'

'And hello to you, Parmesh.'

'Where are you from originally?'

She smiled. 'Sri Lanka.'

Parmesh beamed back. 'Me too! I was born in Palali. It's just a small town way up in the north near the coast – do you know it?'

She shook her head. 'No, sorry, I don't know the country at all. I was just a baby when I left, one of the lucky ones – you know, the war. Countries were taking in orphans. I was adopted by our wonderful parents. The UK is all I know.'

She smiled across at me as Parmesh nodded. He looked genuinely upset. 'Yes, it was a terrible time. Now look at the two of us. Both with very funny accents.'

He got a laugh from everyone, including the Templars.

Parmesh radiated his normal over-the-top big smile and oozed friendliness. For the first time, I wondered if it wasn't only to help with his obsession, but actually genuine.

Charlotte was all smiles and looked pleased to meet him. But, then, she knew it wasn't him the danger was coming from: it was the other two by the settee. Or maybe she felt she was using her heritage to bond, perhaps to help us later somehow.

The laughter subsided and he carried on: 'That is so true, Charlotte. So true. But I think my accent is the funnier. That British accent, you sound so cool.' He stared into her with intensity, wanting more. 'So you never knew your parents? Can you remember anything? Your name? Family name, maybe?'

She shook her head, but not with sadness. 'James and our parents offered to help me find out where I was born, trace my family, maybe brothers, sisters. But there were so many killed, so many families separated, no records. Where would we start?

'But you know what, Parmesh? I didn't want to. Our parents were the ones who'd cared for me since I was a baby. They loved me. They put plasters on my knees when my kid brother here pushed me off my bike.'

That got another laugh, and the Templars joined in again. It was very freaky.

'That's who my parents are, and James is my brother. What more do I need to know?'

There was a lull in the conversation while Parmesh stared at her, his smile still on main-beam. He tilted his head. I was used to it by now, but Charlotte would be feeling his strangeness soon enough. For now, she felt she had to cut the silence.

'So what about you, Parmesh? You escaped the war?'

He came back to us. Memories of the past were getting to him. 'Yes, like you, we lost family – killed. But me, my parents, we were so lucky, so blessed. And in fact I have my own family now.' He waved off to his left as the cheerful Parmesh slowly returned. 'Come on, guys, I want you to say hello to Charlotte and James, two very special people.'

Soon his whole family were gathered around him, waving at us, like one of those awkward American Christmas cards. This was weird: had they been waiting? One of the girls clambered onto his lap and Parmesh began the introductions. He thumbed behind him. 'This is my husband, Kyle. We've been together for ever, and good old CA finally made it legal to marry. It was a great day – even though he's British.'

Kyle was the same age as me but taller, tanned and much better-looking. He carried a small bundle of blankets in his arms, and his accent gave away his birthplace. 'No, not British. Scottish.'

Charlotte and I waved our hellos as the two little girls wriggled about.

Parmesh pointed out Jing. 'James already knows this one, Jing. And this . . .' he pointed to the second '. . . this is A'lia – which is a beautiful Nigerian name that means "glorious and wonderful". Just like she is.'

He thumbed back at Kyle. There was movement in the blankets and I realized he was holding a baby. 'And this is our new addition, Shoba. She is just like you, Charlotte – a war orphan. She was found abandoned in Aleppo and, again just like you, without even a name. But she now has a wonderful Hindi name. It means "beautiful", and she is so very much. We want her to be happy and have a contented life, just like you.'

Charlotte looked invested in the set-up. Maybe seeing the baby, seeing the love she was receiving, gave her a bit of a flashback to her own life and how drastically different it might have been. She was getting a bit emotional herself. 'Yes, you have an amazing family, a wonderful family.'

Kyle waved Shoba's tiny olive hand out of the blanket as he

gently rocked her left and right to keep her settled. The other two were getting big kisses on their heads from Parmesh but he started to move things on. 'I think we have to talk about work now. So I tell you what, wonderful children, I'll see you all very soon. And maybe we will go for a swim.'

The two little ones jumped up and down for joy. No doubt going for a swim didn't mean a trip to the local municipal pool. It would be Dalladine-style.

'Say goodbye now to Charlotte and James, please.'

We got waves as Kyle led them away. 'So nice to have met you both.'

Then: boom, exit left, out of camera range, and we were alone again – even if it was virtual.

I filled the vacuum. 'What a wonderful family.'

He put his hands together in prayer. 'Yes, thank you – I am blessed, and you know what? For the very first time I feel complete.'

It was weird: he was focused solely on Charlotte. 'As you are, too. Loving parents. And, of course, James.'

I had no idea what was going on in his head, but his expression was more sad than contented. Maybe he was thinking back to the war. He would have been old enough to remember. But as quickly as the sadness came, it lifted, and we had the beaming Parmesh once again.

'Charlotte, James, I have a suggestion. Or, in fact, a proposal.' His forearms came down onto his thighs to get closer, as if he was about to include us in a conspiracy. Instinctively, I leant in too, and so did Charlotte. As if it was going to help: the speakers were doing the talking.

'I feel that we are part of a family.' He tapped his heart with a forefinger. 'Therefore, what I want to do is show faith. Not only to you, but to the people you have brought along with you. So, right now, I'm setting out some affairs in New Zealand that will hold fifty per cent of your incentives for all five of you. If you'd be so kind, I would like you, Charlotte, to agree to control those assets. Once you have them, they are yours. No matter what happens.'

The effect it had on both of us must have been clear to see. 'I am sorry if it is overwhelming, but I want to show commitment to you both.'

He swivelled to face Charlotte. 'I am not too sure how much you know of what I am trying to achieve, but it does not really matter for now. What does is that you eventually believe that what we are doing is not only honourable but for the betterment of us all. And that you are part of it.'

Charlotte's gaze was fixed on Parmesh, as if they were the only two in the room. 'James has just explained everything. And I'll do whatever is needed to help him. I'll look after whatever needs to be looked after.'

There was a pause when he fixed into her eyes before coming back to me. 'Thank you, James, for introducing me to your wonderful sister. I see great things ahead for us all.'

He slapped his thighs and stood up. 'Well, clearly, I have to go swimming now. We will talk very soon. Mr Egbers?' He looked over and the South African jumped to his feet as if he could see him. 'Mr Egbers here will make sure you have all the details. That will be done some time tomorrow. Wonderful to see you, James. Fantastic, Charlotte, to meet you. The water awaits. I will speak to you all soon.'

We said our goodbyes and waved, and he exited out of camera range and that was it.

It didn't take long for the Templars to dismantle the holoport. We both sat there, not saying a word to each other, until they left with courteous nods and goodbyes to Charlotte.

I waited for the final click of the door latch before looking across at her.

'Come on, then, numbers girl, what's fifty per cent of four lots of fifteen million?'

Charlotte was already there. 'He is giving us thirty million to start off with. Can it be real?'

She slumped into the desk chair and her head fell backwards. She stared at the ceiling. 'Shit, James, shit.'

39

Wednesday, 5 December 2018

Neither of us had slept. It was the anticipation, hope, I wasn't sure what, really, of all that cash being dropped into Charlotte's lap.

She had called me just after 5 a.m. to see if I was awake and, if not, to wake me and tell me that she was coming to me, so order coffee. Since 5.45 all we had done was drink coffee, talk, and feel excitement and dread in equal measure.

It was nearly 10 a.m. and she was finishing the last of the long-ago-cold coffee and the last muffin before we sorted ourselves out to meet the rest of the team at eleven. We had spent a lot of time talking about what Parmesh was all about, and she still wasn't done. 'He's weird, but I sort of like it. He always like that?'

'He's eccentric, to put it mildly. But there is something about him.'

She sat on the same chair as last night, her back to the desk. 'Let's see if he really means it about the money. That's what's going to focus minds and get everyone on board.'

She was right, of course.

'Certainly focused us.'

She was gathering the muffin crumbs left on her plate with a forefinger. 'What are you going to say, anyway?'

I pumped up the pillows, and rested my back against the headboard. She licked her finger to get the last few crumbs to stick. The first of the day's thrill-seekers screamed across the lake. 'The truth, apart from the crusade part – and you're right, the money will change things.'

Charlotte wasn't too sure. 'You've got to be careful how you approach that. The sums are so big it could boil their brains. Maybe think about offering a smaller number, something that sorts their families out but feels obtainable, something they can get their heads around. Otherwise, why would they believe? We didn't, did we? Then, once the job's done, they can worry about what to do with their big-boy bonus.'

The team might have been her main concern, but that wouldn't stop her thinking about what the money would do for our family, and her own life. I could sense the cogs turning in her brain as it boiled away.

'James, just think about it. What if it's true? What if the money is real – what if we can actually get away with this?'

I shrugged. 'I try not to think about it – and fail, of course.'

As we gave each other a slow nod, my mobile buzzed.

'Egbers wants us in Reception.'

I pulled on my trainers and followed Charlotte out of the room. Neither of us said anything. What was there to say? Besides, we both knew that if we did, it would be the same thing: 'It's exciting.'

Egbers was waiting for us as we exited the lift, dressed in jeans and a light blue shirt pressed to within an inch of its life.

He smiled, then gave Charlotte a nod and a Prussian click of the heels. 'Good morning. Please, come with me.'

We followed him to one of the small business-centre meeting rooms. In it were two men, both in grey suits and one-colour ties, one blue, one red. Both sat on the left of the clear glass desk that seemed to fill most of the small room. Their matching brown leather bags were on the desk, opened, exposing paperwork.

Egbers addressed Charlotte. 'These two gentlemen are here to finalize the account details that Mr Mani spoke about.'

She shook hands with them and I followed suit as Egbers closed the door and stood with his back to it, facing the room, like a club bouncer. Was this really going to happen?

The elder one introduced himself as Theodore Alexandris. He had a strong Greek accent and was maybe mid-forties, something like that. The other was in his thirties, and introduced himself as Lukas Fischer. He had the American accent that Germans always had in the old war films.

Theodore took control in a polite-but-we-are-here-for-business manner. 'Please, Charlotte, sit, make yourself comfortable. This shouldn't take long.'

We both took seats to face them across the desk. Neither of us had said a word since the initial hellos. Charlotte was still shocked at the potential this meeting had to change everything, one way or another. I knew it: I was having exactly the same feelings.

Theodore got down to business. 'So, Charlotte. SIB is Mr Mani's bank. It's more efficient to handle his business and personal affairs in-house, so to speak.'

'What does SIB stand for?'

Theodore mistook my question as concern. 'Subramanian International Banking. But please do not worry. This is a real bank that is certified and regulated by the Federal Reserve.

Please feel free to verify our details. I'll give them to you, if you wish.'

I shook my head. 'Not necessary, but thank you.'

Theodore got back to business and explained to Charlotte, 'It's a simple transfer. You have absolute power over the account. No other signatories are required. Here we have a chequebook for you, which I think you'll never use, but regulations state you must be issued with a physical means of withdrawal and payment. However, you'll also have your card for the account. The PIN is 7890. You can change it to whatever you wish. There's only one card, and it's yours. And, of course, you can transfer the monies to wherever, to whoever, and whenever you wish – even today. I will be your personal account manager. Anything you need, just call me. I will leave all my details for you. Feel free to contact me any time, day or night. I am at your service. Now . . . we have some paperwork for you to sign so that you can control your account.'

Lukas had been busy fishing paperwork from his bag and passed it across the desk. Then he flourished a fountain pen, the lid already removed for her. 'Please, Charlotte, take your time, there is no rush. Any questions, please just ask.'

I could see what she was about to sign, and the amount was exactly what Parmesh had promised: thirty million pounds sterling. She read, she signed, and as she pushed everything back to Lukas, it was Theodore's turn. He pulled out a large white envelope and smiled as he passed it across.

'Welcome to the bank. And on completion of the task, the same amount again will be deposited into this account – your account, Charlotte.'

'Why me? Why have I been chosen? Why not James, or why not make it a joint account?'

Egbers stepped forward from the door. 'Because you are an

accountant, you know money, and Mr Mani knows that James has enough to think about.'

Lukas had finally checked Charlotte's signed paperwork and Theodore closed his bag. They both stood. We got up, and Theodore's hand came out across the desk to Charlotte and they shook.

'I can sense the enormity of what is happening, Charlotte. But please take comfort that Mr Mani has the ability to think on a scale larger than anyone I have ever known. He will touch the world for us. That's why we have dedicated ourselves to ensuring it happens. I know these are early days for you and for James, but Mr Mani has faith in both of you. All you have to do is have hope and believe.'

Charlotte looked as if she still had a bit more shock left in her, and Theodore sensed it. 'Please call me whenever you need to. You have my details. As I said, I'm at your disposal twenty-four hours a day. From this moment, you are in complete control of the account. Do with it what you wish. Like I said, Mr Mani has total faith in you. In both of you.'

He turned to me and we shook. Then they left with Egbers.

The two of us collapsed rather than sat down. Charlotte tipped the card, the chequebook, and Theodore's contact details onto the desk as if she was checking this wasn't a dream.

We both stared at them for what felt like an hour before we came back to the real world, and Charlotte stuffed everything into her jeans. '*Okaaay*. What do you think?'

We had to remain practical. 'I think you need to check the money actually exists.'

Charlotte agreed, but I could see her head was elsewhere. Understandably.

We headed back to Reception, with no sign of the bankers or Egbers. Not only was that meeting one that I would never forget, it had got me thinking.

'Know what? I get what you said about boiling their brains. It's just done mine. So shall we say, like, a million? That's still a lot of cash to let sink in. And once we're out of here, we can tell them about their bonus fourteen? Maybe your new personal banker will help them manage it.'

I threw her a smile, more in relief that the shock had begun to subside and I was trying hard to grab some reality back.

Charlotte joined in with my smile and tried to sound casual. 'Yep. Just a million. Enough brain-boiling for today.'

We couldn't help but laugh as we sat on one of the reception settees to order even more coffees. Tony came through the main door and into the foyer. Warren and Gemma were close behind, and all were heading our way, looking a lot less knackered but still red-eyed.

Gemma greeted us. 'Morning. At least you two got out the funny side of the bed this morning. I'm still fucked.'

We listened to their bad-night, jetlag stories and heard how their body clocks had got them up at GMT so they'd walked around the town. Gemma checked her watch. 'Ten to. Are we still up at your place at eleven?'

'Yep, on our way there now. With you in a tick.'

They headed for the lift and Charlotte jumped up. 'It's no good – I've got to check this is real now. I'm going to an ATM.'

40

Back in my room, waiting for the team to arrive, I sat on the bed and took a couple of deep breaths. I was excited for Charlotte, for me, for all of us. What if it was true? But we weren't exactly drinking cocktails on the beach just yet. And, of course, there was a job to be done first, plus Egbers and his threats. About that, though, I was starting to feel that maybe, just maybe, the threat level had dialled back a bit when Charlotte arrived. Only a bit, of course: in the back of my mind, reality lingered. The images of the Filipino and Richard were embedded. What would happen to the team if they turned down the offer?

There was a knock on the door, the sound of laughter outside and voices. I used the couple of seconds before I opened to steel myself. For their families' sakes, it was up to me to make sure they accepted.

Three smiling faces greeted me, still waffling about what they'd seen around the town.

I beamed back. 'I'll get some coffee.'

Gemma took over, picked up the phone. 'I'll do it. I want a smoothie anyway.'

Warren grabbed the second chair by the desk and Tony walked over to the large patio doors and admired the lake.

It was Warren who noticed first. 'Where's Charlotte?'

I was still standing by the settee where Egbers and the Brit normally positioned themselves. I felt more in control there.

'She'll be here soon. She had an errand to run.'

We talked about the town and I shared the bits and pieces I knew about it. Then Warren asked about the job.

'Let's wait for Charlotte, mate.'

There was a knock on the door. Room service pushed in a trolley of coffees and Gemma's smoothie, with a plate of pastries. People jumped on it like no one had eaten all morning. I checked my watch as they settled down again. Tony got into one of the chairs and pulled apart an almond croissant.

We passed more time. Gemma liked the sound of the boats screaming past: she wanted to go for a ride later, then find a rugby game to watch. Warren was up for a longer wander: soak up the atmosphere, send postcards home, all that sort of stuff, because it was going to rain. He was sure it was: hadn't anyone else seen it on the weather forecast?

Tony wasn't listening: he was too busy looking at a second croissant.

Another check of my watch. 'We'll give her five more minutes, yeah?'

At last there was a gentle knock on the door, and she stood there, face serious. Good sign or bad? The team clapped her in as a late arrival and she gave them a forced smile.

I kept it upbeat. 'All good?'

Charlotte just stared at me. I glanced around the team but they were too busy with their drinks and licking icing sugar off their hands to notice. I glanced back at Charlotte. She was in shock, without a doubt. But shock good or shock bad?

41

I needed to keep those visions of the Filipino and Richard front and centre while I delivered my pitch. They must be the last victims. I clapped my hands to bring myself back to the real world. 'Okay, welcome, everyone.' I took a deep breath. There was no other way of selling this. 'The job's different from what Charlotte will have explained. Basically . . . I lied to her to get you all down here.'

Gemma was first in. 'Lied? What the fuck? There's work here, isn't there? You said you'd pay up front and you're getting no fucking money back.' Her eyes narrowed. 'You getting us in the shit?'

What else could I say? She was right.

'Only if the job goes wrong. Look, I've got you all down here because I need you to help me steal something.'

Tony's eyes jerked up from his sticky bun and Warren stared at me with a slow shake of the head as he reached for the door.

It was pointless trying to stop him or reason with him. I knew him too well. We watched in silence as he disappeared and the door gently clicked to lock.

I turned back to the others. 'That wasn't exactly the reaction I was after. Don't worry, he'll come round.'

At least no one else had followed.

Gemma didn't need to show anything. As always, she just verbalized. But it wasn't me she turned on. 'Charlotte, what makes you think I'm not gonna follow him? When did you know about this shit?'

'After he asked me to contact you. I'm sorry. Look, I'll go and find Warren. Just listen to what James has to say, please.'

Charlotte held out her hand for the key card before she left the room, while Gemma put her feet on the bed and pushed herself back in the chair. She wasn't happy.

I carried on: 'I'm also sorry I lied, I really am. But I had to.'

I told them exactly what I'd initially told Charlotte, about what had been happening down here for the past seven years, and the reasons why. Then, of course, that I'd got caught and been made to steal the ledger. 'Nothing else, just a book.'

I'd had a brain-baby incubating since they'd entered the room, and gave birth to it in that moment. I reached under the bed for the Jiffy-bag and raised it above my head. 'I don't know what's in it, and that's the way it has to stay. As soon as I get the ledger, it has to go in this and stay concealed. We hand it over and we're done. Rich people, rich problems. I don't care. And I'm hoping you don't. That's why I'm standing in front of you now. I need your help, and I need Warren's help. I didn't know any other way to get you down here except to lie – and to Charlotte. For that, I'm sorry. But you still have a choice, even Warren.'

Gemma jumped in. 'Why didn't you tell them, whoever caught you, to fuck off? Or just do a runner?'

I took a breath, about to tell the truth, but she got in there first. 'Who are they? And why us?'

She raised her hand and was about to jab a finger at me, but

I silenced her. 'I can't – I *won't* – tell you. It's better you don't know. Better for you and for me . . . and I can't just refuse the job, or run. They threatened to hurt Pip and the boys. I can't take any chances. I'm here until the job is done, no matter if you're with me or not.'

I hadn't heard the door open, but it was Charlotte who broke the silence. 'I'm with you.'

42

Warren followed her into the room and took his seat by the desk. I continued as if he'd never left. That was always the best way with Warren. He'd always been the same, and even as a kid I understood why. His parents were arseholes compared to ours. As far as they were concerned, Warren was never good enough at school, at sport, or even at just being a kid. Everything he did was shit – even a drawing, the kind my kids had sent me, would be put in the bin rather than on the fridge. Surely he could have done better.

I used to ignore him when he threw a wobbler, and would continue with whatever it was we were doing or playing. I knew he would eventually realize he was being a dickhead and would join back in as if nothing had happened, and I would let it stay that way. I had no idea how Jackie coped with him, but that was love, I supposed.

'I don't know what's in the ledger. Just billionaire stuff. Industrial secrets, who knows?' I checked over to Charlotte and she nodded.

'There's no one to get hurt, no one to avoid. The house is

unoccupied. We just make our way in, take the ledger and go. The end.'

Warren had to rejoin quickly. It was his tactic to make himself feel better, to confirm everything was back to normal. 'If it's that easy, why are we here?'

'Because, mate, I need masters of form – and that's you three. Believe it or not.'

They weren't ready for jokes and it missed the mark, but I pushed on. I explained about the house, the outbuilding, the tunnel between them, the bung, the void, the tiled wall – and, critically, that we must leave no sign of ever having been there. 'That's why you're here. Tony: electrics. Gemma: getting past the bung. Warren: restoring the wall tiles but from the rear of a stud-wall. At first I thought that would be impossible. But then I thought, Maybe I know a man who can . . .'

Warren still wasn't onboard. His eyes were fixed on his boots. 'It's not for me, James. I have family to think about – it's not worth the risk. Besides, I'm not a thief.' He looked up and stared at me. 'And neither were you.'

He was right. We locked eyes. At least he was back in the room.

'What was I supposed to do, mate? Sit back and blame karma for what happened? I wanted to get some payback from the people who took it from us. The same people who took it from *your* families. What can I say? I steal, but I don't feel like a thief. You know me better than that, mate.'

Charlotte was by the bathroom door, one shoulder leaning on the frame. She concentrated on Warren. I couldn't tell who she agreed with on this one – maybe both of us. It didn't really matter: when it came to the crunch she was on my side.

Warren stared, like he was wondering what had gone wrong with me.

My eyes turned to the other two. Tony sat cross-legged on

the chair. Elbow resting on his thigh, he put his chin in his hand. He looked sort of lost or bored but, then, I never had been able to tell what was going on in his head. He was so laid-back he was almost horizontal. But that was why I liked him so much, maybe even loved him. All my life there had been this caring, calm consistency about him. I'd noticed it even more when Dad died, and his kindness had really helped me to take the pain. Warren could have done with an Uncle Tony.

It was Gemma who came back, with enough spark for all three of them. 'I'm with Warren. What the fuck you doing, James? It's far too risky. It doesn't matter what you're nicking. I don't know about here, but that's jail time back home. For fifty grand? Really? Come on, for fuck's sake.'

Now was the time. I chanced a grin. 'What about two million, then? Two million pounds each.'

I looked at each of them in turn, but avoided Charlotte. I didn't know why I'd upped the amount by a million, but it felt right. Anything to get them onboard. It certainly got raised eyebrows from Warren and Gemma. From Tony there was no reaction, no way to determine what was going on inside his head.

'Two million each. That's what you walk away with. The fifty was part of the lie to get you down here. Think about that. Think about what that would mean to your life, and to your kids' lives. Isn't it time we got something back from the people who took it all from us? Isn't that worth the risk?'

I was finding it hard to judge the mood. But I was hoping it was boiling their brains just a little.

'Look, if you don't want to help me, and you hate me for lying, think about Pip and the kids. Charlotte? Me? We've got no choice, they're family. We have them to think about, but you can just think about the money. That's what I do.

I have to think about the upside on this. And I want to share it with you.'

Tony still didn't look interested, let alone convinced. 'How do we know the money exists? It sounds too much. It must be worth so much more to him, to be offering that sort of reward.'

'You're right. But that's not our concern. What I can tell you is that we already have the cash – it's in an account, and it's safe. It can't be handed out, though – it's far too much to go unnoticed by the banks. We'll have to find a way of dealing with that. But the money's there, ready and waiting.'

I kept my eyes from Charlotte: I still didn't know if she had been refused at the ATM.

Warren looked up at me. No words. I hoped he was thinking about how the money would change everything. I hoped he wanted to be dragged into this screaming.

'It's a risk, mate, there's no doubt about it. But what about your girls' future? Maybe worth it. It is for my kids.'

Then it sounded like I was losing Gemma again. 'I'm up for anything, but going to jail? No way. No matter how much the system fucked us up. They are the man with the plan. We're nothing to them. We're just dust. A click of the fingers.'

Tony sat there, brooding.

Charlotte pushed herself off the doorframe and faced us. '*Okaaay* . . . what I think is this. I think it's payback time for everything we've all been through. All our families' work, our labours, fears, the stress and the sheer bloody anger at these people. Yes, there's risk for us all. But you have risk every day, don't you? Getting out there, working, making ends meet, trying to recover some dignity and pride – you take risks all the time.

'And these people, you're right, Gemma, they don't care. But why should they? They always get what they want. So what I think is, we give them what they want – the ledger – and we get their money. Dignity, pride, security. What's worth more?'

She was on a roll and no one could look at her. All eyes were focused on the wall, the window, a croissant, anywhere but Charlotte. It was a good sign? I was hoping.

'We're not like these people. Even the world isn't big enough for them now – they all want to go to the moon or build communities on Mars. It's like now they've defeated the earth, they want to control the entire universe. They've got the ultimate God complex. But so what?

'I don't care how they want to spend their money. Because one of them has chosen to spend it on you.' She looked around the room. 'Look at me. You need to take on board what I'm going to say.'

They did as they were asked. She had something about her that had always commanded the field when it was needed.

43

'It's not two million. It's fifteen. Fifteen million pounds each. And it's real.'

She stopped for effect and looked across at me with a shrug. Fair one: we needed something to get them across the line.

'I already control fifty per cent of the cash. We were worried that if we said exactly how much was on offer it would blow your minds. It did ours!'

The room fell silent, but Charlotte wasn't going to let that happen for long.

'Fifteen – million – pounds – each.'

She let it hang for another few seconds. 'I'll organize some of it to go to you today to cover your debts, the things that keep you all awake at night. But after today they will not exist. I'll make it happen if you come onboard. And I'll do it even if you just walk away now. But, please, the risk . . . fifteen million pounds each? It's got to be worth it, hasn't it?'

Gemma didn't give Charlotte enough time even to lean back on the door. 'Fuck it, what if we just take whatever's there now and run?'

I shook my head, but Charlotte made the answer. 'With their money and their power? We'd never get away with it.'

Gemma gave a shrug, but thankfully there was a smile along with it. 'Fuck it, then, if Captain Calamity's in, I'm in.'

Warren wasn't quite there yet. His question was for me. 'What happens if we get caught? Or fail? We don't get the book? What happens then?'

'Look, mate, if we get caught, we maybe go to prison. Simple as that. But what are we stealing? A book, bits of paper. Breaking into a house. This isn't an armed bank robbery. But what I do know, half of what you'd get is already there waiting for you, no matter what happens. The kids sorted for ever.'

He was getting there.

'Look, the guy who wants the book has faith in me – and he has faith in Charlotte. So if we finish the job, the remainder of the cash will be there. I've looked at the job and it's doable. If not, I wouldn't have asked you down here.'

Warren finally gathered his thoughts. 'But what happens if I just go home now, not taking any money, but knowing what I know?'

With Richard and the Filipino in my head, I'd been hoping no one would ask that.

'I really don't know. It's the same . . .' I searched for the word '. . . *forces* that threaten Pip and the kids. They may do the same. But just think, if we pull it off . . .'

He was looking angry. I had put his family at risk, and I felt a shit for that. I understood. I left him to it for a while.

'What do you think, Tony?'

He nodded slowly, as if he was accepting a late-night cup of cocoa. 'I'm in.'

My relief must have been plain to see, and in case it wasn't, they would have heard my little gasp of delight.

Tony uncrossed his legs so he could lean in to Warren.

'I was in from the start, boy. I don't care, now that Maureen's gone. I'll do it for you lot. Our generation worked their fingers to the bone to try to make your life better than ours. And for what? To be treated like serfs. More setbacks, more tax, then put on the scrap heap once no longer suited to requirements. So it's your turn now to make a better life for your kids. This is an opportunity, a risky one, mind, but aren't they all? Besides, Kiwi prisons might have a lot more going for them than the UK's. If we get put inside, I might finally get to take up watercolours.'

He squashed his nose, which covered half of his face, then let it go. 'And I might finally get this big boy sorted out.'

It got a laugh, like it had done since we were kids.

That still left Warren.

Charlotte hunkered down beside him. 'Tell me how much you need now to clear all your debts and I'll work out a way for that to happen. The problem is, Jackie mustn't know, not yet. No one must know.'

She placed both hands on his arm and at that very moment my head started to burst. What I had said to everyone about Parmesh's faith in me . ... It suddenly hit me: I really did have faith in him. I really did believe him. Was this how these connections, commitments, happened? Was I really having my road-to-Damascus moment, now, in a hotel room in Queenstown? Maybe I was. It felt like it.

Now wasn't the time to dwell, but it changed the way I thought about everything.

'I identified you three, not just because you're so good at what you do but because you're just like us. Just normal people, screwed over. But out of our nightmares, maybe something good comes for all of us. It's the only chance you'll ever get at doing something that will change lives.'

I really *was* having my road-to-Damascus moment. I wasn't

just saying this for the good of my friends and their families, but for the good of the world. I actually believed it.

Tony got up and patted Warren's shoulder while clearing his throat of pastry. 'I'll look after you, son, don't you worry. I'll get you home for Christmas.'

He made a show of checking with Charlotte, now on her feet, and finally strode over to Gemma, who was gagging to know more. 'So how the fuck are you going to sort this money?'

Charlotte was on it. 'I'll organize an account for each of you that you control, today. And I'm going to put two hundred thousand in each account. And, remember, tell absolutely no one about this. Our safety depends on no one knowing. You'll have to lie, and I know it's hard, but it's for everyone's good.'

Tony laughed. 'Lie? Fifteen million lies, more like. No problem here, my girl.'

Warren still wasn't in any mood to laugh.

Tony squeezed his shoulder again, just like he'd done to me so many times over the years. 'That's right, sonny – stealing back from the bastards who stole from us. They're all as bad as each other. Just a couple of billionaires fighting over a few pages of paper. Fair game, I say. Don't worry, it'll be okay. Your family – it's your job to provide for them. That's what you'll be doing. If you were my boy, I'd be proud of you.'

Tony gave me a wink that said, 'It'll be okay.'

Warren nodded slowly, though I wasn't sure who it was for.

I tried not to betray too much relief in my voice. 'Thank you, all. Back at five?'

It went quiet until Gemma brought things back to earth. 'Right – fuck it, then. I'm out to have a good look around. Anyone up for it?'

The other two stood up, and as Tony dusted icing sugar off his jeans he closed up to Warren. 'I could do with a pint. You?'

Gemma turned to Charlotte. 'That lunch you promised is

binned. You two have got that shitload of cash to sort out. Yes!' She pumped the air, then grabbed Charlotte and planted a big kiss on her cheek. She turned to me. 'Resistance would be futile!' She grinned as she wrapped her arms round me and crushed.

They left after we'd agreed to meet up that evening. Charlotte would have some news about the cash.

The room was suddenly quiet. There weren't even any thrill-seekers out on the lake. All I could hear was the hum of the air-conditioning.

44

Charlotte and I stood staring at each other for what felt like an eternity, before she broke it with exactly what I was thinking. 'Shit! This is really happening, isn't it?'

'Think so . . . Warren?'

'Not sure.'

She shrugged, knowing we just had to wait and see.

Reaching into her jeans back pocket, she pulled out a wad of notes and handed me a hundred-dollar bill. 'One each. I'm framing mine.'

I folded the polymer note with its translucent window into my jeans, trying hard not to think of all the bad things that might lie in store for us.

She slumped into a chair, like all the air had left the balloon.

'Charlotte?'

She kept staring at the wall. Eventually she snapped out of it. 'Yessss?'

'I believe Parmesh. I really do believe what he's doing is right. It just happened. I'm going to do it, not just for the boys and Pip, and even if Warren or any of those three change their minds. It just sort of happened. I have hope, and I don't know why.'

She turned to me and leant closer. 'You can be so thick some-times. Come on, he's a strong leader in a very likeable way. He wants to do the right thing, he wants to love, he wants to guide. He's just like . . . ?'

She waited for me to fill it in, but all I had was a blank. Charlotte rolled her eyes and the look on her face took me straight back to our childhood. It felt so comforting.

'Dad, you idiot.'

'What?'

'When Dad died we all felt the pain – but you, Parker, you've been in a vacuum ever since. Lost, no guidance, no point of reference. And all this cat-burglar stuff makes it even clearer to me.

'I know you better than you know yourself, thick boy. Hey, it's not a problem. If it works for you, it works for me.'

We sat back in our chairs, staring out at nothing in particular.

'What did Simon say about you coming down here?'

She exhaled long and slow and stretched out her legs. 'Not a lot, really. I didn't give him time to get worked up. I took the dogs to the kennels and didn't go back.'

'Oh. Sorry.'

'Don't be. He was a crap partner and even crapper painter. I mean, he couldn't even finish the hallway, let alone morph into the next Picasso. Even your boys' drawings are better than his.'

It was true and funny, but we were both too exhausted to laugh.

'Anyway, at least I don't have to worry about my half of the rent. You know he got me to sign an agreement when I moved in, the arsehole?'

Now that did get a laugh.

'What did you ever see in him? I mean, he was always being a dickhead.'

She thought for a couple of seconds. 'We were just two lonelies, I guess.'

I shrugged. 'So I suppose you're going to call Theodore and organize something for the team? Could you call Pip while you're at it? Tell her everything's fine and to say to the boys I love them, can't wait to see them, and I love my pictures. They're on my hotel wall.'

They were. To the left of the TV. They looked fantastic.

45

The five of us were focused on the laptop screen as the drone footage played for the fourth time. I froze the image on the side elevation of the outbuilding and pointed with a hotel pen to where the wall met the roof. 'There – that's where I saw the red indicator. Tony?'

He wasn't looking where I was pointing. His eyes were flicking round the screen, looking, I guessed, for other sensors, power lines in and out, anything that would help him form a picture of how the house was powered up – and, more importantly, alarmed.

Besides the video footage, we'd checked Google Earth, Google Maps, What 3 Words – anything open-source that would help us come up with a plan. We went through the video once more, then the other four peeled away from the screen and found places to sit. Tony and Warren took chairs, Gemma sat on the end of the bed, and Charlotte on the desk. Everyone was everywhere but the spare space on the settee.

I had moved out of the way and stood by the entrance to the bathroom, feeling confident. After all, this was planning, logical, methodical thought. I could do this stuff. What was more, I knew how to keep teams together. On a site, I herded contractor cats to the same point, and I was good at it. Something else I'd inherited from the old man.

I needed everyone's attention. 'So – the aim of this . . . What should I call it? Venture?' I tried it out with air quotes for comic effect, but it scarcely raised a smile.

Warren was still depressed with doubt. But that was okay: it was normal. The main thing was that he'd stayed. I wanted to thank him for being there, for making the right decision, but that would be acknowledging there had been a problem in the first place. So, as normal, I ignored it, just as he liked.

I was concerned that his negativity was affecting the team, but as I looked across at the settee, I realized the room's mood might have been down to the fact that Egbers was sitting there, bolt upright, black polo shirt, grey cargoes, creases in his sleeves and perfectly groomed hair. Humans were good at sensing danger. I knew I was. He hadn't said anything after I'd introduced him as our middle guy and help, but he was so good at creating an atmosphere just by being in a room.

But the way my body reacted to him being close by had changed since that morning. I sensed less danger from him. I got where he was coming from, and even felt a bit of ease from him in the way he'd treated me since Charlotte arrived. Something was different. Was it me or him?

'All right, not a venture – we're here to steal the ledger from Sanctuary.'

That didn't get any laughs, but it wasn't meant to. I pushed on. 'I'm thinking we split the whole job into five phases. Phase one: getting us and the equipment into the outbuilding. Phase two: getting through the bung and into the void. Phase three: accessing the house through the wall. Phase four: finding the ledger. Phase five: retracing our steps, making everything as new and leaving town.'

There was a general nod. Why not? So far it made sense, right?

'Okay, phase one. How do we get to the outbuilding? First of all, we fly to the hard standing, which we can only assume is a helicopter pad.'

Gemma pulled a face. 'I thought no one was supposed to know we'd ever been there. But drop in by heli, what the fuck?'

It looked like there was more scepticism to come so I held up a hand. 'We're going to use two drones. The same ones that took the video.'

I seemed to have their attention. Everyone straightened in their seats.

'All's good. I've flown from one – they're designed for recovering casualties from the battle space. Not much noise, and they're quick and easy. We don't even have to fly them – there's the Js, the pilots, operators, whatever they're called – and we leave no sign outside to show we've been there. You'll love it. Flying past trees – it's great. That lot out on the lake would pay good money to do it.'

There didn't seem much enthusiasm, but Tony jumped in to add some geekiness: 'Do you know the maximum weight these things will lift?'

I shook my head. 'But it's got to be a lot. Wounded soldiers, with body armour, kit and ammo?'

'Well, we need to know the max they can carry, and for how long with a full charge. We also need to know if the battery packs are in series or parallel – I should imagine parallel because it's all about the output capacity, the output voltage. More time in the sky, if you like. Can we find that out?'

Tony didn't bother checking with me: it was Egbers he looked to for the nod.

'Perfect. Then I can work out the ideal payload for them, because we'll have a lot more journeys than one wounded body being brought home.'

I carried on with what else we needed to do with the little information I had, but I needed to manage any information requests from the team carefully – or someone else might get thrown into the ocean. But if the information was essential? I decided I'd cross that bridge when or if I had to.

'So, getting into the outbuilding. It's the intruder-detection systems that are the pain because we're waiting to find out what they are.'

I checked with Egbers, who just gave a nod.

'Until then, we have to assume they exist, and until we know what they're capable of, we need to assume the worst. It could be motion detectors outside, heat-source detectors, anything and everything. How can we cut whatever they have without knowing what it is? Tony, all yours, mate.'

He was at a loss. 'You just said it. If we don't know what intruder systems they have, I can't do anything with them, can I, boy? Even cutting the power to the house, any systems would still work. They got PVs and Teslas.'

He was only getting warmed up. 'But if we can't do anything about the house itself, we need to know where any alert goes to. No point having an audible alarm given where the house is – only the birds are going to hear that. Any system is connected to an ARC.'

We all waited to find out what that meant.

'An Alarm Receiving Centre. For high security it would normally be to a private security company – the police response is always slower. So the ARC could receive the alert via the mobile network, if it's 4G, or even via satellite, maybe even both, dual path signalling. Or it could be even real old-school and via a landline. But the alarm has got to go somewhere, to tell someone that something is up. If we know where it goes to, we might be able to intercept it before it gets there. Then the alarms can shout all they want and no one will ever know.'

Parmesh had the world's resources at his disposal. We could make all sorts of things happen. 'What if the power was down in the whole area?' I asked. 'They have outages round here all the time.'

Tony grinned. 'You're thinking right, boy. You're thinking big-time. The problem is the power in the house. The Powerwalls and back-up power systems will still supply output.'

'Okay. What if we cut the power, cut the landline, and cut the mobile network too?'

Tony looked at me like I was frothing at the mouth. 'Really?'

'Yes, really. Think even bigger-time. I'll get you whatever you need.'

'Mobile towers have back-up power, same as landlines. They need very little juice to keep going. And what if they've got a satellite? They're unrelatable so we just don't know what they've got until we know what systems the house actually has.'

He was right, of course, and I glanced at Egbers, but his face was stone.

'As soon as I know you will.'

That was good enough for planning. We'd have to come up with plan B.

'Can you get all the power and communications cut? We'll need their power back-ups to go down as well.'

I kept looking at him. He didn't move a muscle, apart from the ones in his jaw. 'I will find out.'

Tony wanted the last word. 'The bugger is, we need power.

Do we know if the Teslas are definitely online? If not, we'd better fly in gennies, just in case.'

I got back to the team. 'Okay, we sideline that for now until we get an answer. Tony, think about it. Gemma, think about it. Warren, think about it. So, we get into the outbuilding. Whether there's a door to the tunnel, we don't know, but we'll get past it. We *have* to get past it.'

46

'Phase two: we move down into the tunnel and we get to the bung. Gemma, the manufacturer's spec gives you two hundred millimetres of pre-cast.'

She looked confident. 'I'll spend more time fucking about setting up the kit than cutting.'

I'd have liked her to have thought about it a bit more, but of course she already had. 'Like you said, masters of fucking form, or what?'

That did raise a laugh, from everyone but Egbers.

'I'll cut a core big enough for everyone to push through. Even you, Tony.'

Another laugh, the biggest from Tony.

'On the way out I'll replace the core, then cover the tunnel side with a concrete render. But what about the equipment I'm going to need? Will the drone be able to carry it?'

I looked at Egbers. He nodded. 'Once you know the maximum weight per flight, you'll have your answer.'

Gemma gave him a nod back. 'Nice.'

I wasn't sure if she was talking about the drones or Egbers.

'Okay, so we're into the void. We take in all the kit with us because we're going to leave everything in the void. All we take out with us is whatever kit Gemma needs to render over the bung on the way out.'

What was the point of taking all the kit away with us? By the time they had opened up the void – if ever – they would know the ledger had gone. At least Castro would have the satisfaction of knowing how his ledger had disappeared.

'Phase three. We're facing the block-wall. The other side of that has stud-wall, then tiling, then the basement. The vertical studs have 450-millimetre spacing and the tiles are 250 by 400 mil, laid horizontally and stack-bonded.'

All the stuff Richard had provided in the heli – I fought to keep my head clear of him – his words falling over themselves as he tried to please us all with detail.

'So, Warren, what do you reckon?'

He hadn't laughed as much as everybody else, but when he did, he was doing it in spite of himself. I tried to take that as a positive. He knew what he had to do, and he looked at each of us in turn to make sure that we knew. 'I'll get the block out first and leave the stud in situ, then cut out a section of stud to the tile, work out where the grouting is, and cut a panel of tiles to get everything through.'

He raised a finger. 'But I'm going to need time to re-lay the tiles on a steel mesh, like a trapdoor, and match up the grout when we reverse the action. I'll have all the different colour matchings with me, but it will take time.'

Warren tilted his body to look past me at Egbers. 'Can we find out the colour and type of grout used?'

I jumped straight in. 'No.'

I wouldn't let another body go limp, not for a colour match, anyway.

Warren straightened up, waiting for the reason. He was going to get one.

'You'll have no problem. Once we're inside Sanctuary, you'll have time to match. Even if we get the ledger in quick time, we'll wait for you to get it right. There'll be no rush, mate.'

He nodded, not realizing that he might have saved a life. 'So we take sandwiches?'

He was being serious, and everyone nodded. I'd forgotten: they might be masters of form, but at heart they were trades-people. British tradespeople.

He carried on: 'I'll give Gemma a hand with the bung render and I'll be able to texture it for her. No one will see the cut.'

Gemma held out a fist for a bump and got one. Sort of: Warren had never been street.

'Okay, phase four: we're in the house – where do we go? Where is the ledger? In a safe? Hidden somewhere?'

The team obviously didn't know the answer, but I'd turned my head towards the settee. Egbers made no movement, except with his mouth again. 'We don't know exactly yet. But we're nearly there – and as soon as we do, you must be able to act quickly and retrieve the ledger. It's very important. You must retrieve it as soon as we know. It could be tomorrow, it could be in three days. We don't know how long yet.'

'Does that mean you aren't coming in with us now?'

'I'll be there, but by holoport. I'll be leaving the country as soon as you know when you're entering Sanctuary. I have things to do that will help you. That's why you're taking the holoport in with you. You will need a cell system, but if the towers have to be closed down, we'll fly our own secure rebroadcasters over the house for the holoport to connect to. It's important that we maintain a connection. Without the holoport, it'll be impossible to access the ledger. Do you understand?'

'Got it.'

Egbers at last moved more than his lips as he gave a curt nod. 'Good.'

I turned to the team. 'Okay, then. First round, all good.'

Egbers stood, said his goodbyes to Charlotte, then left.

47

Tony was bursting. 'He's a bundle of joy, isn't he? What's this holy port?'

'Holoport. I'll explain later.'

Gemma wasn't thinking about any details. 'He can hang from my drone any time he likes.'

Charlotte shook her head. 'That's an image I won't get out of my mind in a hurry. Let's talk about money instead. We'll have your account cards for you later today. Two hundred K in each account. Please remember, think carefully about this, everyone. Just move cash around to cover what you need to, no more than ten thousand at a time. Any more, and your banks will have to ask you where you got it.

'Use it just to clear cards, or draw down from cash machines to use for normal life stuff. No big purchases, nothing your life couldn't normally absorb. Not just yet. Once we're done, there'll be help for us all on how to deal with this kind of money.

'You'll also need to buy whatever you need for the job – and, of course, organize your own transport. Please, please, please, tell no one.'

Warren hadn't lightened up, even once Egbers had left. He

was becoming borderline aggressive with Charlotte. 'You've got it all sorted out, haven't you? What are you risking for your fifteen million? Oh, I forgot, you'll be running the books back here.'

Charlotte's eyes narrowed. 'Warren, I'll be taking the same risks as you because I'll be there to help you and anyone else in any way I can. And you know what? I'm not getting paid one single penny. I'm here for Pip and the boys, remember?'

He did. It was clear to see during the awkward silence that followed.

Tony broke it. 'Let's not worry about that, Warren. Let's spend the rest of the night getting our shopping lists together for the knowns we need, while we think about the unknowns we might need. Then we can be up at sparrow's fart with a plan and get on with it. What do you say, son?'

He put his hand on Warren's shoulder and gave Charlotte a wink as he coaxed the younger man towards the door.

Gemma followed. 'I'm going to look at one of those big fuck-off pick-up trucks.'

Tony stood in the doorway as Warren stepped out into the corridor and disappeared off to the right. He had decided to hover over my walking boots, which still had their socks draped over them. He bent down and picked up a sock. 'Can I have this?'

Why would he just want the one? 'Take the pair – they're stinking the place out anyway.'

Soon the room was empty apart from us two, and we took a chair each. Charlotte was worried about Warren. 'You think he'll do it?'

'He will. Don't worry. Tony'll look after him. We'll all look after him.' I pretend-punched her jaw. 'I didn't know you were coming?'

She got up, went to the minibar and grabbed some chocolate

and two Steinlagers. 'Neither did I.' On her way back to the chairs she looked straight at me, as if she was deliberately trying to make me feel bad. 'I'm here to look after the kids and Pip, not just my arsehole bro.'

She smiled as forcefully as she could to underline the sarcasm. She was still angry with me, but it would pass. She sat down, unscrewed the bottle tops and handed a beer over, then unwrapped the foil from the chocolate. 'I was worried about Egbers coming in with us. It'll be harder to copy the ledger.' She broke the bar and passed me one of the halves. We sat there munching, drinking and thinking.

It took a while for me to get through the chocolate before breaking the quiet. 'Know what? It doesn't matter. We don't need to copy anything. All is good.'

She clearly felt that it wasn't, because she didn't bother replying. She just continued to munch at the 98 per cent cocoa and finish her lager.

I got up and headed for the phone as I checked my watch. 'The dinner menu's started. They've got great burgers.'

PART SEVEN

48

The Toyota was parked facing the Mitre 10 Mega on Frankton Road, close to the airport. The 7 a.m. opening time meant the day's preparations had started early. Mega by name, mega by nature, the 'home improvement warehouse' was massive, orange, unmissable. Egbers and the Brit would easily find it, so when they'd called about fifteen minutes ago to say they needed an urgent meet, I stayed where I was and waited for them to come to me.

I'd just bought the final items on my list: a set of hand-held luggage scales, five contractors' boxes of blue disposable decorator's overalls with boot covers and hoods, dust masks, safety goggles and rubber gloves. Plus loads of stuff we might need to try to cater for Tony's 'unknowns'.

The morning had been a frenzy of activity while we waited for Egbers to tell us anything he had found out about the intruder systems and where the ledger was. But the longer he took, the longer we had to prepare.

Gemma and Tony had hired a Nissan pick-up each with a hardtop covering the tailgate.

Gemma and Charlotte were using Gemma's right now for a reconnaissance of Hunter Road and the phone line set-up along it, and eventually to Sanctuary. Tony was in town somewhere with Warren getting more kit and had just texted. He wanted a box of large steel paperclips, not coloured or plastic coated, just steel. I didn't bother asking, just went and got. Warren had been hovering over his different-sized disc cutters and colour charts along with RAL number mixes for the grout since last night.

Both vehicles were crammed with kit. Jerry-cans of water for the render and grout in case we couldn't access water. Gemma's core drill, with a heavy-duty core-drill bit to carve through the concrete. She'd also bought loads of blue plastic tarpaulins to keep dust off the floor, and even a Henry vacuum cleaner and a broom in case they didn't. Tony and Warren had got hold of all the gear they needed, and everybody checked in with me almost hourly as they came up with ideas for the known unknowns.

The one thing we did know for sure from the Js was that, to maximize power from the drones' batteries, which were in series for superior output capacity, they would have to have a lift limit of 97 kilograms for this job. Even Tony came in under that – just – though he might have to travel with a light load. I'd also learnt from Egbers and the Brit how to rig up the holoport, and had walked Tony through it well before Mitre 10 Mega had even opened. He had no problem under-standing the technology – in fact, he grasped it better and faster than I did.

The team were now as upbeat as I was – even Warren had raised a smile this morning when they'd been given their account cards.

I was excited about that, not only for those three but also for Charlotte – and, I had to admit, for myself. Like the team, though, I was getting my head down and doing my job, compiling methodical and boring lists of whatever. I really did feel that this was a mission for good. Nothing to do with the environment or politics, it was much more than that. It might take a while, but my kids and theirs would see the benefits. It made me feel lighter inside, like walking on air. I could almost understand the enthusiasm of Pentecostals, arms raised to the heavens, praying to their God. It was simply because they believed, and I now had hope, too.

With the engine off, the inside of the car was hotting up. The car park was full of pickups and trucks being loaded by men in shorts and boots with trolleys full of wood and bags of sand. The immaculate BMW 4x4 that glided through them stuck out like a sore thumb, as did its well-groomed occupants. They cruised around slowly until they saw my tiny vehicle and pulled up alongside.

The Brit jumped out and opened the rear door for me.

Egbers remained at the wheel with the engine running, air-con going full blast to keep the interior pleasant. I climbed in and inhaled a lungful of new-car smell, just as I had in the Range Rover. That seemed like a lifetime ago.

Egbers didn't acknowledge me, his eyes intent on the screen in his hand on his lap. The Brit got in alongside him and turned in his seat. 'We have someone you need to talk to.' His tone was different. It was slow, low, almost as if he was having a civilized conversation rather than delivering orders or threats. But that didn't stop my new-found confidence shattering. The Filipino and Richard were back in a flash. Shit – another victim.

I leant between the two of them. 'But let's just talk this

time. We don't need to do it your way. I'm with you – I believe Parmesh. I believe that what he's trying to do is right. Your crusade. *Our* crusade.'

Yet, deep down, I knew I needed the information.

The Brit twisted more in his seat. 'How do you know you believe?'

I took a breath, but couldn't think of the words. 'I don't know. I . . . I can't think how to explain, I . . . but at the same time, it can't be denied.'

The Brit smiled at me: a first. 'Exactly. No one ever knows how. Shit, it just happens.'

Egbers was on to WhatsApp the moment it rang. He gave comforting tones to whoever was on the other end, trying to keep them calm, trying to keep them focused.

'It's all okay. Everything's to plan our end. It's all over soon . . . No, you'd know if he'd found out. Just stay safe – I'll be there soon. Just stay safe.'

The Brit came closer and spoke quietly. 'She works for Castro. She's risking her life for you right now, just by making this call. You must not fail.'

Egbers handed me the phone and I put it to my ear. She was nervous. I could hear the erratic breathing. 'Hello?'

I faced down to the footwell, a finger in my spare ear as if it would make the call more secret for her. She spoke in a semi-whisper and was hesitant. It was a young voice and she was American, West Coast twang and high-pitched – but that could have been her emotional state.

'I've found out as much as I can. Yes, the house has back-up power, you know, the batteries. Yes, there are alarms. Many kinds, lots of alarms. I don't know how many, I don't know what type, but they're all connected to the cellular system. Three different companies in case one fails. That's all I know for now, that's all I can find out without—'

She stopped talking and voices filled the background. 'Oh, no! Oh, no!' The line went dead.

I looked up at the Templars.

49

Egbers grabbed the mobile and stared at the screen, like the power of thought could make it ring. For the first time I could see he actually felt emotion: there was human in him.

The Brit was just as concerned. He kept his tone low. 'She – we are willing to die to control the ledger. You say you believe, James? Are you willing?'

The mobile rang and Egbers jabbed the answer icon. 'All good? Great. He's here. Wait.' He handed it to me.

'Hello? Do you know where the ledger is?'

'It's not that easy.' Her breathing was ragged and scared as she gathered her thoughts. 'It's in the basement – I've never been, just heard it talked about. That's all I know right now. I'm trying, trying hard to find out more.'

She stopped, but hadn't cut off. I could hear her heavy breathing as voices, American voices, echoed in the background, then slowly faded. She controlled her breath before continuing.

'Set the holoport up in the basement. It's there, but I don't know exactly where yet. I need to see, need to be with you. I need to put the bits in my head together. You understand what I'm trying to say? You need to help me.'

'I will.'

'Okay. Tomorrow night, your time – you're twenty, twenty-four hours ahead?' She was sounding flustered.

'We'll work it out. But we will be there for you tomorrow night, our time. I won't let you down.'

I glanced at Egbers. He nodded, showing concern for another human being.

'And I need Casper back.'

'Yep.'

I pulled the mobile away from my ear as I sat up, assuming I knew which one Casper was.

We could all hear the mobile now as I pushed it between the front seats.

'*Shit! Gotta go!*'

The line went dead again.

I offered Egbers the Samsung.

'You Casper?'

He nodded as the phone went back on charge via the vehicle's power jack, worry etched all over his face.

'She thinks Castro is on to her.'

The Brit turned to him. 'She'll be okay. She's smart. Not long now, she'll be home.'

Egbers tried to regain some semblance of normality as the Brit settled in his seat. I had eye contact with him in the rear-view mirror. 'What's your name? After all, we're in this together, aren't we?'

The Brit studied me in the mirror. 'Jonathan Drum. Jon.'

There was silence in the cab as they both thought their thoughts. It was very clear to me what I needed to do.

'We'll be ready tomorrow night. We'll meet the drone guys at the same place, just before dark. That's about seven-ish, so six thirty. They need to keep their lights off, coming up the hill.'

265

Casper nodded.

'No need to worry about cutting power and communications or the rebroadcasts. The alarms are using mobile networks. That Faraday bubble on the yacht, can the drone guys, or whoever does it, create the bubble over the house? If we have your Samsungs for communication, then the holoport will be able to send out through the Faraday.'

Egbers nodded. 'You can have whatever you want. *Saraswati* is just off the west coast waiting for the ledger. We are leaving in an hour, back to Atherton. The jet's waiting. We need to be with Mr Mani and we have to be sure Skye makes it to the holoport at all costs. That's one of the reasons Mr Mani chose you instead of us. Without Skye with Mr Mani, and you in Sanctuary, we've lost our chance.' He checked his mobile again, as if he could command Skye back onto it. He returned to me. 'You must find the ledger, whatever happens at Atherton tomorrow. Nothing else matters.'

He paused, waiting for my understanding, and he got it. 'Nothing.'

Everything made sense. These two going to Atherton was for exactly the same reason Charlotte had come here to protect Pip and the boys. I had to ask. 'My family – are they still in danger?'

Egbers shook his head. 'You believe – you have hope, don't you?'

'I do.'

I wanted to ask if he would have carried out the threat, but thought better of it. I'd leave that one alone because, deep down, I knew the answer.

Casper Egbers had a question for me. 'Is Charlotte going in with you?'

I nodded, and they looked at each other, both making sure each other had seen correctly before Casper acknowledged.

'OK. You need to keep her safe.' Casper pushed on: 'Change of plan. Once you have the ledger, you're to take it and Charlotte to the airport. Flavia will be waiting with the helicopter to take it to *Saraswati* with both of you. You are both important to Mr Mani. You need to be safe. The rest go back to the hotel, pack, and leave. Tell them we'll contact them after they're back in the UK.'

I got it and nodded.

'James, once we have the ledger, our crusade will surge. You'll want to be part of that, won't you?'

I nodded again. I did want to build something.

'Good, James, good. I'll see you tomorrow night via the holoport. Good luck to us all.'

I climbed out of the BMW and into my Toyota, not worried too much about tomorrow night. That was going to happen regardless. What stuck in my mind was that Casper, Jon, Skye and Parmesh were willing to risk their lives for the ledger.

A question went round and round in my head. I was strong enough with the words, and the emotion to say them, but . . . was I really strong enough to put my life on the line?

50

Dead on time, just as we were rigging up the last of the bulk bags ready to be airlifted, the Js' 4x4 snaked up the track towards us with their lights off. It felt a good omen.

We'd finished off the final planning that morning. Every-one had decided to check out early and had their passports, cash and personal items on them, ready to leave once we were successful . . . or had to run because we weren't. Questions were answered; some were not. We had all the equipment we thought we'd need, charged up tool batteries, and if we didn't have something we needed, it was too late. We were where we were. All that mattered was that we were on the high ground with what we had, and that we were going to go for it.

As the 4x4 pulled up alongside me, the Js were already staring at the bulk bags through the windscreen. James was at the wheel. His window came down and a fist came out to be bumped. His tone was serious. 'It's a ninety-seven-kilo limit, right?'

'Right.'

Our fists touched. Jamie was already out of the cab and heading for the tailgate. Their mood had changed. No funnies from him: he got out and got on with the job. No more surfer vibe going on. More like a workplace vibe, which made me happy.

James opened his door and was straight into work mode too. 'We have to get the deniability in place first.'

Jamie joined us. 'Have you got any more of those bags?'

'How many?'

'Just the one.' He turned to James. 'I'm thinking: the deniability in the bag – easier to recover?'

James agreed. He followed me to Tony's Nissan while Jamie got on with the drones. He seemed to have something he wanted to say, but hesitated before taking a deep breath, as if he was gulping in all the air before it disappeared. 'I hear you're with us – you get the gig? You're synced up and ready to go?'

I nodded, but my head was on the job, and that was where I wanted to keep it.

James was very happy, and I got a couple of gentle slaps on the back. 'Big day, man. We got *Saraswati* off the coast, we got Flavia at the airport, and Mr Mani at home for Skye to get this done. I'm stoked, man.'

As I pulled one of the still-folded bulk bags out of the Nissan, Tony and Warren had been checking out the two surfer characters, but I knew they wouldn't ask questions. They knew what they were about. They probably just hadn't expected them to look like the cover of a Beach Boys album. Besides, they had their own jobs to be getting on with. They were busy double-checking the weights of the kit inside the nine white bulk bags laid out in a line.

James finally noticed what was missing. 'Hey, I thought there were gonna be five?'

'There will be. The other two are on the road, ready to cut the phone line when the deniable is in place.'

He took the bulk bag from me and unfolded it as he continued checking our cargo. FIBCs, as they were properly called – flexible intermediate bulk containers – were big polypropylene square-shaped bags, with handles, used worldwide for storing or transporting dry goods like gravel, sand or fertilizer. Today they were going to be used as air-cargo containers.

I pointed to the one furthest away. 'They're in the order in which they may need to come to us. But that will all depend on what we need once on site.'

He nodded, checking inside it, more about the weight than the contents.

'Once you've got that deniable in place, the first lift will just be two of us.'

He nodded but his eyes were on the kit. 'Who's going with you?'

I pointed to Tony, and James was immediately concerned. 'With how much kit?'

'It's okay, he's ninety-five kilos. He just looks a solid unit. I'll be taking the tools. Just drop us on the hard-standing outside the outbuilding. Once we're in, we can start calling in the team and the rest of the kit as it's needed.' I pointed at Warren. 'He'll be the last one in, so he can co-ordinate that with you. He knows what's in the bags, so he knows which has to be lifted once we find out what we need. That okay?'

'Cool. We've got no equipment coming out apart from one cargo bag, right?'

I nodded.

'That gives us more juice to keep the babes up there. I'm going to keep one over the house scouting out, so if it all goes wrong and you have police or whoever screaming towards you, I can get the deniable out of there. Sorry, dude, but the kit's out first.'

My face must have told him I had different priorities. 'But hey, I'll let you know, so you guys just get outta there, run towards us and we'll get out there looking to pick you up. These babes don't leave soldiers behind, man.'

A high-pitched buzz came from behind the tailgate and all our heads swung as the drone turned itself into an eagle, releasing its legs from under its body so they could articulate themselves, claws extended, then grab as if they had caught their prey. It continued to gain height and was soon out of audio.

James gave me another gentle slap on the back. 'We are going to change the world, man.'

51

The deniable, as the Js called it, was a dark grey plastic box maybe five hundred millimetres square, surrounded by bed pillows held in place by black duct tape.

'Not quite as hi-tech as I expected.'

Jamie opened the FIBC ready to take it. 'We had to protect it somehow when it came off *Saraswati*. Let's show you that it works, okay?'

He pulled his Samsung from his pocket and I did the same with my mobile.

Three bars of signal.

Jamie shoved his fist between the pillows and powered up the deniable. Instantaneously, my three bars went to zero.

'Give my number a call on WhatsApp.'

I did, and nothing from my end.

He handed me a Samsung that was now mine, showing four bars. 'Call me.'

I did and his mobile rang.

'See? Cool.'

He put his ice-cream tray over his head and got to work. Above us, in the ever-increasing gloom, I soon heard a familiar high-pitched buzz. As the big dark shape materialized above the 4x4s, Jamie presented the four handles of the bulk-bag for the two sets of claws to close around. A metre now above the bag, the drone took up the slack and hovered, motionless and solid.

James glanced up from the screens. 'Time to go. Check your own cell for the signal to return.'

The buzz tone changed as the eagle took the strain, lifting slowly, metre by metre, until the buzz faded into the oncoming darkness and disappeared from sight as it flew swiftly in the direction of Sanctuary.

I watched my phone and it was no more than thirty seconds before the signal returned. I showed both my mobile and the Samsung to James as he concentrated on the infrared images on his screen. Sanctuary came into view in greyscale, and as the drone flew over the centre of the multi-roofed building, the picture slowed. It was an easy choice of landing site for James: on the video I had identified a flat roof protruding over the eastern elevation to protect the veranda.

The flat roof got closer on-screen and the bulk bag came to rest. I watched the grips release, and then there was a moment when the drone sorted itself out, making sure it was free of the bag, before James zipped it skywards at such a rate the screen fast went to black.

James was very happy with himself. 'You wanna cut that landline now?'

I called Charlotte on the Samsung and she answered on the second ring. 'It's me. All good this end. Once you're finished, give me a call, and head back here, okay?'

'No problem. And, James?'

'What?'

'See you in Sanctuary.'

'Yep, see you in Sanctuary.'

I closed down and waited for her return call. Skye might have explained that the alarms were on the cell-net system, but disconnecting the landline was belt and braces. No matter what hi-tech security or underground conduits hid the line going into Sanctuary, it had to come from somewhere along Hunter Road, and eventually branch off specifically for the house. It was the same everywhere in the world. And that was exactly what Charlotte and Gemma were doing right now. They were at the last pole before Sanctuary's line headed off the road and went underground to emerge somewhere in the house. They were unscrewing the junction box and making sure the wiring became loose enough for the line not to work, yet at the same time not look like it had been sabotaged. Pulling just two of the wires loose would do it, Tony had said. Then, once we were successful in Sanctuary, Gemma would reconnect the line on her way back to Queenstown, and, along with Tony and Warren, catch the first flight to anywhere.

While they got on with their job, I heaved my daysack onto my back. It contained all of Tony's odds and ends, apart from a large square lump of something heavy in his jacket pocket. It wasn't that so much that made me curious, it was that one of my socks was half hanging out of the same pocket. I pointed. 'What?'

He pulled at the sock to bring out a shape, maybe 150 millimetres square, where my foot would have been. The cotton had stretched to twice its length with the weight.

'That, son, is a rare-earth magnet – and, no, I won't tell you why, because you're making me go in one of those things.'

Tony had said it with a brief smile but didn't look too enthusiastic as he adjusted the drone's lifting strap under his armpits.

'You're going under it, not in it, so stop complaining.'

The second machine hovered over him in the dark, being

prepped and checked for the next lift. He saw me watching him. 'I suppose you're going to say again that people round here pay good money to do this.'

I pulled my own strap over my head and into position. 'They probably do. But I wouldn't.'

As the drone came closer, Jamie gripped Tony's strap behind and above his head and engaged the claws ever so gently, then signalled to James to take the strain. Tony stared up at his new leader in the sky, not sure what to make of it.

There was another buzz as the first drone returned from Sanctuary and Jamie now held the strap up behind my head. I felt the downdraught, then the strain round my chest as the drone took my weight and waited along with Tony's. The buzz from two machines filled my head as they hovered, waiting for the order to lift off.

I kept watching the Samsung's screen, waiting for Charlotte. It finally lit up and I felt it vibrate. I heard a bit of the ring tone over the drones and shoved my forefinger into my other ear.

'All good, bro. All done.'

'Great. See you there.'

I turned the mobile off, put it into my pocket alongside my mobile and gave the Js a double thumbs-up. They took over. The strap tightened round my chest even more as my feet left the ground. I didn't want to look at Tony in case he was having second thoughts. I lost sight of him anyway as the drones parted and his dropped back to give us both more space.

I gained height, maybe five metres, enough to clear the trees. Below us, as the ground sloped down towards Speargrass Flat, I could see a set of headlights cutting into the increasing darkness over to the left. They had to be moving along Hunter Road. They got to what was the end of the road at the T-junction and the lights turned left towards us.

The wind blew in my face as the drone picked up speed. Soon, what I hoped was Gemma's Nissan passed beneath us, and we were closing on the dark silhouette of Sanctuary.

We began losing height, and were manoeuvring between trees. The weight of the daysack pulled down on my shoulders, and the strap around my chest pulled up.

Sanctuary came into clearer view and the drones slowed to walking pace, eight or nine metres off the ground. I could hear Tony's behind me now, and ahead was the gently pulsing red glow outside the outbuilding, as if it was guiding us in.

There was no point worrying about it. The bubble was in place, and if the plan wasn't working, well, we were about to find out. We were there. We had to get on with this.

We passed the red glow and turned left to face the other elevation of the building, the shutter. Soon, I was being gently lowered onto the concrete hard-standing. My feet touched the ground and the strap relaxed, but the Meccano claws would be retaining the straps for the others to use. I had to wriggle and drop out. James was watching: the moment I was free, the drone lifted and zipped away into the darkness.

Tony slowly approached under his drone and I guided his feet to the ground and helped him out of his strap. Exactly as mine, the high-pitched whine faded skywards and was gone. We were in complete silence, apart from the rasp of Tony trying to get his breath back. He got tight up to me. 'I'm not looking forward to the lift back, boy, that's for sure.'

We stood there in the darkness for seconds that felt like for ever. I touched the steel shuttering that filled the whole side of the elevation, both levels. 'Okay, how are we going to get through this, then?'

'Get that bag off your back, boy, and I'll show you.'

52

Tony helped me ease the daysack off my back and onto the hard-standing.

The side door had turned out to be exactly what we'd anticipated: it would have taken a big physical attack to get past it, and we couldn't have hidden the evidence. There were two chunky locks, a third of the way down and a third of the way up, but Tony hadn't spent much time looking at them when he'd studied the drone footage. His focus had been entirely on the shutters.

He set himself up on the hard-standing with his back against the door, the stonework of the frame and the shuttering to his right. The first bit of kit out of the daysack was a small LED head-torch, which he positioned in the centre of his forehead. Then came a Fire HD tablet that had seen much better days. The yellow plastic was filthy and scratched, the corners dented. It looked like it had spent its entire life with Tony on sites, which it had. He never went on any job without that and a few other essentials.

The tablet's aesthetics weren't helped by the fact that Tony had obviously pulled it apart and made holes and all sorts so he could get some wires into it. They dangled out of the right-hand side, and the whole thing seemed to be held together by silver duct tape.

I crouched next to him as he pulled out the pink kids' toy he'd shown me last night. The plastic Im-Me was small enough for a ten-year-old to get their hands around, yet still had a keyboard and LED display. He'd busted that up as well, and there were leads that Mattel would never have intended coming out of the back of it and into the tablet.

While we'd practised assembling the holoport, he'd lowered his tone and glanced around my empty hotel room. 'They stopped making these years ago, but in my trade they're gold dust. This big boy goes with me everywhere. They were designed for youngsters to be able to text each other – maybe they thought little kids would never have mobiles.'

He'd chuckled to himself. 'The thing is, anything smart is really stupid. They all work on just two things: power and binary code. And that's it. Power on or off. Zero or one – on or off.' He jabbed a thumb to his right. 'Just like that bugger.'

His face was serious now as he laid the device beside him on the concrete floor and the torchlight bounced off the duct tape.

Remote controls, Tony had explained to me, all had to operate in the ISM, the Industrial, Scientific and Medical spectrum. 'Radio-frequency energy, whatever you want to call it, for a framework that is internationally agreed. Otherwise there'd be chaos – we'd all be stepping on each other's toes. Microwaves turning on the TV. You go to text somebody and it starts your neighbour's car.' He'd given himself an even bigger chuckle. 'So things like these shutters, they've all got to conform to ISM rules. It's a disgrace. If your bank account password had only two characters, it would be more secure than most of these things.

'All I've done is taken every code possibility that could be in one of the clickers that would open it, anything from three-bit switches to twelve-bit, and even that's just over four thousand codes. Compare that with two characters in your password, which would give you over five thousand codes. That's how insecure these things are.

'All I had to do was pull down the open-source software and code them up on the pad.' He had hit the screen and opened up a file with lines of zeroes and ones.

'This here is what's called the De Bruijn sequence. He's one clever Dutchman who worked out how receivers can read all this nonsense on the screen really quickly. That's what we have here: every code that that thing can possibly read. And what is more –' he'd tapped the screen '– it will send them all, thanks to our favourite Dutchman, in just 8.214 seconds on Im-Me.'

I watched as he picked up the pink device, connected the leads from the yellow tablet, and the backlight on the LED screen came to life. He pressed send on the keypad, and I waited for the shutters to start rolling up.

Last night in the hotel room, I hadn't been able to resist asking him: 'How did you get into all this tech stuff? I didn't have you down as a big-time hacker.'

His face had lit up. 'It's not hacking, boy. And it's not hard if you know electricity. You have to know this stuff to work modern systems. I've been doing it for years on jobs, working out ways to get access when stuff goes wrong. You have people losing their clickers, forgetting combinations, all sorts. It's experience, that's all. But, like I say, anything called smart isn't. How can it be, if old farts like me can get past it?'

But we were still waiting for the shutter to lift. Nothing.

Tony looked at me. He wasn't fazed, but he knew I was.

'Not a problem, son. They must have a rolling code. The

code changes all the time within the FR frequency range, but it's still within the ISM, and is still binary. It just takes a different way to access it, that's all, random codes that will be interrogated and received, and we'll bluff our way in. I have the codes, but it's going to take longer – maybe ten minutes.'

The Samsung vibrated, and I dug it out of my pocket to check the message. I spoke into Tony's ear as he concentrated on his device, head-torch on and the tablet's screen illuminating his face. 'Charlotte and Gemma. They're with Warren, and all's good. They're asking how we're doing.'

Tony gave me a thumbs-up.

I messaged back: *All okay.*

Before sending another: *Calling now.*

53

I stayed on the hard-standing, but moved a few steps away from Tony so the call didn't distract him. He was still sitting against the door, eyes fixed on the tablet screen, where binary code cascaded like something out of *The Matrix*. I scanned the darkness, as if I was about to see figures with weapons emerging out of the night.

'Well done.'

'Gemma did all the work. I was just on dog.'

'What?'

'Gemma calls it dog. Guard dog?'

'You know what to do if we're discovered out here?'

'Yes, all good.'

It might be at the moment, but what if our luck ran out and heads started to flap?

'Are the Js keeping a drone up? They got one up now? There's no way of knowing if we tripped any alarm we haven't cut. We need eyes up there.'

'I'll make sure.'

'If it goes wrong, tell the other two to drop everything and get back to York any way they can.'

'We know, we're ready.'

'Will you tell them again anyway?'

'I will.'

'Great.'

The police, Castro's security, whoever was alerted, the first warning we'd get of it was when they were speeding their way along Hunter Road or if the drone missed that they'd be banging down the door or crashing in through the windows. If Castro could burn a man's feet over a pair of trainers, I could imagine the sort of people he employed. They would be, like, well, Casper, and that wasn't a good thought. As I stood outside the outbuilding, surrounded by darkness, Tony trying to work his kids' toy to get inside, the reality of it hit home hard.

From behind me came a slightly louder chuckle than before. A split second later, the shutter motors whined and our first obstruction of the night began to rise.

I held out an arm to help Tony to his feet. He put the tablet and Im-Me carefully back into the daysack, then dug in his jeans pocket for a set of our blue rubber gloves.

'Like I said, son, smart is really stupid.'

I wasn't going to call in the drones yet. We had to get to the bung first. Gemma would be first up, but it was pointless bringing her in before we made sure we could get her where she needed to be.

I pulled a pair of gloves from my jeans. The moment the shutter was chest high I bent down and dived through as Tony waited a few more seconds. It was eerie in there: I could hear the emptiness, almost feel it. Tony's head-torch flashed around as he scanned the walls for light switches, and very soon, fluorescent strips flickered into life above us from the ceiling. They revealed a smooth concrete floor, unplastered concrete-block walls, a high ceiling. The overpowering sensation was the new-build reek of concrete and paint. With lots of power points all along the walls, it was definitely a hangar, and it looked like nothing had been added since Richard was there, apart from a large pair of steel double doors at the far end.

As we headed towards them Tony flicked off his light and I soon spotted a rectangular steel box to the right of the double doors. Tony knew exactly what it was.

The box was a telephone entry system. There was a normal steel keypad on the lower right of the panel to code our way in, and to the left of that, a large call button. The top half consisted of a vent for the speaker and mic plus a small key-well.

Tony fished in his back pocket and pulled out a bunch of keys, all shiny-new. He flourished one between his thumb and forefinger and dangled the rest. 'CH 751, son. It's the everything key – plus a few others for luck. I bought all the stupid keys that I could think of, but this one will do the trick. It will even open filing cabinets. Can you believe it? Even toilet-roll holders in hotels. It's the commonest key all around the world for all the stupid stuff. What is wrong with these people? Nobody's updated these locks in thirty years.'

He inserted the key and started a gentle jiggling motion. 'Like I said, boy, anything smart.'

The front of the entry system fell forward and stayed horizontal like a tray. Inside was what looked to me like an almighty mess of wires and circuit boards. Tony saw my reaction, but he wasn't concerned. 'There's lots of stuff going on here, but it's all bullshit. Bullshit baffles brains. All this stuff is froth. The only bit that concerns us is the relay.' He studied the chaos of wiring and tapped one. 'And it's this little bugger here.'

He riffled through his keys and this time produced one of my paperclips, now straightened out. The U end had been placed over the key-ring, then stuck together with duct tape, leaving two prongs sticking out. 'I used to keep boxes of these things in the van. Used them all the time to bridge dry contacts like these. It'll be like we've tapped in a code on the keypad. Like I said, boy, anything smart needs two things: power and binary code. Just like this little jobbie.'

I liked the explanations, but now wasn't the time. There was a downside to being almost horizontal.

'Tony, we've got to get a move on, mate.'

Leaning in, he touched the two ends to one of the circuit boards, and the door quietly clicked open. I ran the two paces to grab it and make sure it didn't close again, as if Tony couldn't redo what he'd just done. I used the daysack to jam the doors open while Tony went inside and looked about for light switches. Just like before, fluorescent lights were soon flickering on to expose a concrete landing and steps that would take us below ground level.

As we descended the ten concrete stairs, checking for power points beyond the ones above, the last of the light strips at the far end of the tunnel illuminated the bung, maybe sixty metres away.

I ran towards it, my boots bouncing off steel-grated duckboards, my head just half a metre from the roof. I stopped after a dozen strides and turned to face Tony. 'I've got to check before we get Gemma in.'

Tony was doubled over, having a fit of coughing. The air stank of construction dust. I could feel it at the back of my throat as I ran again and my boots echoed around the tunnel as they hit the steel grating.

I was soon at the bung, a smooth concrete disc designed to fit the tunnel perfectly. I pushed it at the right side and then at the left, hoping it would move, then kicked. It didn't budge. I checked the signal. Two bars on the Samsung. Good. As I ran back to Tony, I called Jamie.

I got an answer after three rings.

'Hey, man.'

'We're at the bung. Let's get the first wave in.'

'No problem.'

'You got a drone up checking?'

'Yeah, I just told your sister. But you'll lose it while we fly for you.'

I got back to Tony, who was in the final throes of his coughing attack.

I gave him a couple more seconds to finish before we started back up to the hangar. 'You okay?'

He gave me a slap on my arm. 'Just old.'

54

I stood on the threshold where the shutter met the hard-standing, light spilling out past me onto the spot where they would land. I'd been straining to hear the familiar buzz, and it didn't take long. Gemma rounded the corner, taking the same route as Tony and I had, but a lot lower. She was no more than two metres from the ground, and the first of the bulk bags was behind her on the second drone. Both machines slowed and began to drop even lower. I went out to help guide her down to the concrete, just as I had with Tony, but Gemma flew past me with a big smile on her face, her legs air-walking as she went deeper into the hangar. She wasn't taking it seriously enough. But then again, when had she ever?

'Catch up, lard-arse.'

The bulk bag flew past, nudging my shoulder on the way.

I ran behind them; it looked like she was being taken right to the door down to the tunnel.

I caught up just as Gemma's boots touched the polished concrete and she was already unstrapping herself. The bulk bag landed next to us with a metallic clank and we made sure its claws were clear of the bag's handles. The drones turned on themselves in the hover and exited the hangar. Seconds later the buzz had gone and all I could hear was Gemma, very excited, as she bent into the bulk bag.

'That was sick as fuck!'

We lifted out the core drill, and the steel rig that was going to keep it in place at the bung. She'd pre-attached them for ease. The drill was a Husqvarna, reconditioned, sprayed blue, a big lump of steel, and heavy. It would cut out a core of concrete and leave a hole big enough for even Tony to get through. We lowered it down, careful not to mark the polished concrete.

Next out was the diamond core-drill bit, which was basically a bigger version of the DIY hole-saw you use to drill out a hole in a door if you're installing a Yale lock, or make a hole in plasterboard big enough to pass a pipe through. Instead of steel to do the cutting, though, this thing had industrial diamonds for teeth. And instead of the bit being Yale-lock-sized, it was 600 millimetres in diameter and 500 deep, the size of a man-hole.

Tony came up the steps and joined us. He was pleased to see Gemma and the kit I pointed to. 'So, as planned. Me and Gemma, we'll move the drill. You're sorting protection and power, right?' I didn't wait for an answer. 'Let's crack on.'

Gemma hefted the drill and the rig. As she waddled down the steps, the steel echoed as I rolled the bit towards the door, taking my time, trying to avoid scratches or gouges in the floor. When I reached the steps, I got in front of it and bounced it carefully down the first couple.

Tony disappeared to do his jobs. Before the drilling phase, he was to make sure that, while we were on the tunnel side of the doors, going down the steps into the tunnel and to the wall of the basement, we all wore rubber gloves, blue overalls, plastic boot covers, face masks and goggles. We needed to keep the hangar and the main house clean of dust and debris. If Skye was wrong about the ledger being in the basement, we could find ourselves searching for the ledger everywhere else. Every time anyone came up to the hangar, they would have to take off their protection, dump it in the plastic bin bags that Tony was going to leave out, do whatever they had to do outside in the hangar, and then, on the way back in, get their protection on once more, with a new set of coveralls, boots, gloves and face gear. Exactly the same would be happening going through the stud-wall and into Sanctuary: we'd take our protection off, go into the basement or even the house, leave no sign, and once we got back in, it would be kit back on, until we came up to the steel doors to go through the hangar, and then it was kit off. In Tony's words: 'What happens in the tunnel stays in the tunnel.'

This wasn't an unusual practice for the team or on sites, particularly when working in an occupied house.

I bumped the drill bit down onto the steel grating in time to see Gemma finishing positioning the drill. The rig was an aluminium base-plate that held a stanchion, and an assembly made of flat steel, about a metre long, with ball-bearing runners, that the drill was secured to. The drill could then be positioned vertically to drill down into a floor or, in this case, horizontally into the bung.

As the steel rolled towards her and the noise echoed round the tunnel, she turned and gave me a thumbs-up. 'No problems here. It shouldn't take too long.'

The drill itself looked like a DIY power tool, only five times bigger. All it needed now was power, and the drill bit.

Tony was close behind me, dragging the bulk bag with one hand and unspooling the power cord with the other. The bag contained all the bits and pieces we needed, including tarpaulins to keep the dust down and replacement protection for the team once we came back from Sanctuary and re-entered the void.

Tony had connected the cable to a socket by the steel doors, but before we spent time attaching the core-drill bit and making any final adjustments, Gemma still had to check for power. The tunnel's lights working meant nothing: power might have been cut in an unoccupied building for safety reasons.

Tony coughed up some more dust as he pulled out the blue nylon tarpaulins to go under and over the drill.

Gemma connected the power and the drill whined into life. She beamed. 'Fucking excellent.'

The pitch changed as she adjusted the speed. Dry core drilling depended on knowing the behaviour of the material you intended to drill, which in turn dictated the amount of pressure you put on the bit as it was cutting, and that dictated the speed of the cut. Get any of these three things wrong and the bit will become too hot and fracture, or the diamonds rendered blunt so Gemma wouldn't be cutting into anything. She had to get the pressure and speed correct for this type of concrete, and always keeping the core-bit warm, never hot, because that's when the problems start to happen. But that was why she was here: master of form.

I announced I'd go and fetch the next lot in, and left the pair of them to get on with their jobs. By the time I was running back towards the hangar, Gemma and Tony were pulling on their protection. All was good for phase two, getting through the bung.

As I reached the stairs, the first grinding of the bit in contact with the concrete echoed deep down in the tunnel. I called the Js while taking deep gulps of stale air.

'You've still got one up there, checking the area? Checking the roads?'

It was Jamie who answered. 'Chill. All good.'

'I'll chill once we're the fuck out of here. I need Warren.'

'Sure.'

It took a few seconds, but he was soon on the Samsung.

'All's good, mate. We have power, no need for the gennies. So, the next wave needs to be you and Charlotte.'

'Okay.' He sounded more efficient than excited or laid-back.

'You need to show the Js which bags to bring in as soon as they drop you off. We're going to need your bag and the holo-port. The rest can wait until we have the ledger.'

He muttered another 'Okay.' But this second one wasn't sounding so efficient.

'It's okay, Warren. All is good, mate.'

The phone vibrated. It was a message coming in from one of the Templars' numbers.

'Got to go. I'll see you in a couple of minutes.'

I took the call. It was Casper. 'How far are you?'

'We're cutting the bung now.'

There wasn't any time for congratulations: he was under pressure. His tone carried worry. I'd only heard it coming out of him once, and that was yesterday.

'I'm trying to pick up Skye. She thinks Castro's team are watching her and that they're suspicious. I need to get her out of the Bay area. Mr Mani and Jon are waiting with the holo-port. If the pick-up goes wrong, we're going to fight our way back to Atherton. We need to get to Mr Mani. You need to set up your holoport for her. Everything that happens here is for you. Remember – at any cost.'

Charlotte and Warren entered the frame of the hangar and the buzz got louder as they flew towards me.

'I understand. But what does that mean for us? Do they know we're here?'

'The only thing that matters is the ledger.'

I turned away from Charlotte and Warren and had to put a finger in my ear as the drones got closer and the hangar magnified the buzz.

'I've got it. Casper – good luck. I hope Skye's okay.'

There was a pause. 'I do too. She's my wife.'

He cut the call.

As Charlotte and Warren stood waiting for the bags, the drones turned on themselves to leave the hangar.

'When they come in, you need to get them the other side of the door. Keep them out of the hangar. Get your protection on and I'll see you down there.'

I slapped a not-so-happy Warren on the arm. 'That okay, mate? That sound good?'

He sort of nodded.

'See you down there, then.'

Charlotte followed me to the other side of the doors, where I started to pull on my protection.

'Everything okay? Who was that?'

Once I'd got my legs through the blue coveralls and the drill was grinding away in the background, I stepped closer to her. 'It's Casper. Skye is his wife. Can you believe that? She thinks she's been found out.'

Charlotte's face clouded. 'What about us? Are we safe?'

'I don't know.'

'Shit.'

I put my hands on her shoulders and made sure she was looking at me. 'It means nothing yet. We still have to get on with the job. We must get the holoport up, and we must find the ledger.'

She nodded, but I could see the doubt.

'Charlotte, it's all going to plan this end. We have the drones up. We'll know if any problems are heading our way. We've just got to push on. We've got no choice.'

A gentle buzz entered the hangar and Charlotte turned back towards the tunnel. 'I'll see you down there.'

Pulling up the hood of my overalls and placing the shaped fibre mask over my mouth and nose, I headed for the tunnel.

55

From where I stood at the bottom of the stairs, it looked as if Gemma and Tony were in a world of blue tarpaulin and grey concrete dust at the bung. We needed the sheets to keep the dust down as best they could – Gemma hadn't been able to get hold of an extractor and collection bags in time.

Both were dressed the same as I was, in full protection now I had my safety goggles on. As I got closer I could see Tony was trying to make sure the top cover was kept in position to stop the worst of the dust flying everywhere, and yet more tarpaulins were spread out on the steel grating to catch the dust ball. It looked like a losing battle: both of them were covered with a layer of light grey concrete.

Gemma went on to her knees, lifted the top tarpaulin and disappeared beneath it, holding it over her head as she checked the drilling. Tony was well into another coughing bout as I arrived.

I leant into him to make myself heard over the racket of the drill. 'I can do this, mate. Why don't you change over with Warren?'

His words were as muffled as mine probably were. 'Don't

worry about it, son. There's enough of this crap in me already.'

I slapped him on the arm. 'Not long now.'

I ducked under the sheeting next to Gemma to see the core bit turning into the concrete, maybe about 200 millimetres in. It rotated with a high-pitched, crunching screech as the diamond teeth cut their way through, creating plumes of dust.

She had to yell: 'Quarter of an hour tops. Piece of piss.'

As I leant in to her and shouted, she wiped her dusty goggles with her fingers so she could keep focused on the drill bit. 'Bringing the kit down. Back soon.'

I left her to it and pulled myself out of the covering and stood up to have another shout at Tony, who was still almost mantling the drill with the tarpaulins. 'Fifteen.'

I got a nod and a cough in reply as I headed for the stairs.

I pulled off a glove and slowed my run when I was about halfway between the bung and the steps, and sent a message to the Js: *We still have a drone up?*

Within three seconds they replied: *Chill. Still cool.*

Closer to the steps, I could look up and see Charlotte and Warren putting their protection on, with all the kit now stowed our side of the doors.

I took the first two steps up to them and would only have had to raise my voice a little over the distant drill. I shouted anyway: it always seemed harder to communicate with these things covering your mouth.

'Close the doors. Keep the dust in.'

A couple more steps up and there was another vibration. It was Casper. I stopped, pulled my mask down below my chin, and pressed the Samsung hard against my hood. There was a lot of background noise from his end this time. He was in a vehicle. I had to push the hood into my other ear with a finger to hear.

The background noise was Skye. 'Take the right – next right. It's there – there. Then right again. Immediate right. Quick. We've got to be quick, before they turn.'

There was no reply from the driver.

'Casper?'

He was clearly nearer the car's mic but his voice was still hazy.

'Listen in. I've got Skye. We're heading for Mr Mani's but we're being followed. How long have you got left?'

Skye was still giving directions, her voice much edgier than it had been yesterday. 'The blue Dodge – it went straight. Now turn left somewhere – it will take us to the freeway. First left.'

I waited for her to finish. 'We're nearly through the bung. Another thirty minutes, tops.'

'Okay.'

Skye was back. 'Left – go left there, the drugstore. There – there!'

Casper's voice was laboured as he fought to control the wheel. 'Be quick, James.'

The call went dead.

Charlotte and Warren were now all protected up, looking down at me.

I put the Samsung away as I climbed the remaining steps. 'They just want to know how long – all good.'

Warren's voice was muffled behind his mask, but it was clear to him that I was lying. 'All that shouting didn't sound like that to me.'

He picked up his bag as I put my mask back on to cover my lies.

'It's all okay, mate. Couple more minutes and you're on.' I touched his shoulder as he moved down the stairs. There was no answer and no reaction to be seen under his mask and goggles.

Charlotte's face wasn't so hidden: she ripped her mask off to confront me.

'He's right, isn't he?'

'Casper's got Skye. They're heading to Parmesh's now. But they're being followed.'

I grabbed her hands, as if that was going to help anything. 'But it's okay. They'll get to Parmesh's no matter what. I know it. I also know we'll get the ledger. Okay?'

It took a couple of very long seconds before I got a slow nod. 'Good. See? I promised, didn't I? I promised I wouldn't lie to you again. But nothing to the team, yeah? It would freak Warren out. You can see what he's like at the moment. They all just need to keep focused on the money. Whatever happens, we've got to work around it. What else is there to do? We're here.'

We parted hands and she repositioned her face-wear. I got a muffled answer from her. 'So let's just get on with it, then.'

'Yep, exactly.'

She headed down the tunnel and I followed after checking that the doors were firmly closed.

56

By the time I reached the bottom of the stairs and was able to look along to the bung, the drill had stopped and a very happy Gemma was emerging from the tarpaulin.

I ran towards them. Gemma stood up and gave Tony a high-five. 'Fucking sick, or what?' She then dug down into her kit as Tony set about folding up the tarpaulin, keeping as much dust on the inside as he could.

Gemma brought out bottles of L&P, a local fizzy lemon drink.

'We have to keep moving,' I shouted. 'Just a quick swig. Let's go. Got to keep on it.'

By the time I got to the bung I was breathing heavily, sweat falling down the sides of my face. I checked out the cut, or what I could see of it. Just over two-thirds of the bit was inside the bung. Gemma knelt down to join me, drinking with her goggles over her eyes but her mask around her neck.

'Right.' She looked at Warren and me. 'As I bring the bit out, you two get either side of it and take the weight. Once you've got it, I'll take the bit off the drill, then you two get the core out on a new piece of Tony's sheeting. Like I told you, yeah?'

She coughed, her throat still dusty, and took a final gulp to clear it. 'Right, let's get on with it.'

Warren and I gripped either side of the drill, as Gemma put the drive into very slow reverse for a couple of seconds before trying to pull the drill back.

Charlotte had to help her. Dust had collected in the rig's runners, making it difficult to move. Eventually the core-bit started to appear.

Warren and I bent with our arms under the bit as it emerged, and Charlotte gave a final pull as she powered down. 'Here we go – ready!'

And out it came, to reveal a perfectly circular bore hole cut into the bung, and beyond that, the darkness of the void. The bit was still supported by the rig, but the weight of it tugged us down and we had to brace our legs to give some extra support. The concrete cylinder was warm.

Gemma got herself in front of the drill, to disconnect the bit. 'Steady – it will drop once it's free.'

She was right. The drill came away and we took the full weight. We shuffled like badly trained removal men towards a tarpaulin away from the mess and Charlotte began to fold down the drill rig. We manoeuvred the bit onto the sheeting and tipped it upright so the teeth were on the tarpaulin, then pulled upwards and twisted the bit to reveal a perfectly cut core of concrete. It looked like a very fat anti-parking bollard.

I checked my watch. That had taken just over ten minutes. I needed to be inside that basement in twenty. Warren had delicate work to do. Crack a tile and we were fucked.

'Okay, listen in,' I shouted, through the mask, so there were no mistakes. 'Warren's in first with his kit. While he's doing that, we get all this gear into the void. Phase three, let's crack on, let's go.'

Warren nodded, but not as enthusiastically as Gemma did, while Tony folded the dust-laden tarpaulins.

Warren switched on his head-torch before crawling through the bore-hole as I grabbed his bags. Not so much a crawl, more a reach through and over the 300-millimetre cut, then a collapse onto the ground the other side.

The moment he was in the void, I passed through his disc cutter. Next went a battery-powered LED floodlight.

I looked across at Tony and Gemma to give them muffled instructions through the mask. 'You two jump into the void and we'll pass the kit.' I needed to keep things moving and, besides, there would be less dust in there to attack Tony's lungs. He wasn't looking too good, and we still had a long way to go.

As they pushed through to the other side, Charlotte finished folding the dust-filled tarpaulins, throwing in the empty L&P bottles, and scooping as much dust off the ground as she could. She then passed them through the cut for the other two to stack out of Warren's way.

We were all going for it – and at speed, working as a team. It felt good. All now depended on Warren getting a grip and doing his stuff.

The core drill and rig were the last to be passed through. As they disappeared into the void, there was a high-pitched growl from one of the disc cutters as Warren gave it a quick test. I could soon hear the difference in pitch our side of the bung as the disc cutter went in – not into a block, but into the mortar. One by one, the blocks would soon be taken out.

I checked the time. Fifteen minutes until Casper would expect the holoport to be set up. That was if the car hadn't been run into a ditch and the pair of them were slumped in their seats, with heads full of holes.

The Samsung vibrated again. I checked, and it wasn't Casper or the Js.

Charlotte stared at me through dust-covered goggles, wiping them to make sure I knew she was looking at me.

I took the call and jammed the mobile to my ear.

'That you, James?'

57

Parmesh was as calm and upbeat as ever. 'How are you doing there, James? How is it going?'

I pulled down my mask. 'Good. Skye with you?'

'They are on their way.'

'Okay, we're at the basement wall. We'll get through as quickly as we can and call when we're in.'

Charlotte peered at me through her dust-covered goggles, anxious to know who was on the other end.

'James. Mr Egbers had to kill a man to break Skye free. He is fighting his way here, bringing her for you.'

Casper fighting to protect his wife? It would have been brutal.

Parmesh took the pause as shock. 'It is sad, James. I have to take responsibility.'

Charlotte could see little of my face but she knew something was wrong.

'It is tragic. But please do not let it distract you. Just please get into Sanctuary. Do not worry about leaving any evidence now. You need to hurry. I do not know how long we have left before Castro's men will come. They now know Mr Egbers is involved, and they know where to find him. It is just a matter of time. As soon as Skye arrives, we need to get her on the holoport. Time, James – we are running short of it at this end.'

I felt strangely calm as he talked. Maybe it was his own tranquillity. Maybe it was coming from inside me.

'We'll be ready.'

'James, no matter what happens to us here, you must get the ledger. When you do, you will understand. And that is why Charlotte and you must continue the crusade if I do not make it. The ledger will give you the power to do so, you will see.'

'Charlotte? Me? We're just—'

'No, you are more than "just". You are family. You are my family. Charlotte is my sister.'

I turned away from her. I didn't want her to see my eyes. 'Say that again?'

Charlotte moved so that she could look at me face-on once more.

'I have been searching for her from the moment my parents died. I remember her – but my parents had told me she was dead. They did not want to give me any anguish – but I always knew she was alive, out there somewhere. And I have always been searching for her. Sri Lanka, Europe, the US, everywhere, trying to find her. So when Mr Egbers discovered more about you, he naturally looked into Charlotte's history. Where she came from was right, the age was right, so we did what we normally do with possibles: we checked her DNA, like he had done dozens of times, and finally after all these years I have found her.'

And now the pause from me was genuine. It was shock.

'You are both important, James. You two are family. You are the only ones I want to carry forwards with the ledger.'

I was still on pause. I kept my eyes on Charlotte and she

stared back at me, shoulders shrugging, hands held out to her sides. *Who is it?*

'Do you know the original name?'

'Yes. Shoba. Now we have two in the family.'

I looked at her. I knew more about her life now than she did. But there was still something that I could never understand.

'Why me? Why me for the job?'

He laughed, which seemed strange, considering the circumstances, but then again, this was Parmesh.

'James, family are people I can trust. I needed someone who would not take advantage once they had the ledger. Read, copy, even steal it for themselves. I can trust you, am I right?'

'Totally.'

'James, you must look after my family at all costs and carry on the crusade with Charlotte.' He almost begged. 'Promise me, James, promise me. You will continue to build.'

There was no doubt about it. 'Yes.'

I could hear his relief. 'Thank you. Now, please, get into Sanctuary as fast as you can.'

His Samsung cut and Charlotte was in my face straight away.

'What's happened? Who was it?'

'Parmesh. Casper has killed someone to escape with Skye.'

She held her gloves to her dust-mask. I could see the shock in her eyes.

'They're heading to Parmesh now, to the holoport. We need to smash into the basement. Don't worry about the mess, we've just got to get in now. We can't waste any time – Castro's people could be kicking in Parmesh's door any minute now.'

'People killed. Oh, my God!' She turned away, heading towards the bung. The others would have to know. 'No. Wait.

Something else.' She turned back to me. 'Just say we have to move quickly. No reason. Just tell Warren to go for it. See you in there.'

She turned for the bung and I messaged the Js. *You still got one up there?*

Yes. All clear. I'll let you know if not.

Just keep one up at all times.

As I bent down and put my head through the hole, the cutter's buzz stopped. Charlotte was telling Warren to just go for it. By the time I put my hands through to balance myself and push into the void, Warren was already on to me. 'What's happening? Why the change? What's wrong?'

I got myself onto my knees. 'All's good, mate. They just don't care about the mess any more. We now just crash in and get out. They want to do it faster, which is good for us, yeah?'

'Are the police coming? It's all going wrong, isn't it?'

He rubbed his spare hand up and down his legs as his nerves were getting shredded. 'It's all fucked up, isn't it?'

The floodlight shone up from the floor at 45 degrees, and fought Warren's head-torch. It threw dozens of shadows in this small void, which probably wasn't helping Warren and his mindset.

'Oh, no! Oh, God!' He pulled off his goggles and his mask and threw them against the block-wall. He fought for air, hyperventilating.

'Warren, the quicker we get this done, mate, the quicker we can get out. It's okay. You just need to get on – and now.'

He turned and screamed at the top of his voice. 'You said it would work! You said!' He had to stop. He couldn't gulp air and shout. His face had what looked like rivers of tears running down the dust on his cheeks. 'I'm getting out. I've got to go. I've got to get out.'

He made for the hole, but I blocked him, arms up to embrace him, rather than restrain him. 'It's okay. Deep breaths, mate, deep breaths. Not long now. Look, I'll cut, you just sit, relax. Not long now, okay?'

Tony stepped forward and threw an arm round him. 'It's okay, boy. Come and have a seat with me, I've still got some fizzy lemon. Lovely stuff. Come on. Let's have a rest while James cracks on.'

Warren broke down and cried, but Tony embraced and coaxed him into the corner of the void where the tarpaulins were stacked. They sat down on them with a loud rustle of plastic.

Tony carried on soothing. 'Here you go, boy. It's all good.'

There was a carbonated hiss as he unscrewed the top of another bottle of L&P.

Goggled and masked, I picked up the disc cutter and got it up to full speed. I continued to cut where Warren had started, following the mortar between the first two blocks, and then pushed it on one of the sides with my boot so it would pivot out and I could pull. With luck, the rest of them would come out a lot quicker.

I didn't have to think about what I was doing: I was on auto-pilot. The only thing on my mind was Charlotte and, well, shit. I had nearly cocked up: I had nearly told her. But this was the wrong time. Right now, I needed all her focus on the job. I needed to pick a time when she could process it and, also, the right time for Parmesh – if he survived.

I cut through more bonding to loosen the next couple of blocks, then kicked them with my boot. They pushed through and I could clearly see the stud-wall the other side of a 200-millimetre gap. I pushed my arms through the hole and banged against the wall. There was nothing solid behind.

I fired up the disc cutter again and cut into the bonding on the third block as Tony almost cuddled Warren while dispensing words of comfort and swigs of L&P.

Sweat was starting to soak my clothing, a combination of the physical work and the sheer enormity of what was happening, both here and seven thousand miles away in Atherton.

58

My aim was to take out four blocks but in my frenzy I cut out five. The sixth fell out of its mortar of its own accord.

I rammed in and the disc cutter's tone pitched up and down as it hit first the stud-wall, then the ceramic tiling.

Having achieved one horizontal cut and one vertical to make an upside-down L, I tried to kick it out to speed things up, but it held.

I thrust the cutter in again and sliced another vertical to make a three-sided square. My hands were getting pins and needles as I gripped the cutter and the disc vibrated, biting into the tiles.

This time I lay on my back, right up against the block-wall, and slammed the soles of my boots into the stud.

As I kicked, I got everybody ready for the next phase. 'Get the holoport!'

My boots whacked lumps off the stud-wall to reveal the darkness of the room on the other side.

'Gemma, I need Warren's torch.'

Moments later the black hole was big enough to pass through, and as soon as Gemma handed me the torch I threw off the goggles and the mask. I didn't bother putting the torch on my head, just held it as I crawled through the jagged gap and used the beam to scan for a light switch. It was on the opposite wall, set to the left of a steel door.

The torch beam jerked around the darkness as I ran. I hit the switch and instantly the room was lit from office-like frosted panels above. It revealed a very plain room, grey-tiled on all four sides, maybe ten by five metres, a big space. It was empty. Nothing. Just the tiles on the wall and the polished greyness of the concrete floor.

I checked my Samsung. Three bars now. I put it on full ring volume: I didn't want to miss anything coming from Atherton or the Js.

The steel door had two turnkeys, one a third up, the second a third down. I worked them and opened it into darkness the other side. There was enough light to see a wooden staircase leading up to the ground floor, solid concrete either side of it.

Gemma's head appeared out of the hole in the wall. 'Stand by.'

She pushed the tripods through first, then the small aluminium boxes that protected the cameras, associated leads and transformers. I positioned them in the centre of the room. What was it that Skye would see here on these grey-tiled walls that we couldn't? What more had she found out?

Gemma pulled herself through into the room and stayed on her knees as she swivelled and leant almost back into the hole. 'Mate, come on, it'll be okay.'

She helped Warren through while I set about rigging up the tripods. I was sweating from all the bursts of energy it had taken to get me into the room, and powered by adrenalin. All that mattered was getting the holoport up and working.

'Tony, I need you in here. We have to get the cameras up quick.'

Gemma had sat Warren in the corner to the right of the hole and was squatting in front of him, calming him down.

'Mate, there's no drama. Soon be over and you'll be loaded – just think about that, yeah? You want a drink?'

Tony was next through, and looked about the space as he got himself back onto his feet. 'Where does she want this rigged?'

'Haven't a clue. Let's just do the whole room. Each corner, get the cameras covering the whole area.'

We set up the cameras on the tripods and got them at the right angle and height. I left Tony to get the leads into the power points.

I called Parmesh.

He was calm, but urgent. 'She is here – Skye is here. Be quick, James. Please. We have not got long.'

In the background, I could hear Casper and Jon shouting to each other.

'Clear.'

'Move it, move it! Check the gardens!'

Hard, sharp tones, far from Parmesh's level of composure.

Then Parmesh came back. 'Castro's people are here, James. There are cars outside the house. They are waiting for their back-up. We must win the race. So, please, be quick.'

Skye filled the airwaves. 'Oh, my God   Mr Mani?'

I cut through that. 'Not long now. Nearly there. You ready your end?'

'Yes – we have the lenses on, James. We are ready.'

'Okay, wait. Any minute now.' I closed down the phone, and connected the two holoports via the Samsung.

'Okay, everybody listen in, against the wall! We need to keep the space clear for the holoport. We are now connected with Atherton. I'll be the only one able to see them in the centre space – you must keep it clear – but you're going to hear them over the speakers. Okay, stand by, everyone, no noise.'

I avoided Charlotte's gaze as she tried to gauge the drama level of the call. Gemma and Warren were taking off their protection. Charlotte finally gave up on trying to interrogate me by stare, and followed suit. I kicked away the camera boxes to clear the centre of the room, but left the one containing the goggles. Pulling down my hood, I ripped off the coveralls and placed the goggles on my face. I waited as Tony finished the last of the connections and moments later Parmesh and Skye were standing in the centre of the room a metre away from me.

The speakers exploded with shouts from Jon and Casper.

'It's clear!'

'Okay, on me, let's go! Move, move, move!'

I didn't check the team's reaction to the noise. It just didn't matter.

Skye was in jeans and a red sweatshirt. She was a little younger than Casper, with short, dyed-blonde hair and over-large thick-rimmed glasses. Parmesh was in jeans and a blue sweater. The clothing that stood out on both of them, and I was glad the team couldn't see it, was the black body armour that made them look like plain-clothes police about to go in on a raid.

Parmesh had an arm round Skye to comfort her. Her head rested on his shoulder. 'It is okay, Skye. James is here.'

She turned and saw me. There was no time for anything but solid facts. 'Skye. This is the room, yes?'

She checked, she nodded.

'Where do we look?'

She was hyperventilating almost as hard as Warren. Parmesh comforted her again as she desperately looked around the room, but he couldn't stop staring at Charlotte in the corner, as she listened to the speakers, watched me talking to invisible people.

'The door. It's through the door.'

She pointed. Her hand wavered, not convinced by her own instruction.

'There's just a staircase the other side, Skye. It leads upstairs. Do we need to go up to the house? We got the wrong room?'

I'd messed up. I had created doubt.

'Oh, God. I just . . . A door, through the door.'

There was a loud shout in the background. Casper wanted help. 'I've got more at the rear! Jon – you need to back me!'

Jon shouted something back that I couldn't make out.

This got Skye even more scared, along with the team in the room around me. Only being able to hear and not see, their faces were a mixture of confusion and fright. Tony went over to Warren, who had his knees up as he sat in the corner, his forehead on them. He covered his ears, wanting it all to go away.

Skye turned from the door and her head shot round the basement in bewilderment. 'This is wrong! Oh, shit, it's all wrong! They talked about "through the door" – through the fucking door in the fucking basement! There's no fucking door!'

I held my arms out straight and hovered them up and down in front of her in an effort to calm her down.

'Skye, please, look at me. What exactly did they say?'

Casper burst into the camera zone, his hair flat against his head with sweat. He wore the same body armour, carried an M4 assault rifle, and had a Glock strapped to his leg. 'We've got them in the grounds.'

He spun and looked in the same general direction Skye and Parmesh were facing, wanting to make contact with me. 'James, we'll give you as long as we can. I know you'll do it.'

Casper turned to Skye and gave her a long look that seemed to soothe her before he melted away out of the camera zone.

Galvanized, she turned to me. 'There should be another door. All I know is "through the door". Through the fucking door. That's why I need to be here, to make sense of what I think I know. But . . . but . . .'

'It's okay, Skye. Just give me a minute.' For the first time, I forced myself to bring back the vision of Richard instead of pushing it away. What had he said before he fell into the darkness? What did he say he had done down here? He tiled the wall – but only the one wall.

I made myself think of the Filipino guy, and his blood-stained face. He said they had built a toilet or a storeroom or something . . .

Parmesh was staring at me, serene as ever. Maybe the inevitable had finally happened, so he was thinking, Why worry?

'James, we need to hurry, do we not?'

Warren was making too much noise. Gemma and Tony were trying to calm him down. Too much noise.

'Quiet!'

I found myself taking deeper breaths and everything seemed to slow down just enough for things to make sense.

I turned to the team. 'I need help here. There's a doorway in one of those three walls. We need to get tapping – now!'

59

Gemma and Tony were straight on to it, but Warren had relapsed. No matter how much he covered his ears, he could still hear what was going on, and he refused to help. 'I want to leave now! Let me go home!'

I ignored him as I frantically rapped my knuckles against the wall that held the door to upstairs. Gemma and Tony were checking each side of the stud-wall. Ear to the tiles, we tried to detect a difference in tone.

Warren was making too much noise and Parmesh was broadcasting words of comfort for Skye that were doing nothing for us down here.

'Everyone, shut the fuck up!'

Charlotte rushed over to Warren, and Parmesh held Skye close to him, all the while giving his sister long stares that only I could see.

Gemma gave a strangled scream. 'Got it! Got the fucker!' She fell to her knees, her ear still to the tiles, still rapping against the ceramic surface to make sure the change of tone was constant all the way down.

I swung round to Parmesh and Skye, who were now focused

a hundred per cent on what was happening in the basement. Gemma got to her feet, stepped back, and started kicking at the wall without as much as a run-up. It was futile.

'Gemma, cut the fucker.'

She ran and reached into the hole, dropping to her knees, like a touch-down, pushed into the hole and emerged with the disc cutter before running back to the wall. She dropped to her knees once more but the machine just dribbled power.

'You fucking thing!'

I ran to the hole. 'I'll sort it.'

Squirming through into the void, I grabbed a new battery and pushed back into the basement, sliding it across the floor to her. She changed power packs and a loud buzz filled the room.

Gemma ground into the tiles like her life depended on it, and maybe it did.

Jon jumped into the camera zone. He had the same body armour, carried the same weapons as Casper, and fought to regain his breath. His whole head glistened with sweat. He held out one hand as if exhaustion was stopping him moving. His jeans were covered with blood but there were no rips or holes to show that it was his. Thank fuck Warren couldn't hear over the cutter's noise and, even better, couldn't see what I was seeing.

Jon disappeared out of camera view and Parmesh still had Skye in his arms. Her shoulders heaved up and down, her head on his chest. He stared at me, his chin resting on the top of her head while he stroked her hair. He said something I couldn't hear over the din, but I got it. Things weren't going well.

Gemma screamed at the tiles as the disc cutter kicked more and more into the structure. 'You fucking shit!' Tile chips flew off the wall and strafed the ground. Then a plume of dust blew out of the wall as the stud-wall behind it began to cave in.

Gemma was now on her feet and aimed a kick. Her leg disappeared to mid-calf.

I joined her in pulling away the sections of broken stud-wall to reveal a small space, just as the Filipino had tried to explain as he begged for his life.

It was a toilet-sized room – but there was no plumbing. There was nothing but a safe. It wasn't that big, maybe 600 millimetres square, with a keypad and opening handle.

Parmesh spotted it. He looked down at the top of Skye's head. 'Skye, we have it. Look!'

She turned from his chest and a smile spread across her tear-wet face. She recited: 'One six seven four two eight. Or, one six four seven two eight.'

Before I had even entered the space, Gemma was on her knees and tapping away at the digital keypad.

A red LED display responded to the first code.

Error.

Gemma kept her eyes on the safe. 'What's the other one?'

Skye came away from Parmesh and walked towards the space, as if getting nearer could make her voice over the speakers any clearer: 'One six four seven two eight.'

Gemma tapped away.

The red LED displayed again.

Error.

She stood up and kicked at it.

I turned to Skye. She was so close to me that, in the flesh, I would have been able to feel her breath. 'Maybe the right numbers but wrong sequence. Take a moment, think . . .'

She wrapped her arms around herself, eyes closed, trying desperately to remember.

From behind me, Tony broke the wait. 'I'll have a go while the thinking's going on.'

He fished in his jacket pocket and pulled out my walking

sock that held the rare-earth magnet. The large heavy square hung from his hand as he headed for the safe.

Gemma moved out of the way to let him closer. He dangled the sock in front of the door, and the magnet hurled itself against the steel to the left of the digital keypad, slamming into it with a loud metallic clang. Any fingers in the way would have been smashed.

Gripping the loose end of the sock, Tony dragged it along the door of the safe in the direction of the side that opened. He hadn't even finished before there was a loud clunk and the safe sprang open. Tony tugged back on the sock, and that, in turn, pulled the door open.

Gemma came out with exactly what we were all thinking. 'What the fuck? How did you do that?'

I left them to it and turned to Parmesh. We locked eyes.

The door was open, but no one bent down to investigate what was inside. That seemed to be my job. Crouching level, I saw a very bland black book, A4 size, the sort you'd buy from any stationer's.

I placed both hands in the safe to pick it up and expose it to the light, and from over the speakers came the sound of gunfire, lots of it, outside the camera zone. We all ducked, as if it was happening right around us.

60

More screams and shouts came over the speakers and then more bursts of gunfire from somewhere in the Atherton house. The uproar echoed around our basement.

Parmesh and Skye had taken cover. He was on his knees and Skye was over him, trying to protect him.

Casper and Jon ran into the camera zone and stood either side of them as they slickly changed magazines on their M4s, drills they knew so well, both grabbing breath before their barrels were soon back up, pointing and ready to fire once more. Both men were drenched in blood that wasn't their own.

They kept their positions either side of the other two still on the floor, their weapons up in their shoulders, aiming, searching, ready to fire if the echoes out there in the house got closer.

There was no emotion from the two protectors. No panic, not so much as a concerned look: they stood rock solid, weapons in the shoulder, accepting the situation, ready to fight, just like the Knights Templar they were.

Casper filled a brief respite in the shouts penetrating the house. 'James, you there?'

'Yes – and I've got it.'

Jon turned his head to his right, in my general direction. He couldn't see me, but it didn't matter. 'I knew you'd do it. Thank you.'

I took a step towards him. I knew he couldn't see me, but it was instinctive. 'Jon, for fuck's sake, you've got a window, just run! All of you, get the fuck out! Why aren't you running?'

Jon stood rigid, his weapon still up, both eyes open and now looking dead ahead, along his barrel, waiting as the noise drew closer and closer.

It was Parmesh who had the answer. 'James, there is nowhere to run. We have lost at this end. But remember, James – remember what you have now. You have made everything worthwhile.'

I stared down at him. *What?* This was really fucked up. 'Casper! Just go! Take them!'

He didn't answer. He stood as still as Jon, two statues, weapons up, waiting for the inevitable.

The noises and the shouts got much closer and Parmesh called out again, but not to me. 'Charlotte, Charlotte!' He could see her in the corner.

She looked generally in the area where I was, the centre of the basement, her eyes desperately scanning the area as if she would be able to see him too. 'Yes! I'm here!'

Parmesh moved Skye's arm away enough to expose all of his face. He was smiling. 'I'm so happy that I finally met you. You have completed my family. You have completed me. You and James, you must – *must* – continue the crusade. You must, my sister.'

Charlotte's head swung to me and she did a double-take. 'Sister?'

There was a deafening din of more gunshots, much closer

this time, then both Templars fired their weapons on automatic, big long bursts, and the empty cases spewed out towards me and Charlotte. Instinct took over and I flinched, as if they were going to hit me. Long bursts filled everyone's ears through the speakers. The team had now curled themselves up in corners, their hands covering their ears, as if that would save them.

Jon took rounds and fell to the floor, blood gushing from the back of his head.

Seconds later, Casper ran out of ammunition, dropped his rifle and went to his leg to draw his Glock. It never left its holster. Bullets thumped into him and his body jerked, like a ragdoll, as they hit his vest, his arms and his neck. Blood spurted at me like a geyser.

Casper dropped to join Jon.

The firing stopped as abruptly as it had started but Skye's screams filled the void. She pushed herself away from Parmesh and ran the three or four strides to where her husband had fallen. She screamed at him to get up, but there was a burst of gunfire and the rounds slammed into her, spraying her blood in all directions as she collapsed on top of him.

Parmesh lay so still he seemed not to be breathing, a smile fixed on his face.

I jumped up and down in frustration, feeling so close I could have kicked out of the room and run to help. 'Run! For fuck's sake, run!' He was two feet away from me and there was nothing I could do.

He kept smiling. 'Charlotte, continue—'

He didn't get to finish the sentence. From outside the camera zone came a sustained burst of fire and Parmesh's body jolted as the bullets slammed home. Some hit his vest, but others ripped into his neck and face. Blood plumed out of him and mixed with all the other red fluid awash on the wooden floor.

It all fell silent, in both houses.

The only slight sound came from Warren, still caught up in his own world, mumbling and crying to himself.

And then a London accent barked through the speakers and made me jump. 'James? James? Mate, you still there?'

61

He strode into the camera zone. He had the same assault rifle as the Templars and was dressed very much the same, in jeans and body armour. He was about my age – he had long dark brown hair, and a really thick hipster-style beard covered most of his face. 'James, if you're still there, please stay there. We need to talk. Mate, everything's okay, but we do need to talk.'

He bent over Skye and pulled her goggles off her face. They fell apart. They'd been shot up and were covered with blood. He dropped them and carried on to Parmesh. 'Everybody in Sanctuary, stay calm.'

Other operators, dressed and looking the same, came into the camera zone. They checked the bodies on the floor, making sure none of them was breathing.

The hipster eased Parmesh's goggles off his face and wiped some blood off one of the lenses before donning them with a red hand. He looked around and found me quickly. 'James, right? You're James?' He said it like we'd just met in a coffee shop.

I nodded, and he smiled. His eyes were fixed on the ledger, wrapped in my arms against my chest. He was calm and polite. 'James, just listen to what I have to say. Just leave the book on the floor where you are so I can see it all the time. There's been enough killing and we're not going to hurt anyone down there, are we? Mate, all I want is the book, yeah?'

He waited for an answer, but there wasn't going to be one. The team around me were focused on what was being said now the guns and the shouts and the threats had happened. At least they'd been spared having to see it.

The hipster put his rifle on the floor and waved everyone out of the camera zone, as if to signal he was no longer a threat.

'Will you do that for me, James? Just give back what you've stolen. Mate, that's all I'm asking. No one will come to any harm. Will you do that for me?'

I nodded, and he smiled again under a mass of hair. 'That's good, James. Thank you. On the floor, please, so I can always see it. Our people are now on their way. But, mate, nothing's going to happen to your people, all right?'

'You say that?' I waved a hand at the mass of blood and bodies on the floor.

The hipster shook his head. 'Nah, won't happen. Mr Eduardo just wants his book back. So, I get the book, you all go home. Happy days.'

I nodded; he smiled.

'Mate, so all that's gonna happen is people are gonna come, pick up the book, check it to make sure you ain't done a swap, you know, not given us the real one, and then you all leave. Easy, yeah?'

I did what he asked and laid the ledger at my feet, then moved towards the wall to be with Charlotte. She was having a crisis of her own.

'Mate, excellent. Thank you. Not long now. Just wait. As soon as we get the book, you can all leave. Put an end to all this drama, yeah?'

A step away from Charlotte, I bent down towards the power socket.

The hipster knew exactly what I was about to do. 'Mate, don't—'

I pulled the plug out of the wall and my view of the hipster wasn't as good as it had been. Twenty-five per cent of the visual and audio was now lost. The hipster went to grab his rifle, then realized he couldn't do anything with it.

'Fuck, fuck! Fuck you!'

He watched me run to the next lead. 'Don't do it! You—'

I yanked it out. The hipster could do nothing but carry on ranting.

Tony was at the other wall and pointed at the other leads. 'These, too, boy, yeah?'

I nodded, and everything faded away in the centre of the basement for me and the speakers were silent. All that could be heard was Warren's murmurs and crying, his head still against his knees. We had lots to do, so thinking, worrying, getting emotional, all that was for another day.

My shout became the loudest thing happening in the basement. 'Okay, listen in!'

I threw off my goggles and took my phone out to cut the connection. 'Remember, once you get out of here, head towards the drones. Out of the hangar, turn right, keep running and they'll find you. Once you get to the vehicles, change of plan. Go to the airport, find the heli and Flavia. She's waiting for the ledger. Get the drone guys to call her – they'll arrange the meet. All of you need to take the heli to Parmesh's yacht. You'll be safe there. Let's get everybody on that yacht, let's get safe. Let's go – come on, we've got to go!'

Tony grabbed Warren, but he was in a world of his own. He had given up and had become an unreceptive lump, a dead weight, impossible to move unless he could be got to comply. Gemma saw the problem and went over. 'We'll both sort him.'

I retrieved the ledger as they bundled Warren through the hole. All three disappeared but Charlotte stayed. She wasn't budging. She stood waiting for me as I opened the ledger and flicked through the pages. I wanted to know why names and places were worth killing and being killed for.

I saw handwritten lists of people. Quite a few I had read about, or seen on the news. Castro had written details of what they did and what they would do for him when the time came that the CE needed a pope. There were even hand-drawn diagrams of how they networked. On another page, a seating plan for exactly fifty-one people was sketched out, as if they were planning a wedding. But this was no wedding: seat number one was reserved for someone very special.

Turning the page, I read down the list of places and the captions detailing why they were important to the important people.

Parmesh was absolutely right: the cognitive elite really could change the world for good or, as I turned the pages, for bad.

Charlotte had something else on her mind. She dragged my attention away from the ledger, bent down, trying to find my face. 'Sister? Continue?'

I closed the book. 'He's been looking for you for years. He told me on the last call. It was just a chance, a fluke, once he caught me, and—'

The mobile rang. It was the Js. No longer chilled out.

'We got headlights on Hunter. Four sets of them and they ain't just cruising, man.'

'Okay. The team are on their way out now. Pick 'em up. Once they're with you, they're heading to Flavia. Make sure she knows. They need to be taken on board. You got that?'

'Sure. No problem. Hurry, man. Got to make haste.'

I closed down the phone and thrust the ledger into Charlotte's arms. I took the large Jiffy-bag out from under my sweatshirt, which had been tucked into my jeans. The outside was wet with sweat, but the bubble-wrap was keeping the inside dry. 'Put it in this, for protection. You must guard it. Remember: Flavia, nobody else. She'll be waiting. Tell no one you've got it. They'll be looking for it on me. There's work to do with this. We've got to make it safe.'

As she gripped it, I pulled her into my arms and hugged her so tightly the ledger dug into our ribs. I whispered into her ear: 'You really are the real deal. But you always were.'

I let go and she looked freaked out, but I didn't want to explain what I had just seen written. She could do that for herself once she was on the heli and safe. 'Go! Go! Go!'

She didn't move. 'James, what's happening? What are you doing? Why are you staying?'

'I'm not. I'm just checking. I don't want to leave anything that will give us up to these people later. We want to get away with this, don't we? Go! I'm right behind you.'

Charlotte pushed the ledger into the Jiffy-bag before she dropped to her knees and crawled through the hole. As soon as her feet had disappeared I turned and raced up the wooden staircase the other side of the steel door, and into the darkness and echoes of a cavernous hallway. It was empty. What little ambient light there was came from the stars penetrating so many full-glazed walls. Enough to make finding the main door easy.

I threw the locks and pulled, and the huge floor-to-ceiling double doors, so heavy they must have had steel inners, opened agonizingly slowly.

I stood outside, my mind racing, and as I looked up at the stars a buzzing sound filled the night and one of the drones zoomed behind and above me. The pitch of the rotor tone increased as it took the weight of the deniable, and soon the noise was gone. There was nothing but silence again and the stars. It was the first time I'd noticed them since I'd been here, and maybe I was noticing them now because I was trying to take them in. It might be the last time I got to see anything or anyone because it was my turn now to take a stand, and try somehow to give Charlotte, the ledger and the team some space.

I felt at ease with myself, almost calm, as I realized I really was willing to die for what was in that ledger.

I heard movement to the left of the house, and the noise was closing in on me.

62

Hurling myself into the bushes and away from the slabbed pathway, I crouched on the ground and fumbled for anything to attack with. My breath quickened but I tried to control it. The sound was magnified tenfold in my head. Surely they could hear me. My hand moved over the dry soil and I found a stone just big enough for me to feel I was armed. I grabbed it as the noises grew clearer: movement and laboured breathing. My hand closed round the stone.

The body shape came into view as it turned the corner of the house. A male coughed, and an arm went up to steady himself against the glazed wall of the house.

'Tony?'

He looked as startled as I was.

I climbed out of the hedgerow and he stooped, hands on his hips as he fought to get his breath back. He looked at me long and hard. 'What are you doing here, boy?'

'What are *you* doing here? I thought you were taking care of Warren.'

He shook his head. 'Gemma can do that. She's going to put the fear of God into him. He'll be okay. Me, run? That wouldn't happen for too long, boy. I'd drop dead within a minute.'

He gave a slight chuckle, hoping to make light of it, but he was probably telling the truth. 'So I thought to myself I'd try to do something.'

'What?'

'You know. What have I got to lose? I'm on my last legs here, boy. The cancer.' He tapped his chest. 'It's got me.'

I felt like a sledgehammer had hit me, but all I could think to say was 'Shit.'

'Don't let it worry you, boy. It doesn't worry me. Now that Maureen's gone, I've got nothing left. That's why I thought I'd stay and see what's coming up the road – you know, give you kids a bit of a head start.'

He comforted me with a tap on the arm. 'Come on, cheer up, boy. Something gets us all in the end. At least I have a fancy one: respirable crystalline silica. All that breathing in concrete dust since my apprentice days. That's what got me, not Maureen's fags.' He chuckled away as he drifted into his own world, thinking about his wife. 'You know, she got thrown off a bus once because she was smoking and disagreed with the ban.'

I laughed with him. 'Maureen used to get through those B&H like a good 'un, didn't she?'

We took a breath, both staring out into the darkness at the end of the slabbed walkway that led to the drive.

I nudged Tony with an elbow but kept my eyes forward. I was finding it hard to look at him, and I realized how much I loved him. 'I liked that magnet trick.'

He gave another laugh and cough combo, then cleared his throat. 'The safe was controlled by a solenoid. They've been about since the 1820s. That's how fancy that lump of steel was. Magnets, never leave home without one. That's what I say.'

We both fell silent once more. We didn't say it, but we both knew we were waiting for four sets of headlights to cut through the dark.

'Son, I know what you're doing here, and you don't need to. It would be a waste but I'm glad you're here because I need a favour.'

'Anything.'

'Just promise me you'll get me back, scatter my ashes in Dean's Park. Maureen's there – she's behind the memorial in the wall. That'd do me. You'll have to do it without the buggers seeing you, mind.'

I knew the park well. It was part of York Minster's grounds.

'She wanted me to throw her about the grounds as a final two fingers up to the cathedral because they wouldn't let us get married there.'

He played with his nose, pushing the tip up more than most humans would be capable of. 'Not posh enough, don't you know?'

I nodded and put an arm around him. 'Of course. But I need a favour from you.'

He didn't say anything: he waited.

'Me and Charlotte have always wanted to know how you got that nose. I mean, if you were born like that, you would have been in a circus.'

He had a little laugh, which morphed into a hacking cough. 'It was your mother. She hit me smack in the face with a frying pan.' He couldn't control his laughter as he put his hands on his hips, leaning forward, coughing up the contents of the tunnel and having a spit out. I rubbed his back, as if I was winding one of my boys when they were babies.

He finished and stood himself upright. 'I knew your mum and dad from schooldays, when we were like eight or nine years old. By the time we were getting to be teenagers, well, you're thinking about people differently – and I fancied your mother. Fancied her rotten, I did. We all had a bit of a party at her house one day because her mum and dad were out – and I tried to grab hold of her and give her a kiss.' He squashed his nose again with his forefinger. 'But she put paid to that nonsense!'

He laughed and spluttered again, then gripped my arm. Vehicle lights were cutting into the darkness ahead of us.

'You'd better get going, boy.'

I hesitated. This wasn't how I'd thought it was going to play out.

'Go! Get on!'

I grabbed him, hugged him to me, and felt his hands come up onto my back and embrace me. 'Say goodbye to Charlotte for me, will you?' And then I swore I saw him wink. 'And your mum.'

We parted. I turned and walked back towards the house.

Tony was confused. 'What are you doing? Just cut across the grass. Get picked up by one of those drone things. Go! Go!'

I got to the door. 'Not yet. There's something I have to do.'

63

Heaving the huge wooden doors shut behind me and throwing every lock I could find, I sprinted back into Sanctuary and the light spilling round the staircase to the basement. I took the stairs two at a time until I came into full brightness.

The first thing I did was unscrew the black camera from its mount. I wanted the living memory it contained. I shoved it down the front of my sweatshirt and tucked that into the top of my jeans, all the time moving towards the hole in the tiles. I scrambled and crawled my way back through the hole, then the one in the bung, and ran as fast as I could along the tunnel. My boots stamped into the steel grating, the metallic clang each time bouncing off the walls. My chest heaved.

At the far end I ran up to the stairs, two at a time again, almost jumped through the steel double doors and ran out into the bright lights of the hangar. I could see the black triangle of the still-open shutter area, and as I got closer the perspective changed. Beyond the light spilling out of the hangar, I could once more see the glimmer of stars.

Any comfort that brought was soon ripped away as I

ran out onto the hard-standing and heard shouts, screams, gunshots, and the rev of vehicle engines round the front of Sanctuary.

I jinked right, towards the high ground, so far away, totally in the darkness, but it was where the Js were. I ran – that was all I could do until the drones found me and picked me up. I never looked back to find out what or where, who was caught, who was shot.

My throat was parched, my face wet with sweat. I fell and recovered, stumbling, crawling before I could get up and run again as fast as I could. It didn't matter what my body was doing as long as it was moving away from Sanctuary. But that wasn't happening as fast as I wanted. Headlights swept across the ground from behind me, casting weak shadows from trees and bushes. An engine revved, and more lights swept past, right to left, propelling my shadow in front of me. It was stronger than before. They were getting closer, until the lights went static, their bright beams illuminating me.

I heard shots, then shouts: 'Stop! Stand still! Stop!'

The vehicle surged towards me once again, lights still blazing. They had me. My shadow was straight in front of me, and its edges got sharper as the lights got closer.

More shouts to stop, but I kept running. What else could I do? The vehicle stopped. I glanced back and the headlights blinded me, but on the edge of the arc of light I saw the driver's door opening. All I could see was the frame of a body. Just like Casper and Jon's had been, the rifle was up. I ran at an angle to make a hard target and there was gunfire. Simultaneously a sharp, intense pain stabbed at my right leg, a deep burning, paralysing me with pain as well as disbelief, as I tumbled forward.

My face banged into the grass. My arms splayed out, the camera digging into my stomach. Instinct made me keep struggling, trying to crawl away from the danger. It wasn't happening: where did I think I was going to crawl to? I rolled over onto my back, and as I writhed I put my hand down to the hole in the back of my jeans and the source of the pain.

The silhouette had made its way much closer to me, rifle up. I lay motionless. I couldn't do anything more. I accepted my fate. I guessed that my timings and opportunity, my luck, had run out, and it was this guy's time.

A strange calmness came over me. I didn't have the ledger to lose, and that was what it was all about. Eyes open, I fought the pain: I wanted to see him, wanted to know what the man who was about to kill me looked like and what he was feeling. Was he sad? Angry? Or did he not give a shit?

Frustratingly, I couldn't see his face. The shadows with the light behind wouldn't let me.

For some strange reason I tried to get my breath back, as if that mattered or would help. My hand pressed tight over the hole in the back of my leg. Maybe his orders were to keep me alive to question me. I'd rather he spent more time dealing with me than any of the team, especially Charlotte – and the ledger.

Again, at the thought of her I felt calm. She would do the right thing with it. As soon as she'd read it, she would know what to do.

He took another step towards me and the silhouette got bigger. The rifle was still up, aiming at me, and at first the buzzing behind him didn't register.

The sound pushed in from the right and got louder and louder as the drone descended from above. The eagle swooped out of the darkness, its legs down, claws fully extended in the attack as it smashed into the silhouette and took him to the ground. He still had his rifle as the drone hovered over him, but as he loosed off a couple of shots into the air the claws dug into his rifle arm. His screams of pain were louder even than the rotor noise as flesh was torn and bone was crushed. The claws lifted his arm upwards and his body followed. His legs kicked out at nothing but air as the eagle ascended and he tried to break free. The rifle fell to the grass now far below him, and just as quickly as it had appeared, the drone was swallowed again by the darkness. Soon even the distant screams had faded.

I turned and did my best to crawl towards the high ground, dragging my injured leg behind me. It felt like I was trying to pull it away from my body as the wound stretched.

The screams in the sky returned and got louder. Moments later there was a deafening crump. The ground shook. I turned back to see the man once more on the ground, but now a mangled doll.

The buzzing, too, got louder again. As I lay on my back the Js brought their beast down towards me, its claws extended. The arms gave a small electrical whine as they came down each side of me, two metres off the ground, the camera spinning through 360 as they checked the area before committing. Then the lens came down and focused just on me. It was as if the Js' faces were focusing on me, taking me to safety.

Never leaving a man behind.

The downdraught from the six rotors blasted the sweat off my face as the drone hovered, waiting for me to move into the claws' embrace. I sat with my arms up, and they interlocked under my armpits and around my back, then took the strain. I held on and the drone gently gained height. Soon my arse was off the ground. It carried on lifting and my feet left the ground. The pain in my thigh intensified as gravity took hold of my leg and tried to stretch the wound even more. But so what?

The more height the drone gained, the better my bird's eye

view of what was going on at Sanctuary. Lights were on in every room in the house, bathing the building, like a *son et lumière* show. Vehicle lights jerked back and forth; torches scoured the area.

I tried to lift my leg, as if that was going to help it in any way. It didn't. It got worse, and I was dizzy. Pain, blood loss or the exertion of holding onto the drone's arms? I wasn't too sure. All that mattered was that the direction of travel was towards the Js.

I felt that I wasn't alone out there. I looked around, checked left and right, and in the gloom to my right there was the second drone, just a couple of metres away, flying at the same speed and level. It, too, had somebody underneath it. But this body wasn't holding on; it was a solid old unit and it bent at the waist, with its arms, head and legs trailing in the slipstream as we moved forward.

Was Tony's death a waste? It didn't matter whether he'd done well down there slowing Castro's men or not. It was the fact that he'd been willing to. That was what mattered.

I closed my eyes, a stupid attempt simply to lessen the pain, and it didn't work. All it did was accelerate things to the point at which eventually I passed out.

PART EIGHT

64

Akaroa
Saturday, 27 July 2019
12.23 p.m.

The GoPro's eye still stared at me from the coffee-table, but a warning light was flashing red. My new police-inspector friend leant forward to change the big chunky battery. The remains of the cafetière were stone cold and neither of them had asked for more along the way, even though I'd offered. An intermission or two to make sure I'd covered the story would have been handy.

While Lawrence did the change-over I turned to Janet. 'That's it. That's what happened.'

They had been shifting on the settee for the past three hours or so, but now Janet had resumed the position she'd started in, her arm thrown over the rear of the seat, her legs crossed. At last it was her turn to talk.

'And the team? What happened to them?'

'They all made it back to *Saraswati*, including Tony and the Js. In fact, it was one part of the plan that actually worked.'

I gave a bit of a smile but nothing was coming back. I pushed on. 'Tony got his wish. We were all there to scatter his ashes in Dean's Park to join Maureen. Gemma? Who knows? She could be anywhere. She's probably bought herself her very own rugby club and is busy oiling up the team for a match right about now.'

There was finally a hint of a smile, but it came from Lawrence, not Janet. I'd have to try a lot harder to get a result out of her.

I patted my blue cargo shorts. 'And me, of course, I got this big boy.' And quite a worrying-looking scar it was, too. They'd sorted out the wound for me on board the yacht. The rich don't just have their own dietary chefs and hairdressers, they have their own doctors. I pointed to the dark pink keloid scarring on my right thigh. 'That's where the round went in, just there – and out through the other side, no bone hit, just missing the femoral artery. A little more physio, and I'll be back to normal.

'As for Warren, he's still in York with his family. And us two? Well, we're down here, aren't we? So we're all okay.'

Lawrence signalled that the GoPro was in recording mode again, and settled back to join Janet. She wasn't accepting my bland statement. 'Okay? Really?'

I shrugged. 'Of course. Warren and Gemma have their money, and Charlotte and I have the crusade.'

Janet looked about the room. 'You've got a bit more than that going on.' She took in the luxury, but I knew she wouldn't be able to comprehend the extent of the resource behind it. I used to register it, but never really understood the magnitude of extreme wealth – and I didn't just mean the money Parmesh had had access to. But, then, did she even *want* to? I doubted it. A look of something close to disgust burnt out of her eyes. And I could understand that.

She came back at me, seething at what she saw around her, and for the reason that had brought her here: what had happened in Paraparaumu.

'The Rayners' lives have changed for ever. But not like yours.' It was anger, pure and simple.

Richard's car had been found within twenty-four hours of his failure to return home from his trip to the supermarket. The local police could come up with only two explanations as to why all his personal stuff, his mobile, his wallet, had been left behind in the glove-box. The first, and preferred, option, as far as the police were concerned, was that he had run away to start a new life, probably with another woman. The second was that he had suffered a mental breakdown and had committed suicide. That would mean more paperwork, because they might end up with a body to process. Both possibilities, they explained to the Rayners, were quite common with men of Richard's age. So when his bloated body had washed up on a Kapiti Island beach three days later, the police just concluded that his death was option two: suicide, and the currents had washed him about until he landed. They completed the paperwork, filed it away, and that was that.

But the Rayners weren't willing to accept the police's easy route out. They didn't accept either theory for Richard's disappearance. If he was abandoning them, why would he have left his wallet and mobile in his car? Surely he would have needed his cards, and why hadn't he taken money from his accounts? If he had committed suicide, where were his car and house keys? If Richard's mind was so unbalanced and disturbed, why would he throw them away before drowning himself? Why not leave them in the Lexus? Above all, Richard was a considerate man, who loved his family and friends: where was his suicide note? They refused point-blank to believe that he'd run out on them or killed himself, and they decided they had no option but to go in pursuit of the truth themselves.

Their quest got nowhere until early January, more than a month after Richard had washed ashore. That was when the events at Sanctuary were splattered all over the New Zealand media.

It had taken a while for the carnage to be discovered. With the houses on Hunter Road being so far from each other, one neighbour thought they'd heard gunshots during the night, but another suggested that, with so many outages, it could have been crackling power lines. Neither took their theory any further, and most of the other neighbours were overseas. Five bodies lay around Sanctuary rotting in the summer sun, and it wasn't until a power-company helicopter, running a check of power lines after yet another outage during New Year's Eve, flew over and spotted the battle scene that the police had known anything about it.

Curiously, the men's deaths were from multiple head and thoracic injuries. It was a mystery: they weren't shot, stabbed, or beaten to death; these people had died from injuries more consistent with falling off a high building or a parachute failing to open.

Along with the bodies, there were two abandoned vehicles and several firearms. Vehicle tracks had cut into manicured lawns; ammunition cases were scattered like confetti.

To add to the mystery, which was a gift for the media that they lapped up eagerly, was that there were reports of secret tunnels beneath Sanctuary, and the interior house walls had been broken down with sledgehammers. Even more excitingly, two sets of DNA, unaccounted for, had been detected in the grass. Were they from the mystery wall-destroyers? But why? The answer about the DNA, I knew, wouldn't have been that exciting. I was sure it would turn out to be Tony's and mine if it was ever tested.

But just as quickly as the media had found a great story to milk for a week or so, it had disappeared from the nation's screens and its consciousness. Almost as if a switch had been thrown.

The Hunter Road mystery was the Rayners' big break. They put two and two together and wondered if there could be a connection between the five deaths and that of their own loved one. They knew he had been doing his last piece of work down there on the South Island, and it was at a place called Sanctuary . . . so the police should investigate. They pursued the local force once again to reopen the case, but the Rayners were banging their heads against a brick wall.

That was when they'd decided to go national. They battled until they got a meeting with Janet in her Wellington office, and gave all the same statements and the evidence they had given the local force. Their dogged persistence was the reason Janet and Lawrence were sitting with me now.

Part of that evidence was their daughter's dashcam footage of the day Richard had gone missing. They'd checked it, along with the house's CCTV footage, just in case there was something – *anything* – on it that would help the police: maybe a strange car, maybe a strange character walking past. There was: it was me, and it was my hire. No residents recognized either me or the car, and once the Toyota's plate had been checked, it was an easy operation to trace me all the way back to Queenstown, then link me to the four Brits who'd checked into the same hotel as me just days before Sanctuary got shot up. It was my card that was used to pay for their hotel check-out around the time of death of the Sanctuary bodies – and then guess what? We all disappeared.

Janet and Lawrence had made the connection between me,

my credit card, and Subramanian International Banking. And guess what else? The bank's sole founder and owner had been killed within the same time frame, during the course of what the US media called a 'house invasion'. But they weren't here on account of the Sanctuary or Atherton deaths. They were here for Richard's.

But just as all the dots were beginning to be joined, they were called in by their bosses and ordered to pull away from the whole investigation, and hand over all documents and evidence they held. Then, just as the media had been requested on grounds of national security, they were told to drop it and forget. Newspaper, radio and TV editors might have complied, but Janet and Lawrence were made of sterner stuff. They were pissed off, and even more determined to find out exactly what had happened. Richard was a real man, with a real family, and from what I had seen of Janet she didn't seem like a woman who liked being told what not to do.

'You're right, Janet. Their lives will never be the same. I am deeply sorry about that.'

I wasn't sure if she believed me or not, but her eyes were back to looking about the room. I hoped she contained whatever loathing she felt. I didn't fancy being the target of a burst of aggression from her because, no matter what the situation was above her on the food-chain, she was here and she still had power. She could arrest me, and then more people than she could possibly imagine would be in the shit.

I waved my arm. 'All this is Charlotte's now.'

Janet wasn't interested in property ownership. She had more important things on her mind.

'And Atherton?'

I shrugged again. 'There was a cover-up. Just like the one down here.'

No one in the States had been arrested for the 'home

invasion', let alone prosecuted. There had been multiple inves-tigations, or so they had said, but nothing had been found.

'So, now I've told you everything. Am I about to leave here in leg irons?'

No smile from Janet, and she was far from finished. She pushed forward to the edge of the settee and leant in to me. 'What I want to know is: why am I being prevented from doing my fucking job? It's what's in the ledger, isn't it? That's what's keeping everyone's heads down and mouths shut, isn't it?'

I nodded very slowly. I had to choose my words carefully. 'I understand your frustration, I really do. I didn't choose what happened.'

That did it. The finger came up and jabbed the air. 'Nor did Richard fucking Rayner! Why do we have to go back to his family and lie? Why should we leave them in a world of doubt, blaming themselves, for the rest of their lives, not knowing what the fuck happened? Not to mention the Filipino. What is his family going through?'

She took a deep breath but Lawrence stayed sitting back, staring at me noncommittally, probably in case he needed to be the good cop.

She switched her tone and shook her head. 'Why, James? Why do I have to let his family suffer? Tell me, what is con-tained in the ledger? Tell me.'

I sympathized. They were just trying to do their job. But the fact was that Richard's family had been given the shit end of the stick, while Janet and Lawrence had been landed with the job of making them not notice the smell.

65

'Parmesh might be dead, but his dream and his crusade will continue, thanks to the ledger. It's not like cutting the head off a snake and the snake is rendered useless. He managed to bring together people from all over the world to be part of something good and worthwhile, something life-changing.'

Janet couldn't have looked less engaged if I'd been reading her the shipping forecast, but I was reluctant to give them more than they needed. I knew the demand would be landing, though – and it looked like it was going to be quite a forceful one. She pushed herself to her feet and strode behind the sofa. Standing behind Lawrence, she glowered at me for several long moments. Then she took a deep breath and turned away, taking a couple of paces towards the front of the house. Just as quickly, she spun on her heel and was coming back at me, her eyes wide and livid. 'I don't care about your precious Parmesh and his fucking dream. I don't care about Sanctuary, Castro, Skye – or even those two murdering fucks who killed Richard.'

She bore down on me and Lawrence's body tensed. 'So

what is it? What's so fucking great in that book that we have to back off investigating a murder? A man whose biggest crime was earning money to pay for his grandkids' education? I mean – *really*? What have you got there? The Holy fucking Grail?'

Lawrence looked concerned about an escalation. I kept my calm on the La-Z-Boy, tried to bring the temperature down. 'Janet, I know it's tragic. I really understand what his family must be going through – and I also understand your frustration.'

She stormed past the settee towards me, her eyes now lasers. Lawrence jumped up to place himself between us, but the coffee-table was in his way. A split second later, Janet towered over me, then jerked down from the waist to bring her face just centimetres from mine. I caught her lemon scent, and then she shouted with such force that she sprayed my face with saliva.

'Frustration? Fucking *frustration*? Doesn't even come close.'

She poked my chest and I kept motionless.

Lawrence pushed an arm between us. 'Boss, please.'

She wasn't having it. 'You fucking people, you come to my country, you buy up half of it, then you kill, you steal, yet nothing happens to you. Why's that? Why is my own fucking government protecting you and at the same time ordering me to shut the fuck up and go sit in a corner like some fucking interfering schoolgirl? *Why?*'

Lawrence eased her back from my face, and I brought up a hand to wipe away the flecks of spit. She thrust his arm down so she could take a step closer. 'Fuck that. Try this for size. I charge you with accessory to murder. Think on that – think hard.'

Lawrence looked as if he was seeing his career shattering

into pieces in front of his eyes, and he didn't know how close he was to reality. 'Boss, please, stop. Come. Sit down.' He moved his whole body between us, his back to me as he manoeuvred her away to the settee, but he wasn't taking any chances. He decided to stay on his feet.

Her face had dialled back a few shades of red and her chest had stopped heaving so angrily, but she still wasn't interested in ifs or buts or preambles. With both hands she wanted to beckon it out of me. 'So tell me, or you will be going back to Wellington in leg irons, and then we'll see what shakes out of the fucking conspiracy tree, shall we?'

My eyes flicked between hers and Lawrence's, and he agreed with her. 'She's the boss.'

In that instant, I, too, made a decision.

I leant in towards the GoPro, reached out and kept my finger on the top power button until the red light went out.

'You know what, Janet? You're right. The whole situation is wrong, and you do deserve to know. I'm here, protected by the people above you. And you're also right about Richard – he isn't getting justice. His family isn't getting justice. But they can't, and I'm sorry about that. Richard's family must never know, and for your own safety what I'm going to say must stay in this room. No one must ever know.'

I pointed across at Lawrence but kept my eyes on her. 'At least spare Lawrence from hearing this. Once it's known it can't be unknown. If this all goes wrong, why should both of you go down?'

Her jaw hardened and she looked ready to give it to me with both barrels, but Lawrence was in there first.

'I'm staying.' He thumbed at the switched-off camera. 'Best for both of you. You might both need a witness.'

I powered the La-Z-Boy to its upright position to bring me closer to them. For just a moment, they looked more relaxed, but that was probably because they had no idea of the extent to which their lives were about to change.

I studied both their faces long and hard before I spoke.

'So here it is. If America were in flames – from a nuclear attack to the scythes storming Wall Street – where do you think the leader of the free world would be evacuated to so that he could ride out the apocalypse?'

66

Ever since the Carter administration in the 1970s, when the Cold War was still raging, American officials had planned how to keep the government functioning during a nuclear Armageddon.

Only a handful of people in the world knew the resultant blueprint, but I was now going to tell Janet and Lawrence in minute detail not only the White House's plan for an apocalypse but also how those plans had been found to be completely inadequate and ripped up, and why the ground under our feet was suddenly at the epicentre of the new preparations, and finally, because they insisted on knowing, why Janet and Lawrence had now put their own lives at severe risk.

Back when the biggest emergency the USA was planning for was a nuclear attack by the Soviet Union, the administration had built a series of blast-proof bunkers and facilities across the States to house different departments of government if missiles were inbound. The ledger listed them. They might have been built decades ago, but they were still part of the new preparations. I counted them off on my fingers.

'Mount Weather Emergency Operations Center in Virginia,

a five-hundred-and-sixty-four-acre facility, which would serve as a relocation site for members of the executive branch of the government.

'White Sulphur Springs in West Virginia, a massive dormitory for lawmakers inside a bunker originally built for members of Congress beneath Greenbrier, a four-star resort near White Sulphur Springs. The 112,544-square-foot shelter included enough beds and supplies to accommodate all five hundred and thirty-five lawmakers, as well as one staff member each.

'Raven Rock Mountain Complex in Pennsylvania, built in a hollowed-out mountain near Blue Ridge Summit. The facility was conceived as a back-up for the Pentagon and built to house military leaders.

'Freedman's Bank in Washington DC, which connected to the White House via two tunnels – one under Pennsylvania Avenue to the Treasury Building, the second under East Executive Avenue from the Treasury Building to the East Wing of the White House.

'And then there were hundreds of other relocation sites across the USA, including the one where the Federal Reserve has stockpiled billions of dollars in cash, which they plan to use to replenish currency supplies after Armageddon.'

The number-one priority of the bunkers, I explained, was to preserve the president and all branches of government so they could continue to carry out their roles and functions.

The president and his or her team would be helicoptered to whichever site was chosen. They'd lock themselves down and wait out the attack. Then they would emerge after the destruction, backed up by the government departments, which had the institutional knowledge to rebuild with what was left of the population.

'But they eventually hit a problem with that plan. Nukes

were one thing, but forty years on the world has changed. The nuclear threat is still out there, and some would say it's worse than it was back then. But now we have more to worry about. We've got climate and the resource conflict, the discontented scythes threatening the established order, what the ledger calls "uncoordinated sabotage". And it's not just the cognitive elite who are concerned about all these new problems.

'So – where would a president now go to sit out the crumbling of society yet still carry out his or her role when the world goes pear-shaped?'

Janet was on it. 'Here.'

I nodded, but neither of them was showing surprise. Maybe it was police training to enable them to hide any emotion during interrogations; maybe she simply sensed I had more to say.

I held up my right index finger. 'POTUS needs three things to be able to function in any emergency. Survivability: POTUS has to be able to ride out a nuclear war, civil war, uprising, pandemic, whatever it is.' Then my middle finger. 'The second thing is connectivity: POTUS has to be able to communicate to all elements of the US government and, of course, to other heads of state. Where POTUS leads, the rest will follow.'

The third finger went into the air to join the other two. 'Finally, supportability: not just security, but everybody from NASA to the military, from food distribution to the power grid to water sanitation. They need to be with POTUS, not just in their own bunker somewhere in the US.

'So if we fast forward to 2019, the triple requirements of survivability, connectivity and supportability have led to a major shake-up of the way POTUS tries to keep control.

'Instead of the different arms of government having their own locations to bunker down in, each location now has an interagency cadre, a fifty-person team comprising all of the government departments that will be pre-positioned during a national emergency to support the president. The cadres will deploy randomly to any one of the sites, but the president will deploy with his or her own cadre to a purpose-built location that's known only to a handful of insiders. Even the other cadres think that POTUS will be bunkered down somewhere in the US. They have no idea what will happen to POTUS. But now you two do.'

They both waited, and I wondered if they felt even the slightest dread for their own safety as it dawned on them that the genie was out of the bottle, and there was no way out of this for them now.

'So, because none of the other cadres know which cadre POTUS would be with, the first thing they will all have to do is to identify and authenticate the actual president. That will be done via a chip embedded under POTUS's epidermis, which will be amplified by a radio frequency that is only used by the cadres, yet still they won't know where their leader is because the frequency can't be located.

'Janet, Lawrence, those are the first components of the ledger – what happens to POTUS when the cadres deploy – but it's only the start.'

67

'Imagine the meltdown if it was known that the president of the United States was leaving their own country to seek safety on the other side of the world . . .

'It would be taken by the homeland and the world as a sign that the USA had given up, and he or she had done a runner with the rest of the nought-point-nought-one-percenters to save their own skins. They would lose credibility, and if they lost that, they would lose power. And on top of that, down here, your country becomes a target if the cadres are deployed because of nuclear war.

'Whether you like it or not, neither the US nor New Zealand will ever allow this secret to get out. Your government and theirs will stop that happening at all costs. You understand what I'm saying, don't you? You two are expendable.'

I wanted that to sink in, just in case they hadn't come to the conclusion themselves earlier on.

Lawrence was thinking big. 'Not to mention the five million of us that would be vaporized.'

He understood. He got it. Then I did the just-to-make-sure bit.

'So, you appreciate that your government is complicit, as it would have to be. The president leaving the US during times of a national crisis is a very big deal. If this secret gets out there, it could only have come from one of you.'

There was silence from all of us and I let the air clear. It was Lawrence who broke the false sense of calm.

'Why aren't you in danger, and why isn't Charlotte? What about your whole group? Why aren't you just lifted away by the Americans, never to be seen again? What about the ledger? Where is it now?'

I shook my head. 'It's safe – and always will be. That is why we are safe.'

They sat and waited: they wanted more. And it felt right to me that they should get it. They were in so deep anyway.

'The reason why is that the ledger contains the name of every member, of every cadre, the positions they hold within the group, and even where they sit at their respective tables.

'But Castro was only really interested in POTUS's cadre. He had written notes, very detailed notes, on who they are, what they think about life, politics, love, even down to what they eat and why.

'Some of the names were researched in even greater detail after Castro made contact with them. He had detailed their reaction to him expressing his willingness to be the linchpin between the cadre and the cognitive elite. He was nearly there, setting himself up as pope.

'Castro's handwritten notes listed what they have committed to him, and what he has given them in return.

'Interestingly, money wasn't the big motivator for the cadre, it was a view of the new world order that was in line with Castro's – or the possibility of seizing or creating their own power.

'For all Castro was, and wanted to become, I can't take

away from him the brilliance of his planning. No cadre member had any idea that Castro had been talking with any others. They thought they were the only one. None of the cognitive elite knew of the ledger's existence, and what Castro had been planning. It was perfect divide-and-rule that any great politician or military genius would have been proud of. Until, that is, Parmesh learnt of the ledger's existence.

'Casper came to him wanting revenge. He explained about the ledger and a plan to take control of it. But then Parmesh let him see the light, the possibility of a better world, and taking control of the ledger became much more for Casper and Skye.'

I paused, but there was nothing coming from them.

'But I won't give you the names of the cadre, or where POTUS will be located down here.'

Janet flicked that one away with a wave of a hand. 'Don't want to know any more shit.' Disgust was back on her face. For her, this was still about Richard.

But Lawrence wanted more. 'Castro. What about him? He still walking about?'

I nodded and gave a little smile. 'He knows he'll be dealt with the same as anyone else if the secret is revealed – and please remember, that includes you two now. Besides, Charlotte has other plans for him.'

Lawrence frowned. 'He joining Parmesh?'

'No. She's going to show him a better way of thinking about things, by joining us, not opposing. Just like she will with any of the cognitive elite who have leanings to Castro's old way of thinking. It won't be easy, but if it was, it wouldn't be so important, would it?'

Janet hadn't quite moved on. 'Charlotte?'

I nodded, very proudly. 'Parmesh discovered Charlotte. Nothing is thicker than blood. She's got two big jobs to do, bringing the cognitive elite and the cadre on board, and it's going to be hard. But she's the Pope, the linchpin, and in any case, that's what a crusade is all about, isn't it?'

I decided not to add that we had the living memory of the hipster and the crew, and that Castro knew we had it. Charlotte had made contact with him and had told him when she held out a hand in peace. It was enough to stop him jumping up and down too much before he came round to our way of thinking. It would take time, but we'd get there.

The two in front of me were still processing the idea that Charlotte now controlled so much power. I wanted to get them away from that. 'As for me, I'm just an adviser to her. But what am I to you guys? You made up your minds yet?'

I took a breath, waiting for an answer to come back to me. But none did, and that wasn't good.

68

'If you feel you need to arrest me, I understand. I get it. But please, please, please – think first of what will tumble down from above, on your own state, what they will do to you if any of this is revealed.

'Instead, you know what? Why not join us? You're both principled, both want to do the right thing, so why not come and be part of something that's both of those things – and more?'

I looked at them and smiled, trying to be welcoming, trying to be as open as I could.

They looked at each other for no more than a couple of seconds, both raised an eyebrow, and then they burst out laughing. Fair enough, but it was what was going on inside their heads that I was more interested in. I would find out one way or the other soon enough.

I carried on with the pitch. 'You'd be most welcome. We must never stand still because there's much to do. Maybe you could help us.'

I studied their faces. 'Lawrence, Janet, think what you'd be able to achieve with our resources, our connections, for the most powerful person on the planet, who will be in need of us. The chance to change the world for good, eh? A better world for Richard's family? So that we can all say he didn't die for nothing?'

There was no reply, no sign on their faces, so I left it out there in the air.

Janet stood, straightened her skirt, and nodded down at Lawrence, before pointing at the GoPro. 'Give him the card. We can't have any of this morning's shit out there, can we?'

Lawrence leant across the coffee-table to open the camera. Janet turned and looked down at me. 'This is not how it ends. I have a widow to go back to.'

'I know, I get it. But is there anything we can do to ease the family's pain? Maybe organize some way to ensure the grand-children's future? Ensure all their futures? We can do that. We have people who will be clever at creating a legal and plausible way of making that happen for them. We're doing the same for Hector Estrella's family in Manila. Whatever they need, they can have.'

Janet liked that.

Lawrence was up on his feet and the GoPro went into his jacket pockets, along with its tripod, making his suit stick out at the sides. I rose, and limped with them towards the front door. When we got there, I put out a hand to Janet, and she took it, as did Lawrence afterwards.

'I know you had to come. I understand the frustration. I'm sorry that Mrs Rayner will never be satisfied with the explan-ation, but—'

'But nothing. I'll be back.'

Lawrence nodded. 'We'll both be back.'

I smiled. 'Of course, any time. Come and stay here if you want.'

As I opened the door, the sun blinded us. The two of them

reached into their pockets for their sunglasses and headed for their hire without another word.

I closed the door and set off at a limp, back towards the rear of the house. They were good people, trying to do a good job in unworkable circumstances. Just like Richard, just like Hector, they were caught in the middle of something they had no control of.

But at least they were both still alive.

69

I reached the concrete steps to the basement, which were now completely hidden behind a dark wooden door that blended with the colonial décor. It took me longer to get down the steps than it would have done before my injury, but I saw it as a good thing. It gave me more time to think about the first time I had met Casper and Jon. I imagined them running down this very flight of concrete shouting at me to stand still, already knowing what Charlotte was to Parmesh. They must have obtained her DNA from the missing hairbrush in the bag Jon had stolen from her yoga class. Very clever.

When Casper worked for Castro, he wasn't yet married to Skye, but it was serious. It was her rage at what had happened to Casper that made her just as bent on revenge as he was. It was her idea to approach Parmesh and, just like Casper, she'd seen the light. Then she'd come up with the plan to infiltrate Castro's empire to discover where the ledger was hidden.

They married; she infiltrated.

Down here below ground, everything was laid out exactly as planned. The nuclear-proof rooms with their own power, air-conditioned wall supply, communications, everything needed to lock down and be safe. Everything required to guarantee our survivability, just like POTUS, who would be tucked away in a purpose-built bunker just outside Wellington. From here, Charlotte would be the linchpin – the Pope – between the cognitive elite, POTUS and his interagency cadre.

I pushed open one of the dark grey steel doors into our common room. Sofas lined the walls, on which hung dozens of TV monitors, keeping a watchful eye on what was happening around the world.

Charlotte was sitting in one of the two chairs in a corner of the room, set back a couple of metres from the bare concrete walls. This was what we had ended up calling our memory area, and it was here that we had sat to memorize the ledger. Every line, every detail. I could even draw the sketches of the seating plan of who sat where, and why. And the reason? Charlotte had decided there had been enough killing over bits of paper. So, once we were a hundred per cent sure that we had both memorized every detail of every page, she had burnt it. The ledger no longer existed. No one could ever find out where it was, and kill for it.

We had sat here, day after day, and these days we still both came down here to keep that memory on its game. To anyone watching, what we did might look like meditating, but it wasn't. It was going through the secrets page by page in our minds.

Positioned around the two wooden chairs were the tripods and cameras of a holoport. She used it to talk to others of the cognitive elite to make them feel at ease about the changes. Parmesh had gone, but the crusade went on. With the knowledge Charlotte possessed and, more importantly, her blood-line, she was most definitely the Pope.

From the depths of this basement, she had also made contact with members of the cadre to explain the predicament they were in now that Castro no longer held any power, and that she had the details of what they had been getting up to with him. It wasn't a threat, but rather a hand outstretched in peace. The linchpin to the cognitive elite had changed, the purpose of the cognitive elite had changed, but they could still be part of it. She would give them the faith to change: they need not worry. For now, all they had to do was make sure that everything returned to normal. No more police, no more media.

But that wasn't the reason Charlotte was down there today. She was there for something very different: she was watching the living memory of that very first meeting in Queenstown, her brother agonizing as he tried to work out whether or not he should tell her about their relationship.

I sat on one of the sofas, waited a minute or so for it to finish. As I did so, I ran through the first couple of pages of the ledger again in my head.

Charlotte stood and took off the goggles and headphones. I gave her a stupid half-wave, and couldn't help noticing there was a tear in her eye, as there always was each time she watched it. But, as always, she didn't try to wipe it away.

She headed towards me, eager for news.

'How was it?'

I got up and stepped closer. 'It was good. They know. It felt right to tell them.'

I gave her a smile, along with the answer to her next question.

'They'll be back. They're curious.'

She beamed. 'Good.' She walked towards the door, and as she passed me, her fingers pushed into my shoulder. She knew I couldn't keep balance on my bad leg, and as I fell back into one of the sofas she laughed her head off and waved backwards at me. 'You need to sort that leg out, limpy boy. See you when you've finished. I'll make tea.'

70

My memory work took an hour and a half, as it always did. I could have done it in less, but I made sure I went through every page slowly, even if my mind wanted to jump ahead a couple of sentences because I knew them so well. It was imperative I could recall it word for word and every single detail of every diagram.

I was standing on my bedroom balcony, overlooking the inlet that was bathed in brilliant sunshine before a cloud came over and knocked it out for a bit, then moved on, and *Saraswati*, about two kilometres away, glistened in its rays once more.

I smiled to myself as I thought of the crew running round fending off gulls. Although we had access to some of the best brains in Silicon Valley, there still wasn't a device on board to send out some frequency to repel the little shits. Or big shits – Charlotte and I had often laughed about the dive-bombing attack Parmesh had suffered on deck. But even more than that, we knew that in the laughter there was a lesson. We may have everything we needed for the crusade, but we mustn't get above ourselves. If we allowed that to happen, we would fail. We had to keep our feet firmly on the ground.

I thought about the Js and their drones. James and Jamie, or whatever their real names were – I'd never found out but hoped to soon – had long gone. Their armoured drone system had been bought by the US and Israeli militaries, and they were now probably sitting on the very large decks of their very own yachts or balconies at their houses in Atherton, and almost certainly flying mini versions over their neighbours' gardens to check for young couples 'jamming'.

They were still with us in spirit, of course, and now, with their new-found wealth, they were also part of the cognitive elite. They were coming down here in a couple of months to buy a sheep station between them. The rules for foreigners buying or building residential property in New Zealand had changed: in general, only residents and citizens could buy homes to live in, but if you had the right representation and deep enough pockets, other investment opportunities were available.

I had been a very happy man when they told me their plan. I liked them a lot. Well, more than liked: they'd saved my life and made it possible for Tony to be with Maureen.

In other news, Parmesh's family had been in Scotland during the raid in Atherton, a trip Kyle and Parmesh had planned deliberately because they didn't know how it would all play out. Kyle, of course, was part of the crusade – he was then, and he still was now. Very much so. Everything that Parmesh had worked for now belonged to Kyle and, because of his allegiance, also, in turn, to the crusade.

Charlotte and I had bonded with Kyle and the kids these past few months. I'd been worried that Charlotte would take on her own name and start morphing into something different, especially when Kyle gave us joint seats on the board, which was now under his control. I couldn't help wondering: would the old family name help her carry on

Parmesh's dream? I needn't have worried. She didn't even consider it. Just as she had told Parmesh, our mum and dad were her parents, and I was her brother. That said, she certainly had the Subramanian genes. Her life was now focused on the crusade. It was as if she'd found her calling in life, and it had made her metamorphose into this amazing person I admired and felt so proud of. She was radiantly happy, yet she still retained the old Charlotte. The strengths she had in combining and blending her old and new lives kept on astounding me. Simon, for example: she had set him up with a studio, a lifelong supply of paint and canvas, and left him behind. It was just as well: he was going to need the practice. To date, he had sold only a single picture – and that was one Charlotte had spotted on eBay and I had bought anonymously.

The sky was completely clear of clouds and the sun was beating down, so I went back inside to my bedroom to pick up some sunglasses. On the way, I stopped and looked at the wall above the dresser, where the framed New Zealand hundred-dollar bill Charlotte had presented to me now hung. We'd finally got round to having them framed about a month ago. Until then they had sat in glass tumblers on a shelf in the comfort room in the basement, and there was a constant fight between us as to which bill belonged to whom. Of course I let Charlotte win. She was probably right, anyway.

Grabbing my Ray-Bans, I made my way back out onto the balcony to take in the view once more. The green hills and turquoise sea were breathtaking, and I could never get enough of them. I hoped that Pip and the kids wouldn't either, when they arrived. There was still a lot to sort out at the UK end of things, but it was great timing for the boys. They had just finished primary school and could start a fresh year in a senior school here.

Pip and I had met up when we carried out a secret scattering of Tony's ashes in Dean's Park to reunite him with Maureen. Charlotte and I had chucked in a KitKat and a scattering of Fruit Pastilles for good measure, a final two fingers up to the powers-that-be who had thought those two weren't good enough to be married in their hallowed hall – as if the Minster lot would have known true goodness if it had jumped up and whacked them on the nose with a frying pan. As for pissing off the litter patrol, Maureen would have enjoyed the idea very much and we just wished we'd thought to take more.

That was when Pip and I got talking. She had met them when we'd first started going out, and it was as if Tony and Maureen had brought us together again. I asked – well, if truth be told, I begged – Pip to come down here and make a new start. There was nothing in York for the boys. Their last grandparent was with us, to end her days with Charlotte. New Zealand – what a great new exciting life for them. Snowboarding, wakeboarding, screaming around lakes in jet boats, what wasn't to like? If it didn't work for the three of them, I'd do whatever was needed and they could go back to York. That was the beauty of having money: it gave you power, opportunity, choice, and the people who made those things happen. Life was a lot easier on the banks' side of the fence, and my one regret was that Dad wasn't there to enjoy it.

Maybe I wouldn't end up living with Pip and the kids. I was hoping I would, but we'd see what happened. I had high hopes. And now I understood there had to be a balance between life and work.

But for now, my work was for Charlotte and the crusade. I was hoping Pip would come over to our way of thinking and be part of what we're doing. Then our lives wouldn't be as separate as they once were.

There was another reunion. At the spreading of Tony's

ashes I had seen Warren for the first time since we'd got off *Saraswati* in Sydney. They'd all taken a flight home the same day, with Tony, in Parmesh's jet – well, our jet now – but Charlotte and I had stayed on board the yacht. We had a lot of work to do.

Warren had been quiet all of the time, spending most of the voyage to Australia in his cabin, I presumed because he was still freaked out by the whole affair, especially what had happened in Sanctuary. But after we had sprinkled Tony about the park and scattered Rowntree's finest, we all went out for dinner, and that was when I discovered his withdrawal was more to do with embarrassment and shame about the way he'd reacted. I reassured him that he didn't have to feel anything but pride in a job well done. He had just been Warren, that was all, and we would always be mates.

I heard noises behind me as Charlotte pushed her way into my room with a mug in each hand and came over.

'Kyle's just called. He's going to bring Mum and the kids up in an hour. It would be straight away, but you know Mum – it'll take some time.'

I took the mug that was offered. 'And the dogs?'

Charlotte took a testing sip while looking out at the ten-million-dollar view. 'Of course – can't wait. The crew are taking them into quarantine now.'

Mum had always had dreams of travelling the world when she and Dad retired, but she hated flying. Kyle had had her picked up, with a nurse and the dogs, taken to Southampton, and they'd sailed down here. It didn't matter if she remembered where or what she saw during the stopovers: what did was that she finally got her wish.

We both stood there, drinking tea, looking out at nothing in particular, but I knew her mind was racing. She had lots of ideas. Charlotte thought big – on a grander scale even than

Parmesh had. She had decided that humans couldn't go on fighting each other for nothing, rendering millions homeless. She felt there needed to be a single community throughout the world, so why not a one-world government with a single global marketplace, financially regulated by one central bank using one global currency? One set of universal values and a universal legal system. All foreign and domestic policies would be geared to help one another. And the first objective would be a global welfare system. It sounded like a good thing to me – just, like everything, hard work. But, as she kept saying, if it was easy, it wouldn't be worth doing, would it?

I leant to one side and gave her a gentle nudge, just enough to spill a little of her tea.

'You know what, m'lady? If you get this world-peace thing right, in a thousand or so years' time there'll be statues of you all over the show. Maybe even a book about you that the faithful sit around reading once a week. You know, about how you were the one that showed the world life could be different.'

Charlotte gave a big smile and raised her mug. 'Sounds good to me, Parker.'

And as we touched mugs, there was a gull above us that had a different idea when it came to world order. It squawked and flapped in the clear blue sky, and then a big blast of grey and white bounced off the side of her head and landed on her shoulder.

'Parmesh was listening!'

We had to put down our mugs fast so we didn't spill what was left as we laughed harder and longer than we had for the last ten years.

ABOUT THE AUTHOR

From the day he was found in a carrier bag on the steps of Guy's Hospital in London, **Andy McNab** has led an extraordinary life.

As a teenage delinquent, Andy McNab kicked against society. As a young soldier, he waged war against the IRA in the streets and fields of South Armagh. As a member of 22 SAS, he was at the centre of covert operations for nine years, on five continents. During the Gulf War he commanded Bravo Two Zero, a patrol that, in the words of his commanding officer, 'will remain in regimental history for ever'. Awarded both the Distinguished Conduct Medal (DCM) and Military Medal (MM) during his military career, McNab was the British Army's most highly decorated serving soldier when he finally left the SAS.

Since then Andy McNab has become one of the world's best-selling writers, drawing on his insider knowledge and experience. As well as several non-fiction bestsellers – including *Bravo Two Zero*, the biggest selling British work of military history – he is the author of the best-selling Nick Stone and Tom Buckingham thrillers. He has also written a number of books for children.

Besides his writing work, he lectures to security and intelligence agencies in both the USA and UK, and works in the film industry advising Hollywood on everything from covert procedure to training civilian actors to act like soldiers. He continues to be a spokesperson and fundraiser for both military and literacy charities.